The Stickwick Staplers

Bernie Douglas
dictated, not read.

Linnaeus Hoffmann
Publishing

Plainview, TX
A division of Morty's Harpoon & Bologna Dist. Co.

Linnaeus Hoffmann Publishing
A division of Morty's Harpoon & Bologna Dist. Co.
Plainview, Texas, USA
bernie@linnaeushoffman.com

Cover design and author photo: Hazel Douglas
Illustrations: Bernie Douglas

ISBN: 0615490662
ISBN-13: 978-0615490663

DISCLAIMER: This book, and all elements within, are completely fictional and products of the author's imagination, including, but not limited to all persons, places, events, organizations, awards and academies, even those seemingly based on real people or things. All claims made within this book, with the exception of the claims on this sole page, under this sole disclaimer are completely fictitious, even other disclaimers contained within this section. -ED

OTHER DISCLAIMER: If a book is a book of fiction, it's all fiction, right? Not just what the author writes, but what editors write, too. For instance, in *The Da Vinci Code,* there is a disclaimer at the beginning saying that all descriptions of organizations, artifacts and rituals are authentic. That page was fiction. You should assume that if you are reading a book of fiction, it is completely fictional, unless the author, and not the editor, says otherwise. This disclaimer, and not the other one is the true one. -Bernie

CONTENTS

ACKNOWLEDGMENTS

Bellini made me put this section in here. I don't know what I am supposed to acknowledge. I think he thought I would say something about how great he is. Or dedicate this book to him. But why do you always have to acknowledge people here? I wanted to acknowledge the fact that I didn't put a header throughout the book with my name and the book title alternating pages. Some people say that is because I forgot to do it, but since I am writing this before I sent it to print, it is clear that I didn't forget. I just don't really understand why people do that. I doubt any of you will forget what book you are reading or who wrote it in the course of reading it, and if you do, you can look at the front of the book. And it isn't because I don't know how to make it on most pages but not the first pages of each chapter. I also want to acknowledge how funny it would have been if I would have put all the dialog spoken by Bellini in Wing Dings. That's how it was originally. Hazel said it was distracting. I thought it was an artistic representation of my perceptions. Hazel said I was a jerk. I don't know what else to say here. I originally was going to put a dedication page stating my devotion to Nasim Pedrad. Dicky loved the idea. Hazel made me delete that as well. And Dicky dedicated his *Rohonc Codex* translation to her. Now she is going to want to be friends with him, and Dicky won't want to be friends with me anymore.

The Lives of Two Toed Sloths
Book 1
Bernie Douglas: An Autobiography of the Future
Written in Past Tense

This book is written with the necessity of the sequel to fol-low. However, the sequel is the exact same book. Bernie Douglas: An Autobiography of the Future Written in Past Tense *is a very bi-ased, one sided view of what happens in the making of Linnaeus Hoffmann Publishing Company, which will be followed up by* Ed-gar Douglas: An Autobiography of the Future Written in Past Tense, *an equally biased and one sided view of the same happenings, that when viewed in the context of this book will allow you to see the whole story. Plus, it will clean up a lot of the loose ends in this story, such as why Edgar shoots me, how I got the stigmata, and how Linnaeus Hoffmann became successful in the first place.*

Writing this book, I see that it doesn't quite fit into any set genre. I could call it fiction, but there is no actual proof that this isn't an entirely accurate portrayal of the future. Being so, I could call it a memoir, but this story isn't drawn from memories of the past, but of the future. So, I coined the phrase "precognitive mem-oir."

And, I am sure when Edgar writes his book he will call me a liar up and down all throughout it. But I want you to know now, Edgar is an absolute liar.

ED NOTE: In order to maintain a continuance of the story, and to fill in gaps and inconsistencies from the author, selections from *Edgar Douglas: An Autobiography of the Future Written in Past Tense* have been included in this story. Bernie, we are sorry we did not mention this before the publication, and you are just now finding out about it, but your contract specifically gave us this op-tion, and we know how you are. Plus, it was a much needed addi-tion. But I still haven't figured out why the owner of the publishing company felt the need to have a contract to publish his own book, especially a contract with this many holes.

-Chrstphr. Bellini

INTRODUCTION

I know when someone picks up a memoir, precognitive or not, they are always hoping to read about two things: sex and regrets. And this is understandable. People like sex just as much as they like feeling they are better than someone else. And when someone writes about how much sex he has had, he'd better add something in there about his humiliating screw ups, otherwise he would come off looking like a pretentious twit. So I will give you both, right up front.

However, unfortunately, I took a vow of chastity years before I was even married, so the steamy sex chapters are well out of the picture. Even though my (transitional) wife told me for years that chastity vows end at marriage, I had my convictions. (When we got married I only considered her my wife, but then Nasim Pedrad got famous, and at the first sight of her on TV, both Hazel (the wife) and I knew that I would really enjoy being married to her, so we decided that if I ever met Nasim, we could have the marriage annulled so I could marry her.)[1] But anyway, you are probably thinking my biggest regret has to do with this chastity vow, but you cannot be further from the truth.

On 26 December 2006, Gerald Ford died, under what I can only assume to be very suspicious circumstances, being that the ma-

---

[1] Of course Bernie is the only one who took that agreement seriously. Hazel just wanted him to shut up and figured he would forget about Nasim a day or two later. -Edgar

jor news sources did not reveal the cause of death. Around the same time, Orenthal Simpson was trying to get a book published. This man, who had had so much tragedy in his life, merely wanted a source of income to support his children after their mother had died and his career had pretty much been washed up when the US legal system determined he had nothing to do with the aforementioned death. And what little money he did have, he had to give to the Goldman family, a group that publically professed they believed Orenthal killed their son, although their private beliefs I can only guess, because they learned long ago, if you can't have your son back, the next best thing is fame, fortune, and a really cool moustache.

Orenthal (or OJ as he lets me call him) had absolutely no means of making money after the Goldmans (Goldmen?) were through dragging his name through the dirt, and everyone associated OJ with the murder, which, once again, I must emphasize, the US Justice system said he had nothing to do with. What else could he do? He wrote a book about the murder. Of course, he wasn't there, so he couldn't say exactly what happened, so to avoid the James Frey fate, he titled the book *If I Did It,* which of course, is very clear in the fact that he didn't do it. It is there in the title. Pre-orders on this book were astronomical, and in fact, I had already paid off my preorder and was just waiting for it to come in the mail when the Goldmen had the release of it cancelled and obtained the rights to it. One might think it an honorable thing, not wanting any money to be made off your son's death, until the Goldmen went ahead and released it anyway, making sure they got any fame and fortune that the book had to offer. Not surprisingly, in the time it took for the book to be rereleased, the hype had died off, and no one cared about the book anymore. In fact, when I got my money back from the preorder, I splurged and bought a case of really fancy, gourmet catsup, and when the Goldmen rereleased it, it never even occurred to me to buy it.

Don't get me wrong, I did feel for OJ and his misfortune, but as they say, one man's loss is another man's gain, and it just so happened that in between the time OJ's book was cancelled and the Goldmen's wasn't out yet, Gerald Ford died. And as I mentioned

4

earlier, it had to be under suspicious circumstances, because I didn't hear a word about what happened to him on the NBC Nightly News, my one and only news source.

That day, a dream of mine died. I had long wished and wanted to be Gerald Ford's Secret Service security guard, because I figured there was no risk of violent attack on his life, and by the end of it all he was probably just sitting around and napping most of the day. Seemed like an easy gig to me, the only thing that could go wrong and ruin such a great job would be Gerald Ford dying–which he did. But, we all know, when one door closes, another one opens. So, I tried to figure out how to make the best of this horrible situation (you know, my childhood dream dying) and thinking about that poor OJ, finally got published and then he didn't get published, and wondering why Brian Williams refused to tell me how Ford died, and then it all fell together. I should write a book, titled *Gerald Ford: If I Did It.*

It seemed so easy, since I had long sat and thought about what it would be like to be with Gerald Ford in his later years. Sitting around the house, napping, wearing my trousers way too high, tucking my napkin into those trousers, drinking through a straw without lifting the glass off the table–I felt I knew what it would be like to live with Gerald Ford. Of course, inevitably, I would get to his death at the end of the book, but I have already written the book on how to die, literally, and everyone would have to believe my version of the events, because Brian Williams wasn't telling them otherwise.

Of course, at the time, I didn't own my own publishing company, and I didn't have a contract with any of the big New York publishers, so even if I wrote the text of GFIIDI (that's shorthand for *Gerald Ford: If I Did It*) in the span of a week or two, found a publisher, went through all their hoops and hurdles, got the book printed, published, reviewed, hyped and on shelves, it would take months, maybe even years, and if the real book, the actual one written by OJ about how he didn't kill anyone, didn't have the momentum to last a couple of months, mine didn't stand a chance.

Looking back, this is actually one of the charging forces that led to the creation of the Linnaeus Hoffmann Publishing Company, because I never again in my life wanted a situation to present itself where I had the chance to write a book about the death of a former US President, parodying the fake confessional book of a former NFL star, and not be able to do anything about it.

I am now realizing that I did a horrible job with this introduction, because while I told you why I started the company that the book is written about, I did not tell you why I am actually writing the book. I guess that part is a bit more embarrassing. Richard Lewis works very hard to get recognition for coining the phrase "the _____ from hell," as in the date from hell or the sickle cell anemia from hell, and I don't want the same fate to befall me, having to convince people that the common everyday phrase they use without thinking about, I actually made up. So, instead of introducing the phrase into the vernacular, then going back and trying to remind people that I was indeed the one who came up with it, I wanted to stake my claim on the phrase before it is released.

"Like a lactating hobo."

As in, when I put on a suit, I make Charles Gibson look like a lactating hobo. Or, why did Katie Couric cut her hair? Now she looks like a lactating hobo. But this phrase isn't limited to network news anchors, although it would be inappropriate to use it in describing Brian Williams, but it can be used for a wide variety of comparisons. In the early 90's, you could have said, Nolan Ryan makes Bo Jackson look like a lactating hobo. Then later said Dion Sanders makes Bo Jackson look like a lactating hobo. In the same respect, Bo Jackson made Harold Baines look like a lactating hobo, who, as it turns out, makes Jose Canseco look like a lactating hobo. As I ramble it appears to me that I am not doing an adequate job of conveying the wide variety of uses for this phrase, as now I am just showing it can be used to describe MLB players as well. Just keep reading. I think you will get the idea.

ED NOTE: I overheard Bernie telling his friend Dicky that the real reason he wrote the book was in the hope Nasim Padrad would read it and want to date him.

LIFE

I had always loved Bob Newhart. And though had I deep admirations for him and desires to emulate his very essence, it was not one's typical celebrity worship: sycophantic idolatry that plagues most pubescent girls with posters of Hollywood's newest fading fad. Most obviously, I have never been a pubescent girl. Two, Bob Newhart was not a drop in the pan star; he had proven his stardom from the days of *The Button-Down Mind* through the twenty-first century. And also, most celebrity worship involves the congregants viewing their idols having a near godlike stature. I knew Bob Newhart was not godlike, meaning above common error. I had the photograph to prove it. And plus, I never had posters of him strewn across my walls. I merely had a nice portrait oil painting.

And also, it was never so much the man Bob Newhart that I wanted to emulate, but more the beloved character he played in *The Bob Newhart Show* (the sitcom, not the variety show), Robert Hartley. Of course, in the perfect world I would have probably rather followed the career and life of Bob Newhart than Bob Hartley, having a job as an accountant and hating it, then leaving it for a life as a stand-up comic that led to an amazing run with a variety show, two successful sitcoms and two more equally hilarious but appallingly unpopular sitcoms.

I was stuck in a job that I hated, but never had the guts or maybe the confidence to become unemployed and travel the comedy circuits hoping to catch the ear of an agent or producer who could give me the chance to develop a sitcom, praying for the ratings to be favorable–especially during sweeps–because that is when all of the advertisers decide how much to pay, and then doing really well during sweeps, so my show makes the network more money, so I can renegotiate my contract for the big bucks. The David Schwimmer bucks. And so on and so forth. Alright, I digress. I guess it is obvious that I had dreamed it, but I had come to a point in my life where I had to look at where I had come from, and where I was going. The path of normalcy leads to normalcy. If anything is going to change that, it has to be an outside force coming in, not one examining his life and making the conscious effort to change. Of course, the argument can be made that people have trekked their own ways, diverting from their chosen path, but there is always the outside hand, pulling them in. You can't do it alone, and that was where I was standing.

I had long wanted to make a steady income, but not do any actual work. I had read of ways to do it, such as Michael Jackson buying The Beatles' songbook and selling the rights at his will. Of course, this is one of those cases of having to have money to make money, and being on the not having side of the money line, I had to be a bit more creative. I had to get the rights to something that no one wanted, so I could get it cheap. It occurred to me that the Bayer pharmaceutical company might still own the patent and trademark for heroin. It may seem like a dumb, long shot idea, but, come on, every time you open the newspaper and see someone was busted making or distributing heroin, well, you have an instant income with the simple copyright infringement suit.

Well, let me tell you, I had never been so disappointed in my life that the Germans lost World War I. Trying to obtain the patents for this miracle respiratory system medicine, I learned that the trademarks and patents Bayer owned for heroin were "loosened" when the Germans lost, something or another, military crap I really don't understand, heroin's patent can't really be owned by anyone, including me.

I had to be resourceful. Patent something used every day that no one else had yet to think of patenting, that way when it is commonly used I could sue and get the profits. My choice was obvious.

Crystal methamphetamine. Apparently crystal meth is made right here in America, everyday, by Americans. No way to really go wrong there. Of course, this did set my life back two years, because the US Patent Office is completely inefficient, and I kind of had all of my eggs in the crystal meth basket, so I had absolutely nothing going for me and no plan B when I got the rejection letter from the patent office. However, one bright side of this massive failure on my part was I learned the weekly updates I sent to the FBI, including any changes to my appearance and whereabouts in an attempt to die with a thicker FBI file than Sinatra have actually been going in my FBI file. And now I have something else in there. And I got to hear about it in person from the FBI. And they were in my house. And they didn't find my pirated DVDs. And they were probably embarrassed when they showed up at my house and found out they were both wearing the same outfit. And I should have thought this paragraph out before I made it a semi coherent run of sentences each one led off by an unnecessary conjunction.

It was about this time that I went back to watching *Bob Newhart*.

From my run in with the FBI, and my parents' subsequent disappointment, I decided I needed a job that was the literal manifestation of honorificabilitudinitatibus. With extensive viewing of *Bob Newhart*, I knew exactly what I wanted to do with my life. I wanted to put on a suit and tie every morning, don an overcoat and fedora, ride a train, get to my office, exchange pleasantries with the staff, hang my overcoat and fedora on a hat rack, hear a neurotic say a hilarious one-liner problem, say "I'm sorry, but we are out of time," and get a big laugh. Except, you know, in real life, not on TV. My wife told me it was a stupid idea. I told Bob Newhart of my plans in a very detailed letter, to which he replied, inscribed on a signed headshot, "Bernie, Your wife is right. Bob Newhart." This is my photographic proof that Bob Newhart is not godlike or inerrant, as he is very fallible.

An all-wise and infallible god, as any god or godlike figure should be, would be much more careful to not ink such an infinite ambiguity. Even if he was correct in thinking that my wife's naïve opinion that I couldn't get work sitting in an office exchanging colloquialisms–however untrue that might be–a godlike figure would have said something a lot more along the lines of "Hey man, I may agree with your wife that your business plan sucks, but I cannot and will not ever say anything, especially in writing on a black and white photograph, ambiguous enough that no matter what argument you are currently having, she could pick it up, point to it, and say 'Oh yeah, Bob Newhart thinks I'm right.'"

So, walking away from the situation, I decided not to become a psychologist, but I did not give up my dream of having an office and wearing a suit, tie and fedora. Simply, in my plans I replaced doing comedic psychological work with sitting in the lobby of a busy medical office, eating chips whilst being the envy of the overly stressed and busy doctors, who look longingly at me, sitting there, eating my chips, not being stressed or a doctor, and becoming increasingly wealthy while doing it.

EDGAR

I always had the satisfaction of never being able to know what it feels like to ride on my younger brother's coattails through life. That's because I am the youngest of two. The same couldn't be said for my brother, Edgar, who honestly, next to me, looked like a lactating hobo. Edgar was two years older than me, so appropriately, he graduated high school two years before I did. Then I graduated high school, and went straight to college. Four years later, I graduated college. He immediately followed suit, since apparently he was just sitting around the whole time waiting to see what I would do. Clearly, since I had no direction in life, he couldn't find one either. However, he didn't know that I was working on the whole meth patent thing, so he didn't aspire to do too much in that time period. He worked on an oil well as the guy who just sits in a trailer everyday, then occasionally, one of the real oil field workers would bring in a bag of dirt, Edgar would look at it and see if there was any oil in it, and tell them there wasn't and they need to drill deeper. Or something like that. I don't really know much about it because, quite frankly, on the oil well people don't get to bathe everyday, and that is just not my scene at all, so I only occasionally visited him when he came home from the well site to his residence in the yellow city of helium, Amarillo, Texas.

There, he didn't really seem to do much but buy goats, which in itself is not that unusual of a hobby, but he lived in a second floor apartment inside the city, and you just *can't* keep goats there, es-

11

pecially when you spend three weeks of the month a hundred miles away in a trailer in BFE.

So, what Edgar would do is buy someone else's goats, but let that person keep them, and since this other person was keeping and raising the goats, Edgar paid way to much for them, to cover the cost of the food and lodging. Even though the lodging was nothing but an open field, and the food was just the grass that naturally grew there. And to add to that, Edgar did nothing to profit from the goats, I mean, milking them, shearing them, anything. The farmer did that stuff, and with Edgar's insistence, kept the profits. So Edgar would pay a farmer hundreds of dollars for each $45 goat, and not only would the farmer keep the goat and raise it just like any other goat in his herd, the farmer got all of the profits from the goat. So, just outside of Amarillo, there is a goat farmer, who every one of his goats was paid for eight times over by my brother, yet, he still kept all of the benefits of owning them. I do not really know what Edgar's thinking was, but, for a while there I considered raising goats and letting Edgar buy them.

Anyway, one day Edgar and I were talking on the phone, and I mentioned to him that I was considering starting a new business, and he decided that sound like a good idea and wanted to come on board. So, I explained to him that I wanted an office, a suit and tie, and no real work, and that was exactly what he was looking for in life, too. And we both had a suit and tie. Me more ties than Edgar, because I like buying large numbers of things that I rarely even use one of, but that was beside the point.

Now, we are not idiots, and we know that no one will hire you if your entire aspiration was to sit there, not working, while wearing a suit, which was the only reason we even had the aspirations to start up a company. We decided that we needed an employee, and a business plan, but mainly an employee. We looked at the people we knew. I had a wife, Hazel, who was a graphic designer, and I had a former roommate Chris Bellini, who could sell overpriced pork to an Orthodox Jew on a Saturday, and we had Edgar, who kind of owned some goats, and we had me, a guy with no patents to my name, but one previously published book. I still owned the rights to the book (never sold well), but I did not own the rights to the formatting or cover, and wasn't really in the position to market or vigorously sell it, because I didn't have the financial means, or desire. But if we had Hazel format it and design the cover, we would own all the rights to publish and sell it, and we could make Bellini market it, Edgar could use the oil money he hasn't spent on goats to back the venture, and I could write the book. Luckily, I had already done that part, and with one check, Edgar had already done his part, so we were free to sit back and let Hazel and Bellini work their magic. Of course, they weren't technically employed by us yet, because they hadn't made us any money, and it would be ridiculous to pay someone for not making you money. But they weren't employed by anyone else, either, so they didn't really seem to notice.

Well, Edgar and I had gotten the hard work out of the way, so like Idaho and the other gay Lutherans of the town, we were able to get every minute of rest that we could. Edgar had come down to Lubbock to help get the business off the ground, I had recently taken up golfing, because, it became quite obvious that golf is one of the more important skills for a successful business owner to have. And I was able to drag Edgar to the course with me, because all you have to do is sit in the cart with clubs in the back, pretend to hit the balls around a bit, and then incredibly attractive and underdressed women would drive up to you and offer to bring you a sandwich, and, of course, we like sandwiches. One day, after I had shot a ninety-one and Edgar had eaten a Rueben, we saw the one thing from our business plan that we were missing: an office building with a for rent sign right across from the course.

We made an appointment with the realtor to check out the place, and since it was out in the boondocks, far away from potential customers and clients, the price on the space was quite nice, and we weren't picky, so we rented the place, and the next day we were there, wearing our suits and ties, sitting in the office chairs we had delivered that morning. Of course, Hazel and Bellini weren't there yet, we were still waiting on them to make us some money before we wasted office space on them. But, there was a chiropractor, orthodontist and psychiatrist in the same complex, and even though they weren't real doctors, they did have busy receptionists and aides and assistants constantly running through the lobby, which made us feel good about ourselves when we sat there, eating chips, and making them jealous of our laid back jobs: the new owners of the Linnaeus Hoffmann Publishing Company.

goat.

(Like in the
    goat farm.)

GETTING STARTED

As you may or may not know, because I have forgotten what I wrote in the previous few chapters and don't feel like going back and rereading them, once the business started, and my book was completely formatted and ready to be rereleased onto the market, Bellini was the guy in charge of finding new talent. Finally, after weeks of Edgar and I sitting in empty offices bored out of our minds, twiddling our thumbs and wishing we had some form of entertainment, he came to us with a manuscript from an unknown author named Tobin S. Palm. It was a book called *Back Bending Sagas*. I don't quite know what it is about, because it is one of those books that you read, just to read it, but when you get to the end of the page you realize that all you did was read each word individually and didn't comprehend a single thing as a whole, because it was about as entertaining as a Paula Poundstone routine. But, it was the only book we had, besides my book, but, I didn't want to rip my book from its current publisher until we figured out how to actually publish a book, so, we really just needed something to butcher while we figured out what we were doing, and this book was perfect.

I called Tobin up to my office, and apparently Bellini had already worked his magic because Tobin was overly eager to sign away all rights to a book that he had taken years to pen, to a publisher who had published absolutely nothing. Come to find out, all I had to do to get him to sign was give him the contract and let him sign it.

But instead, with Edgar by my side, I decided to give him some helpful advice from an industry insider.

"Tobin, I am not going to lie. You're book can make millions, but it needs a different title."

"But, I am really proud of that title, it's an anagram of…"

"Yeah," I interrupted, "you don't want anagrams. What you need is a pun."

"A pun?" asked Tobin.

"Yeah. You don't think that I sold three hundred copies of *The Good Gatsby* because people wanted to read it. I sold three hundred copies of *The Good Gatsby* because somewhere, out there, there were people who knew that they needed to read *The Great Gatsby,* but when they typed it in on Amazon they had a brain fart and somehow ended up with my book. And they were better off for it. Then they told their friends to buy my book, and they inadvertently bought *The Great Gatsby* thinking that's what their friend suggested, then they kept wondering when they were going to get to the part where Gatsby steals the uretheral sounds, but it never happened."

"You only sold three hundred copies?" asked Tobin.

"Yes, Bernie Douglas! But *The Great Gatsby* sold thousands of copies while my book was on the market, and you can only assume how many of those people mistakenly bought it looking for *The Good Gatsby,* because *The Great Gatsby* has been out for what, eighty years, anyone who wanted it already had it, so I really count it that I sold closer to 30,000 books. And F. Scott Fitzgerald's family is not doing anything to compensate me for that."

"So," asked Tobin, "you are wanting me to make my title a parody of another book's title, which will in turn benefit the other book, but not mine?"

"No, not at all," I reassured. "What do you think got me those first three hundred sales? Bernie Douglas!"

"Plus, Bernie did it wrong," Edgar insisted. "He made a subtle change in the title that people would only pick up on if they typed in the name wrong. What you need to do is pick up on the shortened version of a book's name, and then add to that. See, if you title your book *Chicken Soup for the Oviducts,* then when someone searches for *Chicken Soup,* they would find your book and buy it."

"But," Tobin protested, "my book does not really have the same audience as the *Chicken Soup* books at all."

"We know that," I explained. "Because the *Chicken Soup* books have an audience. You don't."

"Isn't that your job with the marketing though?"

"This is marketing. We are teaching you our secrets. Bernie Douglas."

"Why do you keep saying your own name?"

"I used to go to therapy. The therapist said I need to compliment myself more."

"Bernie thinks his name is a compliment," Edgar added.[2]

"Look," said Tobin, "I will sign with you guys, and I will let you publish my book, but the name stays the same. End of story."

And he signed the deal. Then we got to work. Bellini set up a marketing campaign, got in touch with independent booksellers, scheduling a six state book tour with signings and readings, and since one of the states was Texas, that's the equivalent of maybe 15 non California or New York states. Then he set up an internet advertising campaign, and really got a lot of buzz going. Hazel first designed the cover so Bellini could use it in the advertising, then I believe she designed the advertising flyers and website and everything before she actually formatted the book. Apparently you only need less than a month from the time it is at the printers to the time it is on the shelf, and they had a four-month campaign worked up.

Three months before the book's scheduled release date Hazel had it completely formatted and ready to send it off to the printers. Within a few weeks, they sent us a galley to look over, which was pretty much exactly what the book would be, except not bound. After that she sent the galley to a freelance proofreader named Heath, famed for editing *The Good Gatsby* and making up the game Vikings v. Locals, which is an awesome game—and almost as widespread as the games I made up—and once Heath gave the book his approval, Hazel ordered six more galleys, packaged them up and addressed

---

[2] Actually, Bernie saw William Shatner do it on a lawyer show and stole the idea. I don't think he realizes it, though. – Bellini.

them to six different literary review magazines, which I personally took to the post office.

In the mean time, Edgar and I had bought a resonator guitar and ukulele, respectively, and would play them in the office in between our golf and post office breaks. I also took a few days to decorate my office with Arthur Singer bird prints and a framed picture the size and shape of my television, which was solid black, except for white text in the middle that said "Executive Producer Dick Wolf," that way, whenever I walked into my office I would feel nice and relaxed like I had just gotten through watching a magnificent episode from the *Law & Order* TV franchise. I also did a tour of local community events, teaching people how to play one of the games I made up, which is a lot more fun that Vikings v. Locals.

It's called The Nipple Game (the other one is The Dick Wolf Game, but being how that one is already a huge international hit, I don't see a need to explain the rules, as everybody already knows them), and anyone can play it; every day even, if his or her hygiene is good enough. First, you take a hot shower with out the exhaust fan turned on. When you get out of the shower, dry off and do whatever you normally do, and wrap your towel around your waist, and stand across from your fogged mirror *exactly* an arm's length away, (your arm's length, not someone else's), then extend your arm, and touch the mirror with the pad of your thumb exactly where you think your nipple is, and with one circular motion, swipe a small, nipple sized circle out of the fog. Then put your arm back down to your side, and see if your nipple is visible in the unfogged section. If it is, then go on to the next step. If it is not, make small adjustments to your body position to make sure that your nipple is exactly in the unfogged section. Then, extend your other arm to the mirror, and make another nipple sized circle in the fog where you think your other nipple is. Then put your arms back down at your side, and if you can see both of your nipples clearly in the mirror, you win.

Finally, the day arrived and *Back Bending Sagas* hit the shelves. And though it did not really have a strong shelf presence in the big name chain bookstores, our online book sales were quite amazing. When *The Good Gatsby* came out, its ranking on the Amazon worked it's way up to 32,000 within the first week, but never surpassed it, eventually landing in the hundred thousands, where it fluctuated every which way. *Back Bending Sagas* worked its way up to 10,000 with just the preorders, and throughout the proceeding months, it never failed to hit anywhere from 5,000 to 15,000. We had set it up as a print on demand title, rather than printing a huge first run, because, quite frankly, we figured if we printed up 10,000 we would be paying warehouse storage fees on it for ages. But our first quarterly invoice showed sales much higher than 10,000 units.

So, I ended my contract with my previous publisher and set up to rerelease *The Good Gatsby* with Linnaeus Hoffmann. Per my previous contract, I had to redo the formatting and cover, which as you already know Hazel did quite well, but I decided to skip the whole promotional/book signing tours that Tobin did, because I have seen the authors sitting in local book stores, having no one buy their books, and I just didn't see myself doing that. When the galley came back from the printer, Hazel wanted to send it off to be reviewed, but I was impatient and didn't want Tobin to get too great of a sales lead, so I skipped the whole marketing/review process as well and got my book straight onto Amazon.

Inexplicably, my book did not sell well on Amazon. Almost no copies. Despite my pun name. I knew it was Tobin, that sleaze bag bag who Joey Buttafuoco makes look like a lactating hobo, trying to sabotage me for trying to change his book's title. So for $700, I set it up on Amazon to where every time someone was on Tobin's site, it offered them the chance to buy my book with it, and, for the buyers smart enough to realize it, if they bought Tobin's book with my book, I set it out to be the same price as buying Tobin's book with shipping, but by putting my book on there, it pushed the order over the amount needed to get free shipping, so most people noticed that they are going to spend $26 no matter what, but they had a choice between spending it on one book or two.

So what can I say? My book sold quite well. Not bad, eh?

THE ECTO COOLER/JUDGE JUDY EXPERIENCE

After the success of Linnaeus Hoffman's first two books, I started to have quite a bit of disposable income to spend on small luxuries. One day I was on the phone with a private bidder representing me at a New York City *Hollywood Memorabilia Auction*. They were selling an original Fozzie Bear, used in the movie *The Muppets Take Manhattan*. Fozzie had always been my favorite Muppet, and probably my third favorite comedian, after Carrot Top and Bob Newhart, but right before Joey Bishop, Jon Lovitz and Andy Kaufman. Gallagher is in there somewhere as well, but I am not quite sure on his ranking at the moment.

This was my one chance to own an actual celebrity, because most celebrities are real people and the United States outlawed the owning of people many years back. I was hoping to be able to pick Fozzie up for about $5,000, but Rowlf the Dog was sold right before Fozzie went up on the block, and he had sold for $7,500. This had me nervous about my possibilities of buying Fozzie, because my entire auction budget was $12,500, and surely Fozzie would go for a lot more than Rowlf. It seemed like as soon as the auction started, I was over my budget. I started to panic. I ran to the lobby and started screaming.

"Edgar! Edgar, I need help!"

Edgar came out of his office, looking quite worried. It was obvious that he felt the intensity of the situation.

"What's wrong, what happened?" he asked.

"I need to borrow some money, fast!"

"What happen?"

"The auction started for Fozzie, and it is already over my budget, but I have to get it. Hurry, it's going on right now!"

"How much is it up to?"

"$5,000."

"But you have $12,500 to spend on him."

"I know, but I kinda already bought Rowlf."

"What? For weeks you have been talking about how much you wanted Fozzie, you saved up your money, and now you blew it all on Rowlf?"

"I was thinking about how he used to be on *The Jimmy Dean Show,* and I really liked the Jimmy Dean sausage biscuits I ate this morning, Jimmy Dean donated money to my alma mater, it just felt right at the time."

"You spent all your money on Rowlf because you like sausage biscuits?"

"And he donated to my alma mater."

"But you don't like your alma mater."

"Yeah, but you can never put a price on the nortelrye you received. Look, the auction is going on right now, are you going to give me money or not?"

"Fine, I'll give you $7,500, but that's it."

I ran straight back to my phone, and my bidder informed me that the auction was still going on, I told her to bid up to $12,500. Edgar came in.

"What are you doing now?" he asked.

"Buying Fozzie."

"I'm not giving you this money without a written agreement that you will pay this back."

"Look Edgar, we will write it up later, but I'm kind of busy right now so..."

"No. No contract, no Fozzie."

I pulled out a yellow pad and quickly scribbled out an agreement. "There, just sign that."

"Not without a notary," Edgar replied.

"What! This auction could be over and I could lose Fozzie any second and you want a notary?"

"I am not going to court to get money back from you with the only agreement we have something you doodled on a legal pad unless it is notarized."

"Fine you want it notarized, we'll get it notarized."

I ran into the building's main lobby where the doctors' receptionists were.

"Are any of you a notary public?" I yelled.

"I am," said a small Hispanic lady, who I often talked to while I was eating chips, but honestly have no idea who she was or who she worked for.

"Here, can you notarize this real fast?"

"Sure I just need to see your IDs real fast."

Edgar took his out.

"For what!" I yelled.

"To confirm your identification for the signature."

"We have worked in the same building for months and I have to confirm my identity?"

"It's the law Bernie."

"See, you know who I am."

"It's the law."

"But my wallet's in my office."

"Go get it," she insisted.

"Fine." I started sprinting towards my office. Edgar was following behind me.

"Why did take your wallet out of your pocket?"

"My right butt cheek went numb." I grabbed my wallet and made it back to the notary. She checked our IDs, we signed the contract, she put her seal on it, and I ran double time to my office. My bidder told me that I had won Fozzie for $11,000. I thanked her, hung up the phone, leaned back and propped my feet on my desk. Then I heard a shrilling "BERNIE!" come from the common lobby.

I went out there, and saw that Bellini and Hazel were standing around the receptionist's desk, obviously curious from the excitement, now studying our contract.

"Who wrote this?" Hazel asked.

"I did."

"And did Edgar read it?"

"I don't know, probably."

"Edgar, get in here!" she yelled.

A few moments passed, and then Edgar obligingly came in.

"Did you read this?" she asked, waving the contract in his face.

"I skimmed it."

"Read it."

Edgar took the contract from Hazel's hand and read aloud, "'Bernie Douglas agrees to pay Edgar Douglas the sum of $7,500, received for the purchase of Fozzie Bear, interest free, in either cash or Capri Sun.' Signed and notarized. It looks likes everything is there."

"You let Bernie spend $7,500 on a puppet and you are letting him pay you back with fruit juice?"

"Actually, I just gave him the money he was short. He spent a lot more that."

"Bernie how much did you spend."

"Well, um, about $16,000, but it was a business write off."

"You spent $16,000 on a puppet?"

"N-No, it was on two puppets, but it was a business write off."

"What else did you buy?"

"Rowlf."

"Rowlf? Rowlf? You don't even like Rowlf. You say he is the sham while Fozzie is out there working hard—look, I am not having this conversation. How is that a business expense?"

"Edgar and I can play with them here."

At that point I really stopped listening to what she was saying, because it was angry, high pitched, loud, and directed at me. Later that night when everything cooled down, Edgar came home with Hazel and me for dinner. I fixed nachos. I went to the fridge, and being the generous guy I am, immediately began to pay off my debt by offering Edgar a Capri Sun. He opted to take an Ecto Cooler instead.

Even though Ecto Cooler had been discontinued in 2001, Slimer left the box in 1997, and the Ecto Cooler Edgar drank was one of the original boxes from the 80's with the oranges and tangerines on it. I had purchased it many years ago, and have never been able to find another one like it. I consider it to be priceless, but if I had to put a price on it, I would make it $3,500, not coincidently because that is the amount I owe Edgar.

So, as you can imagine I was quite taken aback the next week when Edgar came into my office and asked if I had any plans for a repayment schedule.

"But I paid you back completely that day."

"You didn't pay me back at all."

"Yes I did. You came to my house, we ate nachos, watched some TV executively produced by Dick Wolf, and I completely paid you back."

"With what?"

"The Ecto Cooler. You can't get that stuff anymore. It's priceless, so we are kind of even."

"No, the contract said that it had to be cash or Capri Sun. Ecto Cooler is Hi C."

"So what's the difference? They are both fruit drinks. If I would have paid you with a check would you have rejected that too because the contract said cash?"

"Bernie, unlike you, I am not some five year old who packs his juice box in his lunch sack everyday and kisses his mommy goodbye on his way to school. No, Capri Sun is the only bagged drink available on the market that feels real but doesn't look like a breast implant with a straw in it."

"Ooh, want to play with my Muppets?"

"Did they come in?"

"Yeah, I got them this morning."

"Ok, I'll be Rowlf."

"Dangit Eddie, I want to be Rowlf."

"You're Fozzie Bernie, you know you're Fozzie. You've always been Fozzie."

"But Rowlf makes Fozzie looks like a lactating hobo. I want to be Rowlf."

"I know you do, but you're not. That's why we had to get you Fozzie."

"Fine, but no throwing tomatoes this time."

While puppeteering, Edgar and I had a long talk, trying to get a feel for where we were coming from. Basically, I wasn't going to pay Edgar any money because he just drank about eight grand worth of Ecto Cooler, and Edgar wasn't going to pay me, because well, he thinks it is uncouth for a person to make you eat nachos then charge you thousands of dollars when you are inevitably thirsty.

We had pretty much decided that since Edgar basically took Rowlf away from me and cared for him as his own to "save me from psychological and emotional damage" we could call it even.

Thank Vishnu I had a TV in my office.

Judge Judy was just going off the air, and just as it was finishing, a quick disclaimer popped up, and it was gone before we could read it, but the only thing we caught was something to the effect that both litigates were paid from a pool and any rulings were funded from this pool.

Jackpot.

Do you understand? If we go on *Judge Judy*, and she says that I should pay Edgar, then they will take the money out of the fund, give it to Edgar, and then split up the rest of the money and give to both of us. If I win, then they just split the money two ways. And to top it all off, free trip to New York.[3] What's better than that? Well, I know what's better than that, but no syndicated court shows film in Sheboygan.

Unfortunately, you can't just call up Judge Judy and request to be on her show. She has scouts who scour small claims courts looking for interesting cases that would work on the show, then the producers have you sign contracts removing your case from real courts and agreeing to go on their show, let Judy make her little decision, take the free money and not sue each other any more.

So we had to start in the small claims courts. Not a problem. Of course I had no idea what to do, but that's ok, because Edgar was suing me, so I got to just sit back, do nothing, and get sued. Then I

---

[3] This is one of those instances in a memoir where author's memories trump actual fact that James Frey keeps talking about. Judge Judy is apparently taped in LA, but I could have sworn we were in New York, plus, the musical theatre scene in LA is nothing compared to Broadway.

had to make good on some connections I had made. Now, this may surprise you to learn, but before I learned it was mainly a pastime for gay men looking to meet other gay men, I did a lot of musical theatre. That introduced me to many people who, like myself, did not want to have real jobs, but unlike myself, had not watched enough *Bob Newhart* to have the desire to sit in an office wearing a suit. So they took daddy's credit card and moved to New York to break into the biz, which I guess is musical theatre. But, luckily, it's hard to get into musical theatre, so they take any job that has anything to do with TV, theatre, and film, which includes scouting small claims courts for *Judge Judy*.

Of course, I knew absolutely no one who worked for *Judge Judy*, but I did once share the stage with a guy who was starring in a Neil Simon remake on Broadway, and he actually was in contact with some major TV producers, who though they had no contact with Judge Judy, were the guys that the Judge Judy producers would love to cuddle up with in front of a fire on a bear skin rug with a bottle of cognac. So, the big TV producers thought our case was hilarious and called and told the *Judge Judy* producers about it. The *Judge Judy* producers thought that the big producers were really, really awesome, so, what do you know, before the end of it Edgar and I were sharing adjoining hotel rooms in New York City waiting to present our case to Judge Judy.

We arrived at the studio, Edgar in his best suit, and me, wanting to share in the holiday spirit, wore a red oversized sweater with a Christmas moose, wearing a red and green scarf. (To save confusion in that last sentence, the moose was wearing the scarf. I was just wearing a sweater. With no scarf.) It wasn't until the producers told me our episode wouldn't be aired until May that I realized I was about to look like a lactating hobo on national television.

We entered the courtroom. We were both sworn in, and Edgar was the first to present his case. In an interesting side note, everyone was quiet, waiting for Judge Judy to enter, and before she did, the producers told everyone to pretend to be deep in conversation so she could pretend to call everyone to order. Edgar's presentation was pretty much straight forward. He gave me a loan, agreed to be paid back in Capri Sun or cash, was paid back in neither, and now wanted some money. Or Capri Sun.

It was my turn. Now, at this point, Edgar and I had learned *Judge Judy* doesn't pay out of a flat fee pool where the remainder is split, they pay a per day appearance fee, so we decided on two things. I needed counter sue, so we could both get the most money out of the situation, we both needed to win our suits, so we could get the maximum money out of this, and I needed to make this last a week.

To ensure this case would last for a long time, I started out by giving a history of Ecto Cooler. I got to year 1984 and a half when she told me to shut up. So I told her that it was an understood verbal contract that the Ecto Cooler would replace the Capri Sun as a payment. She told me that we had a contract stating Capri Sun, not Ecto Cooler. Then she asked me what my counter suit was. I told her that since the Ecto Cooler was irreplaceable, then I was suing for the maximum amount. She said you can't sue for the repayment of a gift, and threw my suit out, then awarded Edgar the full amount he was asking. I had lost in less time than it would have taken me to watch me lose on TV.

It was like we lost on *Big Brother*. After the show over, we were whisked back to our rooms and immediately had to gather our things and leave. On the way to the airport, I asked Edgar what we were going to do with the winnings. He told me to shove it, and also told me he was keeping Rowlf.

STATUE

I was something of a civic leader in Lubbock. At one point, I was offered a pretty prestigious post, but I had to turn it down because I wanted to be free to serve my community, and not held down by litigation, red tape and scrutiny that public office would entail. But I did want to do something to help my community, beautify my city, and bring a sense of civic pride to Lubbock, all the while educating the citizens about the history of our dear city.

Everyone knows downtown there is a statue of Buddy Holly, because he is Lubbock's native son and really awesome. Also, everyone knows that Natalie Maines of the Dixie Chicks wrote in a song that she thinks there should be a statue of her in Lubbock. That won't happen because she is a pompous jerk and Buddy Holly makes her look like a lactating hobo. But Lubbock does love to honor the creative and artistic types that have passed through the city, most recognizably with street names (Mac Davis, anyone?), but, as I said, there is a statue of Buddy Holly.

The thing that has always bothered me is though Lubbock loves to honor the creative spirits who have resided in the city, except for Natalie Maines, because she is a jerk, they have never honored arguably the most successful artist to ever live in this town, Meat Loaf.

Meat Loaf attended Lubbock Christian College, (now University) for a very brief stint in 1965. Although he left town quickly and never came back, surely that is because he hated the university and not the city, because that is very understandable.

Though he only lived in this town for a brief period, I can't shake the feeling as I walk down the streets, that these are the streets Meat Loaf walked. When I sit on a park bench, it is a park bench that Meat Loaf may have sat on. When I use a fork at a long established restaurant, there is a real possibility that Meat Loaf had put the very same fork in his mouth. It's overwhelming sometimes.

That's why I wanted to honor this man. I initially wanted to erect of statue of him right in the middle of the Lubbock Christian grounds, but they said no. Actually, they were quite adamant about it. Then I tried to get the statue built in the Buddy Holly Plaza, but the City of Lubbock said no. Actually, they were quite adamant about it. Now, I must go back and correct myself for calling the area around the Buddy Holly statue the Buddy Holly Plaza, because the name had to be changed because Buddy Holly's widow, who could quite accurately be described in many of the same ways used to describe Natalie Maines, made Lubbock drop the use of Buddy Holly's name unless they paid licensing fees. Also, Lubbock had to drop the use of Holly's name from the Buddy Holly music festival. But anyway, I couldn't build the statue there.

That's the thing that is wrong with Lubbock. They don't like statues. Even when they could have a completely free statue, they said no. I think it is because we are uncultured here. Years ago I had gone to Ireland, and there were statues everywhere. Dublin had multiple statues of the same person all over town, and just traveling around the country, you see a statue of Charlie Chaplin at his favorite beach, Bill Clinton in a city where he golfed, and statue of Bono looking like a smug goof. Well, that last one is just an assumption, but if there isn't one out there yet, there will be, because Ireland understands the importance of statues.

It had become quite apparent that even though I was about to do a great favor for the citizens of Lubbock, I was going to get help from no one. So, I bought the closest thing I could to the Lubbock Christian campus, a small house, tore it down, and began my construction.

Well, actually, I tore it down, then began looking for an artist, which is harder than I had imagined. Like, say, you want a suit. You go to your tailor, tell him what you want, he measures you, two weeks later you go in, he puts what he has so far on you, does another measurement, just to make sure everything is going correctly, and then, another two weeks, you go in, try it on, pay the man, and you have a suit. There is no ego you have to tolerate, tailors don't get all pissy if they are asked to make a suit that doesn't show their Dadaistic roots or tendencies. You go in, say what you want, pay, and get it.

Artists are all quite useless. And by this I do not mean all people who make a living from their creativities, but I mean strictly those whose work can be shown in a gallery. The problem with "traditional" artists (painters, sculptors, etc.), over artists who work in film and word, is that the traditional artists have no studios, or editors, or publishers standing over them telling them when they need to get over themselves and make a decent product. Because, many artists simply think if something has never been seen before, then it is creative, new, and edgy, or something of the sort. But many times, it's just stupid. Absolute drivel. But they keep amassing crap with no one telling them to stop it, and all they are doing is keeping themselves as a community unemployed and living in studio apartments.

If I could take Meat Loaf, put him in a box, fill the box with wax, let it harden, fill it with an acid that would completely dissolve Meat Loaf but not harm the wax, then fill that void caused by Meat Loaf's dissolvation with bronze, let it harden, and then melt away the wax, and have that exact replication of Meat Loaf in bronze, that is what I would want. Exactly. To get an artist agree to give me a statue that looks like this, however, is about as difficult as getting Meat Loaf to agree to sit in my wax box.

But, I found out that the secret was to get an artist who had already been beaten up by the world, had lost all of his ambitions and purpose in life, had his rose tinted glasses knocked into a gutter while living on the streets and fighting with another homeless guy over a half eaten cheeseburger, only to have the glasses crushed under the heel of some heiress to granddaddy's fortune who in all actuality wouldn't even be capable of handling the finances of a Girl Scout cookie drive. Also, he may or may not have a drug addiction. That's the guy who will do anything for money. You just need to find the one with infinite talent who should have been someone but never will. And once you know where to look, that's not hard.

Find a New York City slumlord. To do this, call up any friends that you had when you were doing musical theatre, and ask him for the phone number of his first landlord in New York City. Call up his landlord and tell him you are interested in buying out someone's lease, and ask if there is anyone in a small studio apartment facing eviction. Tell him that you would be interested in talking to the tenant to take over his lease to save the landlord the hassle of eviction. When he gives you the phone numbers, start down the list, and every time a new tenant answers, just simply ask "Actor, writer, comic or artist?" Most people will say they are all four. Trust me, you want to skip them, and go with the one word answers. When you get the artist, tell him what you want, and offer an upfront price that will pay three months' rent. Problem solved.

So after months of hearing complaints about the "eye sore" I created by demolishing a house and doing nothing else with the vacant lot, Lubbock was finally in for the surprise of it's life. But first, I had to have a temporary structure built on the land to hide the statue until it was ready, even though it was sculpted and still residing in New York. But, the residents really seemed excited that at least something was going on at the lot.

When the artist, Will Porter, called me to tell me the sculpture was complete, I immediately printed out a UPS address label and mailed it to him. A few days later Will called me to tell me that he had taped the label to the sculpture just as I had instructed, called UPS to have it picked up, but when the delivery man arrived to get it, apparently he just laughed and left. I tried calling UPS's corporate offices, but they were no help either. So I had to go get it myself. I rented one of those self-mover vans and headed up to New York. I had just gotten out of Texas when I returned the truck and bought a plane ticket to New York.

I am kind of embarrassed to say that I never left the Newark airport, I did all the arrangements by phone. When I arrived at the airport, I realized how I wanted nothing more than to not have to drive back to Lubbock. So I found the yellow pages, called a trucking company, and arranged the pick up and delivery, returned to the ticket counted and bought my ticket home. Besides the money I wasted on the plane tickets and rental truck, I think the thing that I felt stupidest about was the week's worth of luggage that I had packed for a day trip.

Back in Lubbock, I gave Bellini the day off from his regular duties as authors' assistant/talent scout/marketer, so he could get in touch with every media outlet and make sure they knew of the unveiling of the statue. But, of course, it was a highly guarded secret what was being unveiled. In all seriousness, it really shouldn't have been a surprise to anyone, because I honestly asked just about everyone I could think of for permission to build the Meat Loaf statue on their land, but, apparently no one really gave a second thought to my request after we got off the phone, or even took my request seriously.

But on the day of the unveiling there were three news cameras, and one newspaper reporter, plus the hordes of bored Lubbock Christian students and one or two Lubbockites who didn't have the typical nine to five job to keep them occupied on the Tuesday morning. I had draped a purple cloth over the statue so no one could see what was waiting for them. After a pledge of allegiance, invocation and a singing of Herman's Hermits "I'm Henry the Eighth I Am" by Bellini, I pulled the cloth, revealing the statue: Meat Loaf as his character Eddie from *The Rocky Horror Picture Show* sitting on his motorcycle, saxophone strapped to his back, complete with a plaque on the base of the statue containing the complete lyrics to "Hot Patootie–Bless My Soul," which Richard O'Brien happily gave me written permission to use.

The crowd dispersed before the benediction and the singing of "Hot Patootie." In fact, by the time I announced that I was donating the land and statue to Lubbock Christian (in theory, not on paper because they would tear it down) for use as a prayer garden, only a handful of students were left in attendance. All of my subsequent unveiling of Meat Loaf statues attracted increasingly smaller crowds and media coverage.

Meat Loaf
Statue

BERNIE'S FAILED SENATE RUN AND SUBSEQUENT FALL INTO A BITTER DEPRESSION WHERE HE TRIED TO PUNISH PEOPLE WITH STATUES THEY DIDN'T WANT

from *Edgar Douglas: An Autobiography of the Future Written in the Past Tense*

Bernie often times spoke of the "prestigious post" he was offered. The one he turned down out of the goodness of his heart. In truth, he almost became a United States Congressman. He was honestly a shoe in for the position. This made his defeat come with great humiliation. I am surprised he even references it at all.

It started out when Bernie had a chance meeting with the chair of the Lubbock Democratic Party at a luncheon he probably wasn't invited to. Everyone was kind of complaining about how the same person had been in congress for close to a dozen years. He was about to run unopposed again. Now, it was a simple fact around here that if you were a Democrat you would get about 33 percent of the vote. If you were a Republican you would get about 60 percent. The rest was filled by the independent or third party. That was the way it was. I wasn't privy to what went on in the meeting. I just know Bernie came out of it with all intentions of running for congress. Someone gave him all the information to get on the ballot.

He did get on the ballot. I think he realized that he was destined for the usual 33 percent. That is why he didn't do a lot of work to win. He knew he wouldn't. Plus, he was really into the show *Curb Your Enthusiasm*. I mean, really into *Curb Your Enthusiasm*. He would have *CYE* parties where he would invite all his friends over to watch it. He would lock them in the room and not open the door until they were done watching it. All of it. On DVD. Back to back. Every season. Every episode. And it was a long running series. That is several days of straight television for a single program. He brought in gourmet sandwiches every eight hours. Most of his friends fell asleep or became disinterested fairly quickly. Bernie never let his eyes leave the screen. He watched intently. He laughed intensely. Needless to say, he still ran around saying everything was, "Pretty good. Pret-tay, pret-tay, pret-tay good," long after that phrase should have died and gone away.

He still made campaign commercials. He just didn't try. Each commercial consisted of an announcer who would say the name of an issue. Any issue. It wouldn't say Bernie's position on the issue. Just the name. Then it would cut to Bernie standing there saying, "Pretty good. Pret-tay, pret-tay, pret-tay good." The commercials were catchy. I will give him that. People without knowledge of *CYE* would sometimes think they were clever. I would often overhear people in restaurants say "Education. Pretty good. Pret-tay, pret-tay, pret-tay good."

Bernie was well on his way to that third of the votes. Then his Republican opponent was in a car wreck. He was drunk. His passenger was killed. It was too late to put someone else on the ballot. Bernie's main opponent was charged with a DUI and intoxicated manslaughter. Bernie was going to win the election.

With one week to the election Bernie completely changed his campaign strategy. He had a press conference stating he was leaning wholly on the "Our National Anthem Really Sucks" platform. He just got really whiney and complained about the national anthem. Said he was going to try to get all public performances of it banned. He claimed he would do nothing else during his time in office. Unless lobbyists paid him a lot of money to do other things. Then he would pretty much do whatever they said. He also made the promise that next election he would campaign on the bald eagle is a Pollacky national bird platform.

He started this new campaign after the early voting. He got 80 percent of the early voting votes. He got 4 percent of the Election Day votes. The Libertarian won the election. He was the only Libertarian in congress. Bernie was absolutely humiliated. He could understand losing to a Republican in West Texas. But to lose to a Libertarian anywhere? Not easy to handle.

So Bernie was embarrassed and depressed. Anyone would be. He became pissed off at the world. Well, really, he became pissed off at West Texas. He vowed if they wouldn't let him push his ideas in congress, then he would push his ideas on the streets. Literally. And as it turned out, more than hating the national anthem, Bernie really liked the singer Meat Loaf.

ROHONC CODEX

This was going to be big. Before, Linnaeus Hoffmann had no doubt made Edgar and me successful, with the sales of my books and Tobin's books combined bringing in over a million dollars profit for the company, but this one was going to be bigger than any of that.

Oprah put a book published by Linnaeus Hoffmann in her book club. No lie. And, you know who found this book for the company? Me. Bernie Douglas. (Bernie Douglas!) And not only did I find the book, I found the author, Dicky Maloney, told him exactly what to write, and the next day he had a completed manuscript for me. I had come to the point where I didn't even see a reason to keep Bellini around anymore. All he was supposed to do was find authors, sign them to Linnaeus Hoffmann, and get a completed manuscript from them on schedule. After that Hazel does everything. I admit, he did find us Tobin, but that was *years* before this, and once I started giving away free copies of my books, I became the number one selling Linnaeus Hoffmann author. And, it goes without saying, that whenever Oprah put her stamp on Dicky's book, with mine taped to the back, we would sell astronomically more books than Tobin ever did.

I had met Dicky at a local diner I frequented every weekday. Dicky was a college student, asked me what I did for a living, being that everyday I was in a suit or a cardigan, and kind of stood out at the diner.

"Is publishing hard work?" he asked.

"Actually, no, it just all kind of happens," I said, cutting up my Monday usual, a foot long hot dog with mustard and onions.

"So how do you find the authors?"

"I hired a guy who does that."

"And has he found anyone really good?"

"No. He brings us these crappy run of the mill *New York Times* best sellers. You know, they're not funny. No talking animals, I mean, their whole books are all just filler."

"So, what would you like to see in your authors?" Dicky asked.

"Well, maybe something about talking animals, you know? Like Fievel. You know, that was a good movie. I would love to publish a Fievel book."

"Well," Dicky asked, "why don't you write one."

"A Fievel novel?"

"Yeah, you said that you publish your own stuff, why not write a book about Fievel?"

I had to explain this to him carefully. "Well, there are lot of legal issues with writing things using other people's characters. For instance, if I wanted to write a Tom Sawyer and Huck Finn book, I could, perfectly legally, because all rights and ownership issues have long expired, but with characters like Fievel that were created during the latter half of the Twentieth Century, the ownership is still there, and honestly, all the work that you would put into something that can probably never be published, it's just crazy. And with Steven Spielberg producing it, there is no way a guy like me could get permission to use the characters. Even if I were someday lucky enough to get the permissions, I would have to pay so much money upfront and in royalties, that it would never be worth it financially.

"Plus, all the fan fiction I write is based on *The Land Before Time*."

"*Land Before Time*?" asked Dicky.

"Yeah, the animated movie from the 80's, with the dinosaurs, traveling across..."

"I know the story."

"So I guess you know why I have to write it."

"But isn't that a Spielberg production, too?"

"Oh yeah. And George Lucas."

"So what was with this 'It'll never be worth it schpiel?'"

"That was about *Fievel*. He still has his dignity. Spielberg and Lucas both took two craps on *The Land Before Time* years ago."

Then I kind of zoned out. It's not my fault. I had been reading *Slaughterhouse-Five* that morning, and, mmmph, it gets in my head. Dicky snapped me out of it.

"Dude, what are you staring at?"

"Hmm, oh nothing, I just get distracted."

"You are staring at the wall."

"I'm sorry, I'm just kinda out of it."

"What's wrong?"

"Oh, nothing's wrong, I just. When I read books, I really, really visualize them in my head, and usually visualize the main protagonist as me, and then cast famous people as the rest of the characters, as if it is a movie staring me."

"I'm a with you so far."

"Well, usually it doesn't effect me, but I was reading *Slaughterhouse-Five,* and I was picturing myself as Billy, and Nasim Pedrad as Montana Wildhack, and, man, it was just so great, I can't shake it from my head."

"Nasim Pedrad, the hot chick from SNL? I love her!"

"YES! I can't believe you said that! I am completely in love with that woman! In fact, my wife gave me permission to marry her if she ever asks!"

"If she does ever ask you, could you just let me date her for a week or so before you do get married? I won't put the moves on her, but, I just think she would enjoy getting to know me!"

"Same here! I don't even plan putting the moves on her after we are married, I just know I would enjoy getting to know her, and she me."

"Dude," Dicky said, "I just want to hang out with you forever now."

"Me too. Tell ya what. Come work at Linnaeus Hoffmann. You don't even have to do anything except supervise Bellini. It will be great."

"Well, I'm flattered, but I have a different idea. I want to write a book. I'm not creative, I have no ideas, and I hate *The Land Before Time,* but I want to write. Not some fiction that middle-aged women will read in the airport, but something that smart people will read, ya know? Something that will make me be the expert on those shows on the History Channel, like when they are talking about Gettysburg and they have an old guy on there talking about it and at the bottom of the screen, it has his name and says author of some book I have never heard of. I want to write that book I have never heard of."

"You know what," I said, "I know exactly what you are talking about. And you are completely right. You do not have to have a clue what you are talking about, as long as you wrote a book about it."

"Yeah, that's what I want to do!"

"You ever heard of Patricia Cornwell?"

"No."

"Well, she is this woman, and she thinks she solved the Jack the Ripper case. Actually, I don't think she really thinks that, but she wrote a book saying that the artist Walter Sickert was Jack the Ripper. She claims to have developed this theory because she saw a Sickert painting and said it was scary. She has further strengthened her case saying that when he was a baby he had surgery on his genitals that made it impossible to have sex so he became Jack the Ripper and raped people. And of course, the surgery on his genitals was done by a proctologist on his rectum. And, he even fathered children despite the surgery on his genitals that was really on his rectum left him impotent."

"So, your just saying she's full of crap, right?"

"Yeah, but when the History Channel does stories about Jack the Ripper, they have her talking on there with her name on the bottom of the screen and the name of the book she wrote."

"I can do that," Dicky said.

"Well, yeah, *anyone* can do that, but, you want to do something that isn't so blatantly wrong, so that way when you are on the History Channel, they won't have to have someone come on as soon as you are done talking saying why you are wrong." I paused, then spoke, "Do you do good with foreign languages?"

"Yeah, I'm decent," Dicky said complacently.

"If you can figure out codes and foreign languages, I know something that will guarantee you get on the History Channel."

"What?"

"There is a book called the Rohonc Codex that was found in Hungary, and it is written in some ancient language that to this day no one has decoded. If you can figure it out, I will publish that book."

And that was it. The very next day Dicky came into my office with a completely translated manuscript of the Rohonc Codex. Since it was more of a historical/culturally significant book than the usual stuff I churn out, I told Hazel that I wanted it done with the most basic format and a plain, text only cover with the author's picture. It was no problem for her, and it was basically already formatted, and within an hour she had it back to me and on the way to the printer.

It was less than three weeks after my initial meeting with Dicky that his translation of the Rohonc Codex, dubbed *Rohonc Codex: The Complete English Translation* was available for online sales. However, at the Linnaeus Hoffmann office, it went by almost unnoticed. In fact, I don't think Edgar or Bellini even knew we had published it, and we spent no advertising dollars on it, which is why it came as such a surprise to us all when we got a call from Harpo Productions saying Oprah wanted the book to be in her book club. And, honestly I am thankful that Hazel answered the phone, because Bellini or Edgar would have denied publishing it, and I probably would have said something offensive. Anyway, apparently Oprah was tired of "discovering" new books that had been out for a hundred years and already read by millions. So, apparently now, she wanted to be the first to discover a book that had been out for hundreds of years but read by no one.

So, I called Dicky and told him the news. He was actually going to be on Oprah the very next week, because she was sure that the book was going to take off any day now, and she wanted to make sure that when it did, everyone credited her for discovering it. Anyway, I was ecstatic, because Oprah was going to guarantee that we would have a book that would outsell anything Tobin Palm or anyone else Bellini found wrote, and not only did I discover the author, I was his inspiration and muse, and I told him exactly what to write.

Dicky was off to Chicago and we had the printers severely bump up the production of the books, and put the little Oprah sticker on the front of it.

The day of the filming went smoothly, and after the show aired, the internet sales of the book immediately surpassed anything Linnaeus Hoffmann had ever sold, and even though I couldn't bundle in one of my books free when I sold it, it still had that "buy it with this book and get free shipping" link on the page, so my book was selling like wildfire too, with over a third of the codex buyers buying my book as well. And, as quickly as it started, it ended.

The book wasn't in bookstores yet, so everyone who bought it bought it online, and received it about three to five days after they ordered it. That was when the trouble began. It was quite obvious to almost ever reader that the book they were reading was not an accurate translation of Twelfth Century Hungarian writings, partially because it was set in England during the turn of the Twentieth Century with personified animals being the entire cast of characters, but mainly, because it was an exact, word for word, replication of *The Wind in the Willows*.

I honestly don't know how it went this far without anyone noticing that. Of course, I know how I didn't notice it; I didn't read it. Bellini usually does that. And I had Hazel rush the formatting, and told her to do a text only cover, so she didn't have any time or reason to read it. I suppose that Oprah's people did read it, I guess they had just never read *The Wind in the Willows*.

Needless to say, we had millions of the books returned, at our cost, which we sold to dollar stores, with a disclaimer on the cover stating it was *The Wind in the Willows,* trying to just break even. On a brighter side, my books that were sold with the codex were not returned, because they weren't marketed fraudulently, making me once again the top-selling author signed to Linnaeus Hoffmann, and because of our immediate refunds, we avoided any legal problems. It would be *months* before I would be arrested for fraud.

ME BEING ARRESTED FOR FRAUD

Since I was a little kid, I loved comic books. It started out mainly with *Archie* comics. In fact, the first place I was ever published was the club page of an *Archie* comic. Later as I grew up, I became increasingly interested with the old EC comics, *Tales from the Crypt* and such. Then in the mid 90's I became enthralled with Mickey Spillane's *Mike Danger* and the newly rehashed *Aquaman,* but there was one comic book I found that I truly fell in love with, Marvel Comic's *The Life of Pope John Paul II.*

It came out in 1982, but I didn't get my first copy until the early 2000's, and I just fell in love with it. There was only one issue, but it was my absolute favorite comic of all time. Every time I saw it for sale, I couldn't help myself, and I bought it. I could go to a comic book show and walk out with thirty copies of the book. But, it actually isn't as redundant as it sounds. The comic was printed in every country and language you can imagine, so, actually, a lot of the comics are different from each other.

Anyway, I had been doing this for years. It was only really bad when I would get on eBay. At times I could buy a hundred copies a week. I didn't think much of it, I mean, I love comic books, and it was my favorite comic, I just couldn't pass up buying it.

For years it was no problem. I could almost always get the book for less than five dollars. But then, it became harder and harder to find. I could go to two or three comic book shows before I found one, and eBay was maybe giving me one a week. Then, there were just none. And when I did find one, it cost well over a thousand dollars.

I tried asking the comic book dealers that I knew what was going on, but none of them really knew. They said that it wasn't a very popular comic, so they didn't pay much attention to it. In fact, the only reason they ever kept it in stock was because they knew I would buy it.

I had talked to another dealer, this one a Catholic who still had his copy of the comic from when he was a little kid, he told me that supply of the comic had completely disappeared. The people who did own it regarded it as a religious item, and didn't want to sell it, and all other copies had just completely disappeared.

That night I went home, and realized that 99.99% of my comic book collection was *The Life of Pope John Paul II*. I felt like I had spent enough money on this comic, and if there was money to be made, I might as well make it. So I sold them. I sold them all, except one copy, the first one I bought. I figured I would see a lot of them again someday, and I would buy them again, and that was the fun of it, finding them and buying them.

I sold them all in one week. Needless, to say, it made me a significantly richer man. For a while I was seeing them on eBay and at the comic book shows for thousands of dollars, but they weren't selling. Over time the prices dropped again, and I was able to start buying them once more, and this time was even easier because I knew exactly where each one was, and I had thousands to spend on them because I was literally buying them for pennies on the dollar for what I sold them for.

Then I sold them again. And honestly, if I had any other job in the world, I would have quit it right then and lived off of my comic book money for the rest of my life. I made way more off of the comic then Tobin Palm ever made in gross sales.

And then I got arrested.

Apparently, it was the second time I sold the comics and bought them again that did it for me. Something about price gauging or fraud or something or another.

And you would think that comic book fraud wouldn't be that big of a deal, but it was a federal case, because, I had sold the "price gauged" comics in 49 states. (And my lawyer made me put the price gauged words in the previous sentence in quotes so you know that I am saying that it was the alleged price gauged comics, not me saying that I price gauged them. But, I think the more interesting thing in the aforementioned sentence is that I only sold the comic in 49 states. Can you guess which one I didn't sell it in? Utah. That's right. Apparently, and I did not know this myself, *The Life of Pope John Paul II* is intended for a primarily Roman Catholic audience. With me being a poorly reformed Protestant myself, and the number one fan of this comic book in the world, I think they missed their target audience.)

Here's what happened. I was sitting in my office, making a ball out of my rubber bands when two police officers came in. I immediately thought, "Thank God, with Bellini in prison I can fire him without him filing unemployment against me." Then the officers walked straight by him and towards the back offices. Now, I am going to skip all of the suspenseful "where could they be going" and "who are they going to arrest" schtick because, as I already told you, it was me.

And then with a surprise twist in the story, I am going to do all of the suspenseful "where could they be going" and "who are they going to arrest" schtick. The officers stopped Hazel and talked to her, the whole time she was glancing nervously back at Edgar and me, who were sticking our heads out of my office door watching the officers, much the same way we stare with curiosity while passing by a car wreck or rubberneck when we see the police questioning someone on the street.

They walked into my office and told me I was under arrest with charges of fraud, and of course, me, naturally assuming that this was about the whole Oprah fiasco insisted that they take Edgar in as well, because he is an equal partner in the business. The officers insisted that this had nothing do with him, and took me downtown for booking.

I do not know if it is a common myth, or if I was just grossly mistaken, but probably the worst thing I could have done during the police interrogation was a filibuster. I thought that if they couldn't get a word in, they couldn't charge me with anything. So I talked about everything I knew. Recited poetry that was hidden in the back corner of my brain that I didn't even know was there, rattled off chapters from Dickens and Hugo, I even told the officers my Miranda rights before I realized it was all a waste of time. Mainly, because, they don't have to stay there the whole time, they have new people coming in round the clock, but they don't have new suspects. Just me. The longer I drew this out, the worse it was for me. Finally, I broke down, and actually listened to their questions, and I was floored. I admitted to doing everything they said I did, except for intentionally doing any of this. Well, I intentionally bought the comic books, and I intentionally sold them, but I had absolutely no malicious intents, and I sure as crab meat didn't mean to raise the prices.

Even though I didn't give them the answers they wanted, they were satisfied enough that I spoke on subject, and they led me back to the holding cell. The next morning I awoke to a cup of Kool-Aid, which was quite good, and then a meeting in front of the judge to determine my bail, which I would have just called a bail hearing, but I had already typed the "meeting in front of a judge" bit and I didn't want to erase it.

Apparently, they set bail based on the crime committed, and I had made a LOT of money off of this comic book scam, their words not mine, and my bail was quite high, but I didn't want to lose the money that I had made off of the comic book deal, so I refused to pay it.

After my hearing, word apparently got around that I was locked up and my lawyer came to see me. And, he was actually quite pissed that I had not contacted him or had him present for the inter-rogation. He also told me that I was allowed a phone call so I could have called him before the interrogation even happened and I could have skipped the whole events of yesterday. But he had listened to the recording, and I had said nothing incriminating, and my total lack of understanding (even as I am penning this memoir) of the crime had convinced him that I had not committed any sort of crime, as the very nature of the crime would require me to plan it, execute it, and actually know what I was doing, and if I go on the stand and he shows my record, there is no doubt about it–any jury would see that I have absolutely no idea what I am doing.

He encouraged me to post bail, promising that when I was found innocent that I would get my money back, plus I would be much more productive not locked in the cell. I pointed out that it wasn't that bad I and I got free Kool-Aid, but he still insisted that I go ahead and post bail. So I did.

Then my lawyer called me up because apparently Hazel or Edgar told him that I bought plane tickets to go to New Orleans and then Honduras to hide out, and apparently that was a violation of my bail. So I promised him I wouldn't leave the state, and then I immediately fired him, beginning my quest to defend my innocence in court.

I bought a new three-piece suit, a light blue pinstripe, and bought a pair of those thirty dollar socks that you always dream about being important enough to buy but don't know if you ever will be, and I bought a bright green tie, same color as my socks, which I forgot to mention were green but I think you picked up on that by now.

Then I custom ordered an attaché case that matched the brown leather in my shoes, filled it with cans of Dr Pepper and summer sausages, and prepared for my day in court, only to learn that I hadn't been indicted by the grand jury, because of total lack of evidence, and rather ambiguous charges, so I was free to go, all charges dropped, which was when I found out I was one of the best lawyers in Lubbock, getting a guy accused of committing fraud in 49 states off without even a trial, so the next day I had the sign on our building changed:

Linnaeus Hoffmann Publishing
Wm. Bernard Douglas, Attorney at Law

I guess the sign on the building wasn't too big of a deal, because it wasn't until I started advertising on television that I was again arrested for fraud. I acted as my own attorney and was sentenced to six months in prison. I have since rehired my lawyer, which is why I mentioned things in this chapter saying I took his advice and didn't admit to anything, because since I never went to trial in the comic book case, I could still be charged, and a confession from someone previously convicted of fraud would probably be enough to sway the jury.

EDGAR IS A JEALOUS BASTARD
AND HE SHOT ME

It had always been a dream of mine to win a Grammy. I didn't care which one, I just wanted the phrase "Grammy Award Winner" written in my obituary. So, I thought being the author of a couple of books that had sold decently well, I could narrate the book on tape versions of my books, any of the half dozen books I publish that sell well, but none of my recordings were ever even given Grammy consideration. So, Edgar and I decided that all the time we spent in the office playing the resonator guitar and ukulele, respectively, that we could make an album that definitely would be given Grammy consideration.

Doing research, we found that for the past 23 years, there has been an award for best polka album, and all but six of those awards have been given to a guy named Jimmy Sturr. So, we figured, to win best polka album, we didn't have to do much, just beat Jimmy Sturr, and honestly, of the thousands of rock and hip hop albums out there competing for Grammys, how many polka albums could be submitted for a Grammy in a given year?

Well, I don't know how many there are every year, but that year there were 52 extra, because every week Edgar and I put out a new polka album, with me singing and playing ukulele, and Edgar doing his best to make a resonator guitar sound like an accordion. And we had some good ones too, probably the best one was called *Francis Ford CoPOLKA!* That was the one I was almost positive would win a Grammy.

In the mean time, at the advice of Dicky, I submitted my *Land Before Time* scripts, and eight of them were actually picked up to be made into movies: *Land Before Times 14, 26, 30, 35, 39, 41, 44, and 58.* They credited the gaps in between my movies to the disconnected storyline that apparently took 44 movies to piece together. Luckily for me however, the other talented *Land Before Time* writers cranked out the manuscripts for 15, 16, 17, 18, 19, 20, 21, 22, 23, 24, 25, 27, 28, 29, 31, 32, 33, 34, 36, 37, 38, 40, 42, 43, 45, 46, 47, 48, 49, 50, 51, 52, 53, 54, 55, 56, and 57 in about two weeks, and it only took another two weeks for the complete production of all the movies, and within a month all 45 movies were completed. Of course, they didn't release them all at the same time, but, I'd say within three months they were all on the market, and after another three or four months they were all in the bargain bins.

But to record 52 albums in one year was not an easy task. Of course, I wrote most of the lyrics and ukulele lines during my six-month stint in prison, and usually we would just turn the recorder on, I would start singing and playing, and Edgar would take off on his resonator guitar. After about three or four takes, we would have something we liked, and put it on the album. This was how we spent our Mondays. Tuesdays we would take pictures of ourselves for the album cover, and the next two days were generally spent trying to come up with a pun name for the title (i. e. *World Series of Polka, Jews Can't Eat Polka, Polka: the Other White Meat, Polka Chops and Apple Sauce, I Don't Know What Technically is the Difference Between Ham and Polka, Jews Can't Eat Ham Either, I Wonder if Jews Can Eat Frog Legs, Probably, Unless There is Something about that Plague in Exodus that Prevents It, But if they Can Then The Plague Wouldn't have been so Bad Because They Wouldn't Have Gone Hungry, Taenia Solium is a Parasite Found in Polka, Polkay Pig, Polkay's Was a Movie Made in 1982 with a Gratuitous Shower Scene, Texas Barbeque is Made with Beef Instead of Polka, Polka Bears are a Species of Bears Found in the Arctic, Polka Bears are Becoming Increasingly Endangered, Pope John Paul II was From Polka, People From Polka are called Polish, I Don't Know Who James K. Polka Is, There is Also an Ohio Congressman Named James G. Polka, Turns Out James K. Polka Was a President, Joseph*

Lieberman Doesn't Eat Polka, Neither Does Dennis Kucinich but That is for Different Reasons, etc.) of course with our best being *Francis Ford CoPOLKA!,* and to be honest, the reason we expected this one to win the Grammy was because it had the best name of them all.

There is no telling how many albums we could have made if we weren't constantly having to stop our sessions to keep Bellini on track.

The morning of the Grammy announcements Edgar and I were literally walking on nails, waiting to hear if we had been nominated. Most people wait for the call from their agent or producer, but since we didn't have either, we were waiting for a call from a friend who interned for an agent, who would probably hear the nominations way before we could. As I got the call, Edgar was just coming in, resonator guitar case in hand, and stopped dead when I put the speakerphone on and he heard Sam Galloway (the intern friend I spoke of)'s voice. Now, this call was very important, not only because it would solidify a year's worth of hard work, but also Edgar and I had a $5000 bet on which album would be nominated, my money on *Francis Ford CoPOLKA!,* and his on *Jews Can't Eat Ham Either.* But what Sam said came as a surprise to both of us.

From the speaker, I heard, "Well guys, I actually have better news than I expected."

"It's *Francis Ford CoPOLKA!* isn't it?"

"No, it's not."

"So it's *Jews Can't Eat Ham Either?*" Edgar asked excitedly.

"No, there is no Grammy for polka albums. They stopped giving Grammys for those in 2009."

"So we didn't get nominated for a Grammy?"

"No, you did, at least, you did, Bernie."

"For what?"

"Best liner notes for *Land Before Time 34: The Official Motion Picture Soundtrack.*"

"But I didn't write number 34."

"No, but apparently, they took one of the scripts that you wrote that wasn't made into a movie, and just kind of chopped it up and turned it into the liner notes for the soundtrack."

"But, it is a real Grammy, right? I am really nominated for a Grammy?"

"Yes, it is as legitimate as Best Polka Album was."

And then Edgar shot me.

Now, he shot me in the shoulder, and I must have blacked out because the next thing I can remember is being in the hospital, bandaged up, with Bellini, Hazel and my brother in the room.

"Bellini, what are you doing here?" I choked out softly.

"I thought you were dead. I wanted to make sure you were okay."

"Are you still on the clock?"

"No."

His face didn't look like he was lying. "Then I guess you can stay a little while."

He sat down and I looked over at Hazel. I could tell she had been crying. So had Edgar. I didn't know if it was because I had been shot, or if it was a culmination of all the hard work that we had put in to the fifty plus polka albums over the past year finally being behind us, and we failed. Well, Edgar failed. I was still nominated.

"You know what's ironic?" I asked.

"That people continue to put religious symbols on gravestones, even though basically they are just a commemoration of the moment when that person finally became an atheist?" Bellini suggested.

"What?"

"You know, if a person is religious his whole life, and he dies and nothing happens, he's pretty much got it figured out," Bellini explained.

"No, that's not what I meant at all, and you need to go to church."

"What were you going to say?"

"I don't even remember. Know what? I changed my mind. You can leave. And I am going to pray for you when you are gone. Seriously, go to church."

They kept me in the hospital for a few days, and during that time, I meditated on what had happened, and what had led Edgar to shoot me. Edgar, Hazel and Bellini all swear up and down that it was unintentional, and that Edgar had brought the wrong resonator guitar case to work that day, and instead of a resonator guitar in it, there was his Tommy gun. And the news that I had been nominated for the Grammy was such a shock that he dropped the case and the gun went off. Of course it was a lie, a lie that I am sure he will explore in his portion of the book, but I decided not to press charges against him anyway, because I liked being the only guy in the office who'd gone to prison. Kind of the office tough guy, you know?

But I realized the reason Edgar shot me, and the reason he was crying when I woke up, is because in that moment, right before he shot me, he realized, we were changing, and I was becoming Grover Cleveland, and he was becoming James G. Blaine. That is to say, we are both here, right now, contemporaries, going for the same thing, but in 100 years, everyone kind of thinks they know who Grover Cleveland is, at least the have heard that name before, but they have no idea who James Blaine is.

I decided that I would forgive Edgar, because, as you know, my favorite Marvel Comics' superhero, Pope John Paul II also survived a vicious assassination attempt, and if he could forgive the guy who shot him, I could forgive Edgar.

I got better and went to the Grammy's. Well, not really the Grammy's. They cut all the small awards out of the real ceremony so they can have more time for the pop stars to sing their little songs, but there is a nice banquet beforehand where they hand out the non-televised awards, and as you have it, I won. I made sure I thanked Edgar in my acceptance speech, and to this day he has never shot me again.

SO, EDGAR SHOT ME BUT I STILL WAS THE NEXT PERSON FROM THE OFFICE ARRESTED

You ever get a thought in your head, and you can't stop thinking about it until you figure it out? That's all that happened. I heard Brian Williams telling a story about someone being poisoned by arsenic, and it occurred to me that I had no idea how to even get arsenic. Now, I had no intentions of poisoning anyone with arsenic, or killing anyone in general, I mean, not even the littlest twinge in me wanted to murder someone, but it really bugged me not knowing how to even get arsenic.

Not that I wanted to get arsenic, but, really, it bugged me not knowing how to get it. I didn't even know if it was illegal to have. I mean, sure there still has to be arsenic out there, because people are still feeding it to people, but where does it come from? I mean, for the love of Ganesha, I could find any illegal drug if I wanted to, probably in just a few days, any of you could, but arsenic? No idea.

And I felt like I couldn't even Google it because I am pretty sure that the feds monitored that kind of thing, maybe just by keywords or phrases, but I bet "where can I buy arsenic" is one of those phrases. And you can't just go asking around, because someone would definitely get suspicious, and even if they aren't suspicious, the next time Brian Williams talks about someone being poisoned by arsenic, they will think back to the conversation. And Keith Morrison will say something about the neighbor with the warning signs that they always turned a blind eye to, and then when someone showed up dead they all rallied around and went against that guy. I didn't want to be that guy.

But I really wanted to know where people got arsenic. I had once gone to an antique store and they had an old timey pharmacy set up, and one of the empty bottles said arsenic on it, so it made me start to think that maybe arsenic was a prescription drug. Of course, it didn't make sense to me that any doctor would prescribe a straight up poison for any ailment, but then again, the FDA approved fenfluramine, ticrynafen, benoxaprofen, thalidomide, and heroin, so I guess they do prescribe straight up poison.

I really wanted to ask Edgar if he had any ideas about where or how to get it, because he took a lot of chemistry in college, but this was not long after he shot me, so the trust factors were really not all the way built back up yet. And of course Bellini would have no idea about it, because he is kind of dumb, so I decided to try to get a prescription for it.

Now, I don't know if I really want to broach this subject, because I don't really like bringing up my failures, but I did work towards getting my masters degree in literature a few years back, and I did all the coursework and everything, but my thesis was rejected, and kept being rejected, and there was a seven year time limit on getting the degree, and that time came and passed and I never got it. And I really don't want to share this with you, I mean, I made up that arsenic bottle at the antique store thing so I could explain how I knew it was used in prescriptions. But then it occurred to me that I couldn't explain how I knew what ailments it was used to treat without Google.

The deal is I wrote my thesis over the effect of syphilis in literature. I took the early writings of famous syphilitics, and compared them to the later writings of the same people, and isolated the elements of the later writings that were most likely caused by the psychosis of advanced syphilis. Then I showed how those elements were used in later writings by non-syphilitics, thinking that they were literary advancements, and not just psychotic ramblings of an advanced syphilitic.

My advisor was apparently highly offended by it. I mean, there is a chance that she had some pretty bad syphilis and I either embarrassed her or whatever, but then again, more likely the thing that offended her was the fact that she finally realized the things she drew from others' work to incorporate in her own was just psychotic syphilitic ramblings, and not the genius she thought it was.

Anyway, during the research for my thesis I learned that arsenic was used in treatments for syphilis before the discovery of penicillin and other antibiotics. So, I did what I had to do. I went to the doctor's office with "a case of some syphilis" a list of the medications I am allergic to, which was conveniently penicillin and every major antibiotic that had come out since then. The one kink in my plan was the fact that apparently they have tests for syphilis now and I didn't have syphilis. Well, he discovered that and told me I didn't need any medication. So I told him that I was in a high-risk group for syphilis (Bernie Douglas) so what treatment he would use on me when I eventually got it, being allergic to everything on that huge list. He told me since the introduction of penicillin there really weren't high risk groups for syphilis, but if I were to get it he would probably give me a third-generation cephalosporin, because it wasn't on my list of known allergens. At this point I was under the assumption that there was some kind of doctor patient confidentiality, so I asked him where I could get some arsenic if I ever needed it. He looked at me weird and asked if I was serious. I said I was. He said he didn't have the foggiest idea.

Did I mention we gave Bellini a company car? We did. Anyway, that has nothing to do with this I was in my own car. But after I asked the doctor about where to get the arsenic he kept me around for more exams. Real easy stuff. Blow into this, pee onto that, let some people draw my blood, and then I got to go home.

Less than a block away from the hospital I was pulled over by a police car. And then another police car came up right behind him. When the officer came up to my window he explained that from his vantage point it looked like I wasn't wearing a seatbelt, because my seatbelt was connected at the top to my seat instead of the door or wall of the car, so when I drove by he was expecting to see the seatbelt coming off the wall and over my shoulder, and since he didn't he pulled me over. He realized his mistake and we kind of laughed about it. He ran my license just for good measure. That was when he discovered a warrant out for my arrest for thousands of dollars in unpaid parking tickets.

I became quite belligerent, being that I couldn't even understand how someone could get a parking ticket in a town with no parking meters. So I was taken downtown, fingerprinted and booked. Later I found out Bellini always ate at the same sandwich spot on Tuesdays, and since it is across from the college campus, it has a thirty minute parking zone. And since Bellini is fat he ordered two or three sandwiches. And it took him way more than a half hour every day. And since it wasn't his car, and he is a fat jerk, he just threw away the tickets. I paid the fine and left.

THE ACCOUNTANT WE HAVE HAD SINCE ALMOST THE BEGINNING BUT I HAVEN'T FELT LIKE MENTIONING UNTIL NOW

As you have probably imagined, there were more people in our office than me, Edgar, Bellini and Hazel, but quite honestly, I don't know what they did, and from what I could see, they had less output than Bellini. There were about three other people who basically had Bellini's job, and he was their supervisor, the pianist (if I haven't mention her yet I am sure I will in a paragraph or two), and then there was the accountant, Maggie Toole. I didn't think much about her, because she didn't really do anything as far as I could see, except, giving out paychecks every two weeks, and authors' royalty checks quarterly, which seems like very little work for a full time salaried employee. Except for two days a month, all she did was put my receipts from lunch in a filing cabinet. And in a computer. And I also made her polish my Grammy, and every Monday she pulled on the pinecones on my cuckoo clock.

Some time back, Edgar and I had torn the wall out between our offices, because we were tired of running back and forth between offices whenever we wanted to practice ukulele and resonator guitar, or work on an old Fozzie and Rowlf routine, and now that we were in the same office, it was a lot easier to push our desks together to play Alamo. What we would do is set up a miniature replica of the Alamo on our desks, complete with tiny Texas Army men, then we would take the rubber bouncy balls I had in a bowl on my desk and just bombard the Alamo until all the Texans were dead. Then we would have Maggie set it back up for us.

We added a spinet piano to our office, for accompaniment to our resonator guitar/ukulele shows, and also, of course for Rowlf during our Fozzie and Rowlf shows. But no one in the office knew the slightest about playing piano, so we hired a piano player, named Claribel Colby. Her whole job was to play the piano all day. Of course, during our skits and routines and songs, she played along, but the rest of the day, she softly played background music, just quiet enough that Bellini couldn't hear it from his cubicle.

But then, it was kind of an inconvenience having a constant stream of piano music in an office occupied by two people who have a tendency to spontaneously break into song. To remedy this, after her first week of working with us, we gave Claribel a songbook of the 45 songs we are most likely to break into at any given moment. We alphabetized it, and put a labeled tab on the first page of every song so she could quickly flip to whatever song we currently were singing.

After a while, though, she just played through our songbook all day, which made it even more difficult for Edgar and me to work, because every song she played we sang along with. If anything suffered it was definitely our Muppet routine. And you cannot believe how much she butchered Run DMC.

And I am sorry if that last part was off subject, I really meant to tell you about Maggie. It wasn't until years after she started working for Linnaeus Hoffmann that I realized I could save work for myself if instead of giving her the receipts after Edgar and I came back from lunch, she could just go to lunch with us and pick up the receipt herself. But when we got to the restaurant, she didn't order anything. She said she only ate organic vegetables. I had lost my appetite.

I realized that I had been paying a woman for years, and the money I paid her was constantly being used for stupid purposes (buying organic vegetables). I went back to my office to call my lawyer, even though when I represent myself I don't go to prison and when I go with my lawyer I do go to prison, Hazel decided to start paying him all the time to keep him on a permanent "hold" or something for me, so I might as well call him to get some advice since I am paying him anyway. And plus, Hazel said if I make big decisions without consultation, I can't eat at Home Plate Diner for a week.

The hardest part was getting my attorney to understand that I wasn't discriminating against anyone; I just lost all respect for her.

"Look, I don't really care what she eats, that's not the problem, my problem is I can no longer respect her judgment."

"Because she eats organic fruit?" asked the voice on the other end of the receiver.

"No, there are 'farmers' who are too lazy to properly maintain their fields with pesticide, so they lose over two thirds of their crop to insects, as well they deserve to, and instead of suffering foreclosure and starvation like they deserve, they have convinced idiots to overpay for their produce so they make even more than if they weren't lazy."

"Bernie, I think they are more concerned with the health issues associated with the pesticides..."

"That's not true. Well, they may be concerned with it, but that's because they are too stupid to do any research on organic food to know that the FDA has categorized many pesticides as organic, so their 'pesticide free' fruit is just as tainted as everyone else's"

"So, are they lazy and don't use pesticides, or are they dishonest and use secret FDA pesticides?"

"Look, I had my obligatory consultation with you and I am going to hang up now. Bernie Douglas."

As soon as I put down the phone Edgar looked up from his desk and said, "Alright, I'm confused. Are the farmers too lazy to use pesticides or do they use FDA approved pesticides."

"There are a little of each."

"So, you really want to fire Maggie?"

"Yes."

"It's a bad idea Bernie."

I sat there. Everyone was saying it was a bad idea, but it was my company, the only reason anyone was there or had any money to their name was because of me. It was my insight and ideas that built this company, so why now would my insight and ideas not be amazing? There was one person here who would agree with me. I hit the intercom, "Bellini, get in here."

He stuck his head in the door.

"Sit down."

He obeyed.

"Should I fire Maggie?"

"If you want to."

That's my boy.

"But I wouldn't."

That fat bastard.

"Why not?"

"Because then she could file unemployment against you, or sue you for improper termination."

"Then what am I supposed to do?"

"Well, you just need to get her to quit. If she turns in a two week notice, and you have that on file, there is nothing that girl can do against you once she is gone."

"Well, how would we get her to write that?"

Edgar looked up from his desk, "Bellini could have sex with her."

"How would that help?" I asked.

"If I had sex with Bellini, I sure as Shawshank would never want to see him again."

"Well, I do completely agree with that."

"Hey, what if I already had sex with her?"

"Well, if that is true, which I doubt, she obviously came to work afterwards, so, it totally blows the whole theory."

"Well, she is my superior, and the company handbook does state that is means for immediate termination."

"We have a company handbook?"

"Yes, your wife made your lawyer draw one up a couple of years ago. Everyone has one in their desk."

I opened my desk. Son of a grape, there it was. The only thing in my desk, a company handbook.

"Ok, but that gets me to fire her, but it doesn't get me a two weeks notice."

"Well, it gives a reason for termination, so you don't need one, but if you still want one, just to be sure, just bring her in, tell her that when she leaves this room, she will no longer be employed here. She can either turn in her two weeks and be immediately escorted out, or she can be fired for prostitution in the office," Bellini suggested.

It seemed like Edgar and I were fighting to get the first word out but neither of us could say anything coherent. Bellini broke through our gibberish, "After I cut her off, she would come by my desk with a ten dollar bill, we would leave for five minutes, come back, and the ten bucks would be mine."

"You had sex on company time?" Edgar asked.

"Only five minutes?" I exclaimed.

"Look, if you want to skip this whole conversation with her, I can go outside, pretend to pack up my stuff, act like we got caught, and I quit to avoid having charges pressed, beg her to come with me, and tell her it would keep her from jail too, not to mention a ridiculously embarrassing conversation, she will no doubt come right in here with her two weeks notice, I will pretend to leave, and then come back, hopefully ten dollars richer."

I looked at Edgar. "Is this legit?"

"I think it can work."

"Bernie Douglas."

And, yeah, it pretty much happened just like that. Another author or memoirist would probably spend the next few pages spelling out exactly what was previously planned out as it actually happened, but that is just a waste of everyone's time, and it's just filler to make the book longer and more expensive, and I would never do that.

ROHONC CODEX, PART 2

Ed note: The book, as Bernie sent it to the printers, had the entire text of *The Wind in the Willows* in this space. He said it was to give the readers a better understanding of the *Rohonc Codex* chapter. Really, it was just filler to make the book longer and more expensive. It was removed without Bernie's knowledge or consent.– Bellini

AESOP'S TABLES

I don't think this has been mentioned thus far in the book, but any biography of me would need to mention my most remarkable trait. A physical quality of mine far above any other person's I had ever seen. Of course, I am talking about my fingernail color. It is quite remarkable. A lovely dark hue of pink. But very vibrant. I know Hollywood stars usually become famous because of how good looking their faces and bodies are, but if instead of faces and bodies it was fingernail color that made you rich and famous, well, let's just say I would have left Jennifer Aniston for Angelina Jolie.

But on to *Aesop's Tables*. I was still pretty high from the success of my book after it was tacked onto Dicky's book, but I was ready for another blockbuster book to come out, and I wanted to ride on the coattails of the two previous books, so I decided to team up with Dicky for this one. But I didn't want to write another fiction book, too much work, thinking, and coming up with stuff. And I kind of wanted to write a travel book, because that is really just getting a free vacation by letting people read my diary when I got home.

So I met with Dicky, and he liked the idea of a free vacation, because it was pretty cool when he got to go to Chicago to talk Oprah about his last book. So the first thing we did was pick a pun title for the book. We wanted to go with a classic that everyone knew and might accidently misspell on Amazon to come across our book, so we Googled classic books, and the first one that came up that we could easily pun was *Aesop's Fables,* because you know, alphabetical order.

But then we couldn't decide where we wanted to go. I mean, we wanted to make it a very long trip–year long free vacation–but we didn't want to go anywhere that didn't speak English, because we didn't want to learn another language. And as far as we knew, the only countries that spoke English were us, Australia, Canada, UK and Ireland. And maybe South Africa. We weren't sure. But to explore every inch of all of those countries would probably only take three weeks, and we really wanted to stretch out this free vacation, so we had a plan. Or I did. Dicky was just along for the ride.

I decided to take two hats. In one hat I put the name of every state capital in the US. And despite having had to memorize every single one in fifth grade, and making a perfect 100 on the test, I could probably only think of twenty of them. So I had Bellini write them down. Then in the other hat, I put fifty fun activities. Then I would draw a piece of paper out of each hat. Completely randomly. Except for Salt Lake City. I cheated on that one, because it wouldn't be nearly as fun to convert a Mormon to Islam anywhere else.

And basically the plan was to travel to each capital, and stay there until we had successfully completed the task we were given inside the capitol building. We would have to go into the capitol building and stay there the entire time it was open to the public until the task was completed. I would be the one actually doing the task, and Dicky would have a tape recorder on him archiving everything I said, so I could take it home and turn it into an accurate masterpiece of American Literature.

So we started off going to Honolulu, because honestly, there was a good chance that we would lose interest in this project pretty early on, and we wanted to make sure we got the good one off before we quit. All we had to do was teach a child the art of ventriloquism. So we went inside the capitol building, and I combed my moustache down so it completely covered my mouth, and I sat on a bench in the lobby with my dummy until a kid sat next to me. And I said "Hey kid, can you see my mouth moving?'

He said, "No."

I said, "That's because my moustache is covering my mouth."

Done. Chapter one complete. It was an awfully short chapter, but that's ok. I only needed to make the book 50,000 words, and I am pretty sure it will take me months to convert a Mormon in Salt Lake City to Islam, and that would have to be at least 48,000 words. The next one would be a bit more difficult, though.

We caught a plane to Trenton, NJ to give someone a tattoo of the state of Texas. Our first task was trying to figure out how to sneak a tattoo machine into the building. So we made a battery powered mobile one, hidden in a backpack to look like every other sloppy, fat American tourist's backpack, and headed into the capital building. And as soon as we got there we were greeted with a metal detector and x-ray scanner. And, as you'd have it, the whole thing kind of looked like a bomb. They kicked us out, kept our tattoo machine, and we might or might not have spent a night in a Mercer County jail.

So we had to revamp our plans. As per the rules of the book trip, we could not leave the city limits of Trenton until we had completed the task, and we also had to spend every possible hour inside the capitol building. So the next day we went up there again to scope it out. I shaved off my moustache as to not be recognized as the terrorist from the day before, and we also put on suits to look more professional, because, in all honesty, the day before we kind of looked like lactating hobos. And then we just scoped the place out. It did occur to us we could just use a sharpened paperclip and India ink and make a prison tat, but that would be harder to convince someone to let us give it to them. Of course, I wanted to just give Dicky a prison tat of Texas, but he pointed out the strip of paper said "Give a stranger," so I couldn't.

We had had the original portable tattoo machine made by a tattoo artist in Lubbock from some parts of his old machines, so we called him up and asked him to make us another one. He used some choice words with us that he probably learned at his tattoo shop, and then we told him we would wire him some money, and he said he would make another and overnight it to our hotel. Well it took him like four days to make it, or to get around to making it, whatever the case was, and then another three days for the over night package to get to us, because he sent it off after business hours on a Friday.

In the meantime, we still had to sit in the capitol building from 9-5 every day plotting our plan as we waited for the machine to come in. There was a men's room on the east side of the building with an openable window right above the corner stall. Luckily for us, the New Jerseyans had some class because they had full length doors on the stalls, so I could sit in the stall in privacy while Dicky on the outside pushed the backpack through the window. So, the day came and we got the backpack tattoo machine, and we did just that.

We had the machine in the capitol, and then we just went around asking everyone if they wanted a tattoo of Texas. And no one seemed to. So we decided to just ask the people who had visible tattoos. And most of them were pretty adamant about just getting tattoos in licensed shops and by people who had given a tattoo before. Finally we found a 17 year old kid who just really wanted a tattoo but had no money and couldn't legally get one done in a shop. I free-handed a Texas on his ankle, which honestly it looked more like a star missing its bottom left point, and we packed our bags and got the heck out of New Jersey. We flew straight to Salt Lake City, where we stayed from March 26 all the way until April 13 of the following year, when we decided 13 months was all we could take in Utah, and we scrapped the project and went home. And as it turned out I forgot to tell my wife and Edgar where I went. Bellini didn't seem to notice I was gone, though.

The worst part was not only did we waste all that time writing a book that wouldn't be written, Dicky and I also wasted an afternoon both becoming ordained ministers so one of us could perform the ceremony when the other one married Nasim Pedrad in Springfield, Illinois.

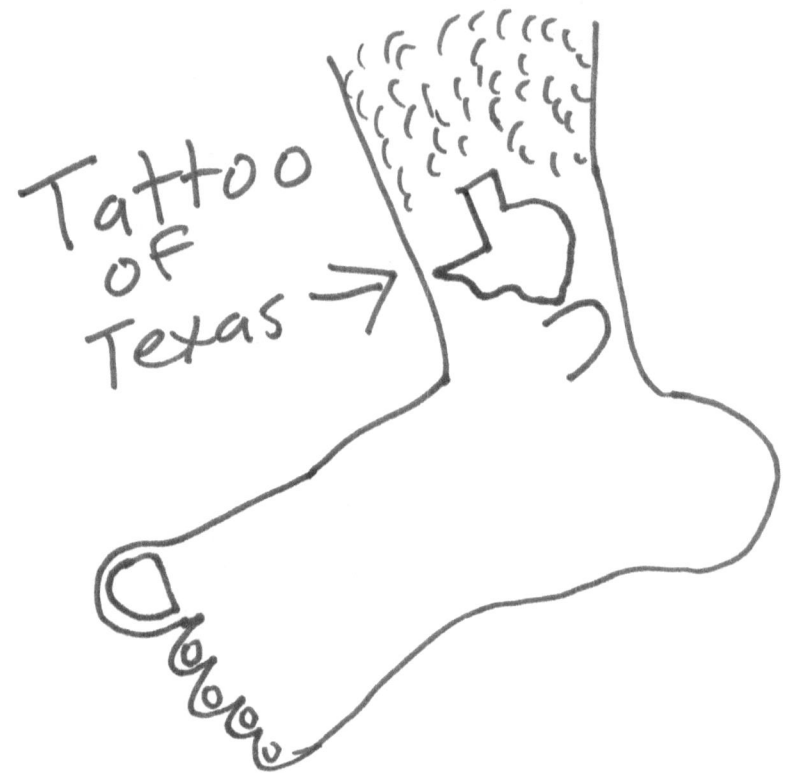

Tattoo
of
Texas →

CHAPTER FULL OF BOWLING BALLS

Ever since I had declared myself an English major in college, people would come up to me and want to talk to me about the book they read, because they had read one book in their lives, and me being an English major had read tons of books, it only makes sense that their one book would be included in the vast numbers of books I had read. But truth be told, I had never read *Catcher in the Rye.*

It was never assigned to me in high school or college, and at those points in my life, with such an overwhelming amount of things being assigned to me to be read, I didn't really read anything that wasn't an assignment. And after that point I really stuck with reading things that would be either short or funny, or both. Except for the time I read *Atlas Shrugged.* That really broke both rules. And a third unspoken rule (don't read books written by women). So I really don't know why I read that. Completely uncharacteristic of me. At one point I convinced myself that I read it because I really liked choo-choo trains, but, in all honesty, I didn't know there were any in the book until I started reading it. I think the real reason I read it, and this is going to be hard to explain in a book because it is more of a visual gag than anything else, is because I was in the book store and I saw *Atlas Shrugged* on the shelf, and I pictured myself as a staff writer on SNL at the pitch meeting, and when it got to my turn to pitch an idea, I would say, "Ayn Rand trying to pitch her book to her publisher, and them saying they loved it but it needed a title change, and Ayn insisting it be called "Atlas Goes 'Eh'" (and picture me shrugging and throwing my hands up and making a high pitched "Eh" sound). So, yeah, I had that thought, and it made me laugh a little and feel good, so I bought the book. And as I read it, every couple of pages someone would walk by me, and I would put the book down and throw my hands up and shrug and say "Eh" in a high pitched voice, they would look at me, I would say "I'm Atlas," then I would laugh and feel good. So that is why I read *Atlas Shrugged*. See, not completely uncharacteristic of me.

But, anyway, point is, I had never read *Catcher in the Rye*. I just felt like I would get into it, and it would be all angsty and not funny, and I wouldn't like it, and then it would be long. But it did stay in my mind that I should read it, and that wouldn't go away either. It was like the arsenic thing, but you know, instead of faking syphilis I would have to read a book. But then, I heard about a little story called *The Ocean Full of Bowling Balls*. It was written by the same guy as *Catcher in the Rye*, kind of as a companion story, set in the *Catcher in the Rye* world, based around the *Catcher in the Rye* family, all that, and it was only 17 pages long. And not 17 book pages, where they make the font all small and cram as many words onto a page as possible to make the story fit on fewer pages (something I would never do), but 17 double spaced typewriter pages. That's like, the length of three pages of one of my books. And, everyone has read *Catcher in the Rye*, and they all think they are so wonderful because they have, but very few people have read *The Ocean Full of Bowling Balls,* because there is only one copy of it, the original typewriter written manuscript, and it is kept under lock and key in a library at Princeton. And the text is not reproduced anywhere else. Not on the internet, not in a book. You have to go to Princeton to read it, and Princeton being in New Jersey, not many people want to go there. And once you get there, they only let one person read it at a time, and they put you in a small room, and frisk you to make sure you aren't taking anything in there with you that can record the story, and a bodyguard watches you read it the whole time to make sure you don't copy the story in any way or steal it or tear it or anything.

But, all that being said, I really felt that if I read it, not only would I have the nagging to read *Catcher in the Rye* go away without reading it, but I would have a one up on all those snobby people who had read *Catcher*.

So I went to Edgar and told him how awesome it would be to read it, and he agreed that it would be awesome to read it. So we went to New Jersey. On the plane we were so excited about reading it we could hardly contain ourselves.

"I think I am going to read it out loud," I said. "That way the bodyguard can enjoy it, too."

"Oh, that's a good idea. I am going to, too. And read it really slowly, one word at a time like a second grader would."

"And you should ask the guard for help sounding out the long words."

"Then I will get frustrated in the middle and start all over a couple times, to make my time in there really worth it."

"Oh dang it," I said. "We should have brought our own bowling balls."

"If this book isn't literally about an ocean full of bowling balls I am going to pitch a hiss fit. I am going to yell and throw things."

At that moment I knew what I was going to do when I read the story, but I didn't want Edgar to steal the idea, so I slightly changed the subject.

"What college would you want your presidential library built at?"

"I don't know. Where do you want yours?"

"Murray State," I said.

"Why?"

"Well, Dad went there, and so did Ernest before he went to camp or jail, and the good colleges in Texas already have one."

"Baylor doesn't."

"Eh. They lost the 'good' title when they hired Ken Starr."

"Good point. But if you did it at Lubbock Christian you could have it with all your Meat Loaf statues."

"Yeah, but I bet Murray State would let me build Ernest statues if I gave them a presidential library."

"Good point."

"You know what's bugging me though?" I asked.

"What?"

"If I was to have had my head chopped off with a guillotine, how would they have hoisted it up for everyone to see?"

"Where would you get your head chopped off by a guillotine?"

"France, but they always held their head up to show it off by the hair. I keep mine buzzed short."

"You're bald."

"Well that's why I keep it buzzed short."

"They'd hold you by your ear."

"But then my head would be lopsided. I look best straight up and down."

"Your face is asymmetrical. You would look much better held lopsided."

"Really think so?"

"Yes."

"Well, thanks. That makes me feel better."

Anyway, we got to Princeton.

Edgar went in first. I couldn't hear anything that was going on, but I could see the guard's face through the slat window in the door. He wasn't a big, buff, muscular guard like I was expecting. He was just some scrawny library geek. Probably working on a masters in library science. He started out looking fine, even maybe a little amused at Edgar. But then he started to look irritated as time went on. Every once in a while he would disappear from my view, probably to help Edgar with a big word. And after an hour or so, he started to look really angry, and even appeared to be shouting. At this point I knew the book wasn't literally about an ocean full of bowling balls, and Edgar was pitching his hissy fit. Edgar stormed out of the room and the guard invited me in. The audience was warmed up, and it was my time to shine.

I decided on the plane that the story was going to be boring, and I didn't want to read it anymore, so instead of reading it out loud to the guard, I would use the opportunity to test out my new duck novel, see how the audience responded to it, and maybe get a few pointers. All the while, pretending to read the story.

I sat down at the table, and there was a short stack of yellowed, typewriter written pages. I looked at them, looked up at the guard, then once again focused my attention on the pages.

I cleared my throat. "*The Ocean Full of Bowling Balls.* Chapter one. Albert's Hardware store was one of the last little bits of nostalgia left in Marris, Kansas. The big box stores had come in with their discounts and the lot, and pretty much shut down Main Street. Frank's Pharmacy was the latest causality of progress, and lately downtown had begun to look more like a ghost town than the heart of a thriving community. As Walter Murphy walked past Frank's empty shell on his way from his usual seat at the Main Street Diner to Albert's Hardware, he lost what little of a skip he had left in his step.

"Walter's wife, Beatrice, had died about six months earlier, and being a man of his late seventies, he knew he wouldn't find companionship again. He and his wife never had kids, never wanted them, but now, in his loneliness, he sees how they now would be nice to fill the void. He had spent most of his afternoons following Beatrice's death sitting on a bench in the city park near the pond, feeding the ducks. And even though he never spoke a word to the ducks, he felt his sessions at the pond did more therapeutic good than hours on a couch moaning to a shrink ever could. But as strong as his sense of companionship became with the ducks, he began to feel that if he truly wanted to fill the void, he needed to do more than throw bread at wild ducks, who only care about him until the loaf is gone. One month after his wife passed, he dug a hole in his back yard.

"Soon he had the hole lined with plastic, upon which he laid smooth river stones. He filled the hole with water, and planted cattails and water lilies around. As the hole was now a pond, he filled it with ochiba koi, which were a nice conversation piece that peaked the neighbors' curiosity, but were just the building blocks for what Walter's heart was aching for, ducks of his own.

"As Walter entered the hardware store, donning a brown fedora, which perfectly matched his suspenders, holding his trousers up mid belly, a style he had been accustomed to since the mid forties, the door scraped against the horse bells hung a top the frame. A burly old man, with a white moustache, khaki apron and blue bow tie looked up from behind the counter and smiled. 'How's the algae growing business going?'

"At the mention of his pond, the life well in Walter sprung again, and warm joy flowed throughout his veins. 'It's ready. I got the ducks on order from Pittsburgh. Should be in in a couple of days.'

"'They're shipping them in the mail?' Albert asked, as if it were an unheard of possibility.

"'You'd be surprised what they can do nowadays,' Walter replied, with a twinkle in his eye.

"'What are you growing algae for?' asked Albert's assistant, a young high school boy who worked in the shop during the summers trying to save up money to impress a young lady he'd been eyeing.

"'Well,' said Walter, beaming with joy, 'in less than 48 hours, I will be the proud owner of two genuine American bufflehead ducks. But the peculiar thing about the bufflehead is, they only eat when their head is under water. So I have been letting my pond grow for a couple of months to get a good layer of food for them at the bottom.'

"The boy didn't respond. A couple of seconds passed and he looked as if he were startled by the fact Walter had stopped speaking, and he hadn't paid enough attention to the conversation to know an appropriate response. Albert stepped in.

"'What can we do for you today, Walter?'

"'Well,' said Walter, thumbing through a book he had picked up from the library, 'I need to make me one of these shelters.'

"Albert looked at the plans in the book. It was a simple birdhouse, designed to simulate the hollowed trees buffleheads inhabit in the wild. An easy build for even the most modestly skilled craftsman, but maybe a project outside of Walter's means. It was no secret that Beatrice had done all the 'manly work' around the house, and Walter, being an accountant by trade, came closer to getting calluses from his adding machine that he ever did from a hammer or wrench.

"'Looks like a couple of pieces of spruce, quarter inch nails and some wood glue is all you need,' said Albert.

"'What about that hole in the front though, how would you go about making that?' asked Walter.

"'A jig saw should do the trick,' replied Albert.

"'Do you think I could get one of those here, or is it a specialty item?'

"Albert pitied the frail man in front of him, and he knew how much making this duck pond perfect meant to him. He smiled at Walter and said, 'You know what, I think I have one at home. Let me get my things together, and I will come by after I close up shop, and we'll see what we can do.'

"Walter was grateful for the offer, and gladly accepted any help he could get. Albert helped him gather the spruce and wood glue, and Walter paid out, with the promise of help in the evening."

That was about all of the book I had memorized, but it was a good chunk of the first chapter, at least enough to get a good read from the guard to see if it was working as an introduction to my novel or not. I looked up at him and smiled. He wasn't paying attention to me. I cleared my throat rather loudly. He looked over at me and smiled.

"Well, what do you think?"

"About what?" he asked.

"The story I just read."

"Oh, to be honest with you I have never read it myself. Haha, go figure. It's like a New Yorker who has never been to the Statue of Liberty. I am here every day but never got around to reading it."

"I didn't read *The Ocean Full of Bowling Balls*. I was giving you a preview to my next book, *Buffleheads*."

"Oh, I'm sorry. I just kind of zone out while I am in here. I am sure it was lovely."

I got up and left. Total waste of my time.

THE TIME I REALIZED EVEN GOD THOUGHT I WAS BETTER THAN EVERYBODY ELSE

I got the stigmata. Yes, the real stigmata. Bernie Douglas.

BERNIE NEVER GOT THE STIGMATA, NOR DOES HE KNOW WHAT THE WORD STIGMATA MEANS

from *Edgar Douglas: An Autobiography of the Future Written in the Past Tense*

Bernie came into the office. He walked around just spouting his own name for a while. He then announced to everyone, "Well, I was going to wait until after lunch to tell you this, but I can't wait any longer. I need ya'll to come in an hour early tomorrow."

There were moans and groans from the office. Bernie pressed on.

"I got us all tickets to a donkey show in Mexico, and if we don't leave by 8:00 we will never make it on time."

Bellini's eyes lit up. "You got us tickets to a donkey show! Awesome! Oh my gosh, this is so great! I have to call my dad! He will never believe this! I'm going to a donkey show!"

He immediately got on the phone and called his dad. This was the most ridiculous thing I had ever heard. I had to protest. "I'm not going to a donkey show," I said.

"You have to, we are all going. It's a work trip, and it's on the clock."

"Then I will just call in tomorrow," I said.

"If you call in you can't eat at Home Plate Diner this week."

"You call in all the time."

"No I don't."

"What about that week you were in the hospital because you ate nothing but peanut butter sandwiches for three months to see how long it would take you to get scurvy."

"You couldn't expect me to come to work, I had scurvy!"

"You got scurvy on purpose."

"I had scurvy!"

"What about yesterday?"

"I had to take a sick day."

"You said you had the stigmata."

"I did!"

"He really did," said Bellini, just off the phone with his dad and obviously trying to playing the "yes man" to get the ticket for the best seat from Bernie at the donkey show.

"Well, I can see by the lack of holes in your hands, and I am assuming feet, that you are all better," I said.

"I never had holes in my hands or feet."

"Then why did you think you had stigmata?"

"Because I did!" Bernie insisted.

"How can you think you have stigmata if you don't have holes in your hands or feet?"

"The doctor said I did!"

"What doctor?"

"Dr. Valentine."

"Jimmy Valentine?" I asked.

"Yes."

"The optometrist?"

"Yes."

"He didn't tell you that you had stigmata, he said you had astigmatism."

"Yeah, a stigmata-ism."

"Stigmata is where you bleed with Christ's wounds, astigmatism is when your eye is misshaped."

"Yeah, that's what the priest said."

"You went to a priest about this?"

"Yeah, where do you think I got the tickets to the donkey show?"

"You didn't get tickets to a donkey show from a priest."

"Yes I did, and I have the stigmata."

The next day we all showed up early to go to the donkey show with Bernie. Bernie came in several hours late. We confronted Bernie about the donkey show. He said it had been cancelled. He assumed we knew this already because it was on the news. We told him it absolutely was not. Lubbock news doesn't cover donkey sex shows in Mexico. He told us that the tickets were to a Don King promoted boxing match in New Mexico. He didn't know how we made the confusion.

On a side note—Bernie was not lying about his fingernail color. It is absolutely amazing. If a fingernail polish company could copy that color they would not have to produce any other color. And every other fingernail polish company would go out of business. They really are that remarkable.

RIO DE JANEIRO

Edgar and I could tell that Bellini was becoming disenchanted with his job, and his job performance suffered. Well, on paper and the charts, it was pretty steady, and did show some signs of improvement, but he did stop listening to our Rowlf and Fozzie routines, even when they were required office meetings, he didn't stay to listen to them, and his feckless attitude was apparent. Plus, he stopped going to Home Plate Diner with us, just sitting there at his desk with a sandwich he brought from home, so when he asked Edgar and me for a sabbatical, we knew he needed it. Also, we knew that we weren't going to give it to him, so we found the next best thing.

As owners of a publishing company, we frequently get invitations to publishing and book conventions. Of course, we never go, because, hey, we're doing all right on our own, why take anyone's help, right? But, we did get a brochure for a conference in Brazil. And as you know, Brazil is deep in the rainforest of South America, where there's nothing but small villages of tribes of indigenous natives, who live off of the land, each person having their own hut, and when white people come in, they are scared because they have never seen one before, and they might kill them. So, naturally, we thought it would be hilarious if we sent Bellini down there, especially if he didn't die.

Apparently, the tribal village where the "convention" was going to be held was called Rio de Janeiro. We sent Bellini off, trying our best not to burst into total laughter on the drive to the airport, saw him off, then went for lunch at the Home Plate Diner. That is when we started to feel kind of guilty, and there wasn't even any way for us to check up on him, because there is no way there are cell phone towers in Brazil, and even if there were, I am guessing Maggie must have been the one in charge of paying the cell phone bills, because for some reason all the company phones were shut off last week, and unlike the electricity, which was cut off the week before, Hazel hasn't found out yet and gone and paid it for us.

As the week went on and it became increasingly more obvious to us that Bellini was dead, the worry started to melt away, and it was more of a feeling of just acceptance. Being the owner of an original Fozzie and Rowlf, I came to know the other puppet connoisseurs in the country, and I bought the original H.R. Pufnstuf to set in Bellini's cubicle, as at least a visual replacement. Of course, since our other puppets are Jim Henson Muppets, Pufnstuf, being a Krofft production, was somewhat out of place, but that is what we felt about Bellini while he was there, anyway.

So, after two weeks, I don't know who was more surprised, me that Bellini was back, Edgar that Bellini was back, the rest of the staff that Bellini wasn't fired, or Bellini, that he had H.R. Pufnstuf in his chair. I immediately called the bank and put a stop on the check I used to pay for Pufnstuf, and contacted the seller for a return.

Bellini was kind of acting weird and distant, and when we talked to him, he really acted like he was hiding something. Then after we promised we wouldn't make fun of him, make jackasses out of ourselves, embarrass him, or try to ruin it for him, he said he would tell us.

"Okay, while I was in Brazil, I got married," he told us.

"What?" I exclaimed.

"You were only gone two weeks," Edgar noted.

"I know, but while I was there, I met the absolute girl of my dreams, and I just knew that she was the one, and, if I didn't do something then, then I never would. So, I asked her to marry me, she asked when, and I said right now, she agreed, so we went to a church, found a priest who agreed to do it, and we are married now."

"You're kidding," Edgar said.

"Really? The have churches in Brazil?" I asked.

"Yes. They are mainly Catholic," Bellini said.

"And are these churches in real buildings or grass huts?" Edgar asked,

"Real buildings."

"So they must be really easy to find," I said.

"Why would you say that?" Bellini asked.

"Because they are the only buildings that aren't grass huts."

"There are no grass huts there."

"Then where did you go?" Edgar asked.

"Brazil."

"No, you didn't," I said, "and we paid for you to go to Brazil. Where did you really go?"

"Brazil."

"So the tribes people make buildings now?"

"You do know that Rio de Janeiro is a tourist resort, right?" asked Bellini.

"What?" said Edgar and I in unison.

"What?" said Edgar again, to make sure he was heard even though I was louder than him when we said it in unison.

"I stayed in a luxury hotel. Why would they have a literary conference in huts?"

"We thought it was a chain letter scam," I admitted. "We actually thought you were dead."

"Why would you send me on a trip that you thought would kill me?"

"If you were stupid enough to go..."

"Don't you want to know about my wife?"

"Not really," I said.

"Is she hot?" Edgar asked.

"She's cute," Bellini affirmed.

"Now, is she cute for what you can get, or would she be cute even compared to what Bernie and I have dated?"

"She's cute."

"So she's ugly?" I asked.

"No she's cute."

"So she's Bellini cute."

"What's that supposed to mean?"

"That's what we call the girls who are way too ugly to date, but would probably be a little bit out of your league, but since their self confidence is so low, because, obviously she is so ugly, that she will date you, anyway," Edgar said.

"Bernie Douglas."

"You guys do that?" Bellini asked.

"Yeah, so when do we get to meet her?" I asked with a giddy enthusiasm.

"Look, guys, I don't know, she doesn't know English that well and she's not adjusted to life in America."

"How about at lunch?"

"I don't think that would be a good idea."

"No, it's a good idea."

"I don't think Shaista is ready..."

"Did you say Shaista?" I asked.

"Yes."

"Her name is Shaista?"

"Yes."

"No freaking way, that's awesome," I said. "Let's go now."

As Edgar and I made our way to my car, Bellini ran his fat butt down to his station wagon as fast as I have ever seen him run, then he jumped in and absolutely peeled out of the parking lot.

Edgar and I casually made our way down to my car, and got in and adjusted ourselves, and took our time leaving the lot. About halfway to Bellini's house Edgar broke the silence.

"If she doesn't know English that well, then mostly what she will be saying will be simple sentences, and she is expecting a yes or no answer, but if we say something that native English speakers will understand, but she doesn't, then we can ask Bellini what is wrong with her and why won't she talk to us."

"I don't get it."

"Like, if she says 'How are you,' and you say 'Okie dokie Mr. Smokey Pants,' everyone will know exactly what you are talking about, except her, and that will be hilarious."

"Okay, I got it."

As we walked up the sidewalk to Bellini's porch, Shaista (I still can't believe that's her name) was standing outside to greet us.

"Welcome to our home," she said. "Would you like some oranges juice?"

"Well scrape my fanny and call me Shirley," I exclaimed. "Orange juice!"

She looked over at Bellini, and he nodded his head indicating that we did indeed want some orange juice, and she left for the kitchen. Edgar and I helped ourselves inside, sat on the couch and made ourselves comfortable. Bellini came in looking quite irritated.

"What's your problem, bro?" Bellini asked.

"What do you mean?"

"You think she has a clue what the flapjacks you are taking about?"

"Probably. And that is a very offensive word. I am going to replace it with flapjacks in my memoir."

"What are you talking about?"

"Well, honestly, this is one of the more entertaining moments of my life and I am sure I will include it in my memoir."

"And she did know orange juice," Edgar said.

"Now what are you talking about?" asked Bellini.

"Well when you said flapjacks..."

"Edgar! Language!"

"Sorry Bernie. When you said *flapjacks*, you were saying Shaista didn't know what we were saying. But she left to get orange juice when Bernie said he wanted some."

Then she came in with a big jug of Pepsi and two glasses.

"Well, I take that back," Edgar said.

"Excuses me?" Shaista said.

"Oh, yes," Edgar said, "Je suis perdu. Où se trouve l'ambassade américaine."

"I sorry?" Shaista said, flashing a perplexed look at Bellini.

"I don't really know what he is saying," Bellini said.

"Bellini doesn't know English very well," I explained to Shaista.

"Le salle de bain," Edgar concurred.

"You enjoys your juice?"

"Slit my nostrils and slap me confused, I just can't get enough," I said.

"Bernie, enough with the slit my this or scrape my that crap," Bellini said.

"Plus lentement, s'il vous plait.'

"And Edgar, she speaks Portugese not French."

"He's speaking English," I said.

"Hehehe," Shaista laughed. "Edgar sound like girl name."

"Yes, well Bernie has a crush on 1975 Lorraine Newman; he thinks he can date her," Edgar confessed for me.

Bellini and Shaista look at me.

"That was before I heard of Nasim Pedrad. And in the third grade at a school assembly, Edgar though he had to fart but instead had explosive diarrhea all over the himself. It went everywhere."

"Bernie cried at 11 o'clock every morning in kindergarten."

"When Edgar was in high school he was supposed to do a research paper on the book *Jane Eyre,* and it was his main project for the semester, and he had to have an outline, the report, 50 index cards from his study and research in literary journals, and a lot more stuff, but he didn't do it and he never read the book then on the day it was due he got to class and told the teacher he forgot it at home, so she said he could bring it after lunch, so he spent the entire morning trying to figure out what he was going to do, but he had no ideas, so he figured he would just go fess up. But when he got to the teacher's room, there was a girl already in the class, because she was in a wheelchair, so they let her go to the classes early so she wouldn't get stuck in the crowds in the hall and be late for class, and when Edgar saw her there, he walked into the classroom and talked to her so she would remember that he was there, and then he told her that he forgot to turn his paper in during class and he was going to do that now, so he pulled a stack of blank papers out of his backpack and acted like he was putting it on the teacher's desk, then when the girl wasn't looking he dropped them in the trash and left. The next day the teacher told him since he didn't turn in his project, she was going to have to give him a failing grade, and he said he did turn it in, and the handicapped girl saw him. The teacher asked if he had another copy saved on a floppy disk, and he said no, he turned it in with his report because that is what she told him to do. So the teacher called in the handicapped girl and asked her if Edgar turned in the project, and she said he did, so the teacher searched for it for hours, and then decided that she lost it, and apologized to Edgar profusely, and gave him a 95 on the project."

"I never did that. That was you and the book was *Northanger Abbey*."

"Edgar had a boyfriend in college."

"Bernie doesn't know math."

"Edgar still keeps a picture of his college boyfriend under his pillow."

"Our parents didn't let Bernie go to medical school because they knew that he would say he was going to be a proctologist to be funny, would keep at it, and sign up for the proctology program, and would end up being stuck as one."

"Look, I always found it interesting that you could be paid six figures a year to look into other people's bottoms. And have you ever seen the first season of SNL? How would you not want to date her?"

"I tried to watch the first season with you. But then the Christmas episode came on and you kept playing the cast singing *Winter Wonderland* over and over. Probably for a good two hours. And you cried."

"It's a very sentimental sketch. I want it played at my funeral."

"And you buy Lorraine Newman's canceled checks on eBay."

"Any document like a check is the best way to verify a signature is authentic."

"You spent three years writing a screenplay that you wanted to star in and direct just so you could have a gratuitous make out scene with Lorraine Newman."

"You know Hazel made me throw that away when she found out about it. If she hadn't I would have an Oscar right now."

"You do have an Oscar."

"Seriously?"

"It's right next to your Grammy on in our office."

"What did I win it for?"

"Best Original Song in a Motion Picture."

"For what?"

"*All My Breast Milk.*"

"Why didn't I go to the awards?"

"I don't know. We sent you on a plane to LA and you didn't show up."

"I had no idea why you sent me to LA, so I caught a ride with a guy to San Diego."

"How did you not notice when you got the Oscar in the mail?"

"I thought that was a gift from you."

"No."

"Then what did you get me for my birthday last year?"

"That Picasso."

"That was real?"

"Yes."

"I thought it was a joke."

"Why would that be a joke?"

"Because I'd never seen it in art books before."

"Of course it's not in art books, if it were famous I couldn't afford it."

"Whenever people come over to my house and ask me who painted it I always say you did."

"Why did you go to San Diego?"

"I wanted to see Jon Lovitz at his comedy club. I figured if I met him it would get my foot in the door in Hollywood."

"More than going to the Oscars?"

"I didn't know I was supposed to go to the Oscars."

"They interviewed you about it on the local news. Multiple times."

"I thought we those were rehearsals for a sketch comedy show that never got off the ground."

"You know I still have your Lorraine Newman script."

"Really? We have got to get that made. The only reason Hazel didn't let me is she was pretty sure if Lorraine Newman ever met me she would try to date me. Bernie Douglas."

"She would never do this movie."

"Why not?"

"It's a rather poor parody of *Being John Malkovich* called *Being* With *Lorraine Newman*."

"I thought it was a clever script."

"You have thirty scenes in it with the only text written saying 'snuggle time.'"

"I wonder how hard it would be to change it to *Being With Nasim Pedrad.*"

"All you would have to do is a find and replace. The script had nothing to do with the actual Lorraine Newman, and you wrote it as if she was still in her twenties."

"Wait, how did *All My Breast Milk* win Best Original Song? It was a George Strait parody."

"You really messed up on the chords and tune. It was unrecognizable."

"I am glad I didn't regift that Oscar. I was thinking about giving it to Bellini until I found that train set at the dollar store."

"Why were you at the dollar store?"

"I was putting some of Tobin's books in their dump bin, so people think he's a hack."

"You know we can just sell books to the dollar store and they would still be on the shelf and we wouldn't lose as much money as just putting them there."

"We should really start doing that. Oh, and I also wanted to go to the zoo."

"What zoo?"

"In San Diego."

At that point, Edgar and I looked around, and noticed that Bellini and Shaista were no longer in the room, and looking out, Bellini's car was no longer in the driveway. So, we locked up Bellini's house, and went back to the office.

OSTRICH

I had called up my local taxidermist and asked her for a conservative estimate on how much it would cost to stuff an ostrich's head and neck and breast, and put it on a wall mount to hang in my office. She said in all honesty it shouldn't cost more than $400 dollars. I thanked her for her time and promised to be in as soon as I could.

Then I flipped through the phone book to the "O" section, but I couldn't find anything along the lines of an ostrich farm. I did manage to find a petting zoo within a few hours' drive on the Internet, so I called them up and asked what they did with their dead ostriches.

"Excuse me sir?"

"Yeah," I said, "I just need an ostrich, and when I get it, I'm just planning on killing it anyway, so I thought if I could find a dead one, then it would save everyone time."

"We don't give out deceased animals."

"I understand, but I don't need the whole ostrich, just the head and neck, and enough of the breast to look good on my wall."

She hung up on me. That was about all the work I wanted to do on that project, so I called Bellini into my office.

"Chris, do you know where to get an ostrich?"

"Africa?" he said, sounding a bit confused.

"Hmm, but how would we get a dead one?"

Claribel, who had been listening in ever since my first call to taxidermist chimed in, "You could have Bellini go over there and shoot one for you."

"That's an awesome idea," Edgar said.

"And very doable," I agreed.

"I really don't think that would work," Bellini said.

"Sure it will. You have your passport from your Brazil trip, now all we have to do is get you a little safari outfit, we will arrange for you to go on a guided hunting tour, and you will be fine. Don't worry. Bernie Douglas."

As Bellini walked out of the room, I could hear him mumbling under his breath. "Good lord. One brother is collecting goats trying to buy a African bride, the other makes me go to Africa to cut a head off of an ostrich."

I looked at Edgar. "Is that why you have all those goats?"

He just stared at me before replying, "In third grade you pretended a fish swam in your ear."

I got up and left the room.

Now, breaking away from the narrative, I wanted to interject and tell you, and I think this will come as no surprise to anyone, that by the end of it, Bellini's wife left him and he died. Not the end of the safari, but the end of his life. In fact, she left him the very day he died, but before his death, and she really told no one of it but me and then when he died, she was seen as the grieving widow and not the lady who may very well have led him to his death. I tell you this, only to say, that after his death, which by the way is still decades away from this point in the story, she gave me his travel diary from the safari. The following are excerpts from that. The only changes I have made I put in parenthesis, and it is strictly to preserve his dignity in death, and changing the extremely harsh and offensive language into something everyone can enjoy. Here are excerpts:

I am here in (lovely) Africa, and Bernie's
cheap (self) wouldn't spring for a real safari
guide, and somehow hired a ten year old boy.
I had never shot a gun before in my (entire)
life, and it is just me and a ten year old kid.
He led me out to this open range, and there

were, I'd say, fifty ostriches there. So I held up the gun, and closed my eyes and pulled the trigger. When I opened my eyes, all the ostriches were running rampant, and one lay dead in the middle. I was kind of surprised that I had killed one, but, not entirely, since all I had to do was shoot in the middle of a (big) herd of the (birds) birds.

After I killed one, the little safari guide informed me that we were in a protected wildlife reserve, and that we had to get rid of the ostrich immediately. I called Bernie on the satellite phone and asked him what to do, and the (Bernie) asked how I got my clothes to Africa, and I said in a suit case, and he told me to put the ostrich in that. I told him that an ostrich wouldn't fit in a (regular) suitcase, and he said all he needed was the head, neck and breast, so cut that off and roll it up. I had no other choice, so I took a knife from the tour guide and separated the breast from the rest of the God forsaken bird, and drained the blood, put it in my suitcase, and mailed it back to the (Linnaeus Hoffman) Linnaeus Hoffmann offices, so I wouldn't get caught with a decapitated head at customs.

There must have been some kind of airport delays or something, because I received the ostrich head a week before Bellini arrived, and it was very nearly completely mounted by the time he returned to work. Then Edgar found a news report of a poacher slaughtering half an ostrich in a wildlife refuge in Africa on the Internet, printed it out, and posted it all over the office. Bellini was freaking out because he was pretty sure he would get caught and extradited to Africa and be imprisoned until he died, but he didn't, and my ostrich mount looks awesome, so it worked out for everybody.

Ostrich
Mounted

JIMMY CARTER SIGNING

I can say with some confidence that by this point I have made clear my compulsive tendencies when it comes to buying Marvel Comic's *The Life of Pope John Paul II* comic books, but I have failed to mention one of the other areas where these compulsive tendencies take control of my otherwise rational nature, Jimmy Carter books.

As you may or may not know, for a former president, Jimmy Carter is quite the prolific writer. He has dozens of books under his belt, from a fictional novel, to religious devotions, to calls for world peace and a nice little children's book. You may be thinking, "Why are you so impressed with someone writing books, Bernie? After all, you've written quite a few, and you own a publishing house, so you have seen many people who have written several books." True as that may be, everyone else I know writes books for money. You know, some of us can't land successful jobs, so we have to resort to such means, but this Jimmy Carter guy is a former President of the United States, so he gets a six figure salary for the rest of his life just for keeping that title, a title, I might add, that cannot be revoked. It seems as though he is writing these books because he feels the content there within can be a benefit to mankind. This is a writing philosophy that I, until hearing of him, had been completely unaware of.

Sadly though, by the very nature of his books, their shelf life appears to be set to expire the very day his newest book is released, and his previous one is drastically discounted, often put in "bargain bins." (Or at least, that has been my experience here in West Texas, where a degenerate could beat the pope in a city council election, as long as the degenerate has an "R" next to his name, and the pope is a Democrat. But the pope seems like he might be one of those one issue prolife voters, so this scenario may not work, but the thought there is true.)

But it pains every sense of justice in me when I see a Jimmy Carter book sitting in the bargain bin or on the shelf of a used book store, so when I see them there, I buy them. All. Needless to say, I have an entire wall in my library dedicated to Jimmy Carter books. So, when I heard about a book signing Mr. Carter was doing in Atlanta, I figured I, more than anyone else, needed to be there. Edgar agreed.

I walked onto the sales floor of Linnaeus Hoffmann and announced, "Pack your bags, people. We are going to Atlanta!"

Of course, the uninspired question of "Why?" seemed to come from all over the room.

"Jimmy Carter wrote a book that was released today, and he is having a signing at his library tomorrow."

"Do I have to go?" whined Bellini. It was just like him, always trying to get out of work,

"Yes, everyone is going."

"Why?"

"Because he is a former president, Bellini! He is publishing a book with a rival publisher and the responsible thing to do would be to be there at the launch. We could learn something. Bernie Douglas."

"His book is being published by a very large New York publishing house. You can't very well call them a rival publisher. I bet you anything apart from Tobin's book or the Oprah fiasco they haven't even heard of us."

When Bellini mentioned Tobin's name I stormed off. Luckily Edgar was there to fill in the details.

"Bernie has approximately 150 copies of books written by Jimmy Carter. He contacted the library, and they told him that as long as he purchased a new copy of the President's newest book each time he goes through the line, he could get four books from his personal library signed, as long as they are written by Jimmy Carter. Of course, it would be ridiculous to think Bernie would have time to go through the line enough times to get all the books signed, so we are all going. With ten people there, Bernie can buy forty copies of the new book, everyone goes through the line three times, some of us four, we will have all the books signed and we can go home."

"How are we going to get the books there?

"You will each take some in your carry on. And you are allowed no other luggage."

"Bernie said to pack our bags."

"Figure of speech, Bellini. We are taking the first flight out in the morning and we will come back on the red eye out of ATL tomorrow night. All expenses will be paid."

"But I have calls scheduled with clients all day."

"Well unless Tobin got an offer from Simon and Schuster this morning and you think you can talk him into staying with us, I don't think you being out of the office one day, Bellini, will really hurt us."

"Tobin got an offer from Little, Brown and Company and I was going to present him with a new contract tomorrow to try to get him to stay."

"Really? Ah pretzel can, forget him. Bernie says he's a hack anyway. But team, double time today. Deadlines don't just go away because you take a day vacation."

Well, the trip to Atlanta itself was pretty uneventful, with the exception of seeing the former president, which immediately caused me to change the company dress code to allow executives to wear bolo ties. I had honestly never seen anything so distinguished in my life. Sure, when the guy was president he wore a traditional tie with a Windsor knot, but when he was on his own, getting money for not having a job anymore, that boy learned to dress, and dress to impress he did indeed. It was like he had a belt buckle adorning his neck, and he didn't even have to wear a belt to display it. I mean, imagine that you could wear suspenders and a belt buckle at the same time. I don't even know why this idea hasn't taken off more than it has.

Anyway, now that I had the books signed, I figured I was set for life, gift wise. First of all, it is a book, which is the perfect gift in and of itself. Secondly, it is signed by a former US President, so instantly it will become a priceless family heirloom. I mean, imagine if 130 years ago, your great great great great great great grandfather was given a book signed by James Garfield, and he had passed it on to his son who passed it on to his son until it got to you, you would no doubt have a priceless family heirloom that would go on for generations to follow. I am giving people a chance to start that heirloom. And no doubt they were appreciative when every year I gave them a new book out of my Carter library. In fact, the idea caught on so well, that that many people started giving me signed Carter books every holiday, after years of me giving them to them. And each one of these books I put on the mantle to one day become heirlooms passed on for generations themselves. I knew how important it was to the people who gave them to me that I cherish them, so I never give a signed book I was given as a gift away as a gift, just as I know my friends and family did the same.

DON KNOTTS AWARD

When I arrived in my office one morning, I noticed an envelope had been deliberately left on my desk. Hazel mostly dealt with the mail, so it was no surprise to me that this one had been opened, but that didn't explain why it was sitting there. I had specifically stated that I would not accept any form of written communications without prior knowledge of the content, so that when my correspondences are gathered for archiving in literary museums, there would not be any stupid stuff in there that I don't want associated with me. The one exception was telegrams, but the new accountant, who like the last one I feel only needs to be mentioned in this book for necessity, and because of that has not been mentioned before now, abolished the use of telegrams completely.

The whole thing started when the new accountant began looking into unnecessary spending and saw that Edgar and I were spending on average $300 a week on telegrams. So one week she decided to watch us, and noticed on Monday Edgar received a telegram from me stating simply "Knock knock."

The next day I got a telegram from Edgar saying, "Whose there." (sic)

Wednesday, I telegrammed Edgar saying, "Herring."

Thursday the accountant met the telegram delivery guy at the door and instructed him to never return. She stormed into the office and threw the telegram on my desk saying "Herring who?" and demanded an explanation.

"I was telling a joke," I said.

"You are spending $60 per telegram to tell this joke."

"Is that a lot?"

"Yes it's a lot. Why don't you just send emails? They're free."

"It would really screw up the timing of the joke." I said.

"The joke is really funny," Edgar explained, "because instead of an immediate response, each line is separated by a day."

"And a work week is made perfectly for knock knock jokes," I added.

"Then why don't you just wait a day and then send Edgar an email with the next line of the joke."

"We have always just done it this way. That just sounds like a lot of work."

"And how would I know I can read the message if the telegram guy doesn't bring it to me?" Edgar asked.

"You sit right across from each other in the same office. Just ask him if it is ok."

"I still don't know about this," I said. "I really like it when someone else brings us the jokes."

"Then just write down the rest of the joke, and tomorrow I will come in at this time and give it to Edgar, alright?"

"Fine," I said. This definitely couldn't be a permanent arrangement, but until we can think of something else, it would do for today. As I was writing down the punch line, Edgar spoke up.

"Are you just mad because we spend more on telegrams than your entire salary?"

"No, I am mad because this is a ridiculous waste of company resources. And no one sends telegrams anymore. That is why they cost sixty dollars a pop. The company probably had to hire someone whose entire job is just to bring you your little knock knock jokes."

"But you have to admit, that is a pretty sweet gig," I pointed out. I handed her the joke. "Now, don't bring this back until tomorrow. Bernie Douglas."

She looked at it, and yelled out, "Herring in a white wine sauce? That is the joke? Herring in a white wine sauce?"

Edgar died laughing. I was quite miffed.

"You totally ruined the timing! He wasn't supposed to know that until tomorrow."

"How is that even a joke?" she asked.

"Because it is a food!" Edgar howled, between fits of laughter. "Food can't talk!"

Edgar continued to laugh, but the accountant left the room. She must have made a phone call or something because from then on the telegram service refused to deliver our messages. I also think they went out of business.

But that leads to the very curious question of how in the world this envelope ended up on my desk. I demanded Hazel give me an explanation, and she simply told me to open it up and see.

It was a congratulatory letter from the O. Henry Club telling me that I had won their prestigious short story award for a short story I had published in a light-hearted horror magazine. I finished reading the letter, threw it in the trash, and went on my way.

"Why did you do that?" Hazel asked.

"Eh, I don't really care."

"But O. Henry is your favorite writer. You won his award."

"If that were true, I would gladly accept it, but O. Henry is long dead and there is no chance that he is coming back to give me an award for a story I wrote about talking wombats."

"But it is his society that is honoring you, Bernie."

"That means nothing. It is just some people who have no business giving out awards so they attached a famous person's name to it to try to give themselves some validity, and all the while it is completely meaningless."

"You know, sometimes you just need to learn how to say thank you instead of being a complete jackass all of the time."

"Fine, why don't I just start an award with some famous name on it and give it out and see if people think they are a corn dog on a stick when they receive it."

"That's not the saying, Bernie."

"You just know I am right."

"That's it, you got me. I am just pretending to be mad because you are right," she said leaving the room.

Edgar, who had been listening in, was eager to ask me what our plan was with the new award we were making.

"We aren't going to make any award. Plus if we did and put some dead celebrity's name on it, his estate could sue us."

"What if they aren't dead?" Edgar asked. He was really starting to sound like Bellini here.

"If they aren't dead, then they could sue us."

"So how are we going to do this?"

"We could find someone who has been dead over 100 years whose name and likeness are public domain, which wouldn't work because no one would care about someone who has been dead that long. Or we could find a famous person with our names, because we can do whatever we like with our own names, as long as they aren't really good lawyers like in the William B. Douglas fiasco,[4] but we do own our names so we can use them how we like."

"Do you know any famous people named Edgar or Bernie Douglas?"

"There is a soccer player named Bernie Douglas."

"No one cares about soccer though."

"Yeah, that's true."

We both sat silently in thought for a minute, then I had one of my top three best ideas of the day.

"Why don't we find someone who is not famous and ask them to be the name of our foundation and award, and then we wouldn't even have to mess with the famous people?"

"But if they aren't famous, why would anyone care about the award?"

"Because they aren't famous, but have the same name as someone famous," I said, "it's perfectly legal, and we can have whatever name we want."

"So are you thinking of who I am thinking of?" Edgar asked.

---

[4] This is one of those stories that I did not want to include in the book because it is one of the sources of deep embarrassment to me, but since I mentioned it, I guess have to explain. The next chapter will just be a simple explanation. Not a full-fledged chapter. My apologies if it does not flow with the rest of the book, but from what my editors have already told me, the rest of the book doesn't really flow with the rest of the book, either.

"I think I am. Bellini's uncle?"

"You know it. Let's do it."

I called Bellini into the office and explained everything to him, and he seemed to understand it well enough, until we asked if his uncle would be on board with the plan.

"Which uncle?" he asked.

"Your uncle Walter."

"Walter? Walter Mondale? Why would you ask him?"

"Because he has the same name as Walter Mondale," I explained to him as plainly as I possibly could.

"There's another Walter Mondale?"

"Yes."

"Who is he?"

"Jimmy Carter's vice president."

"The second vice president ever from the Democratic-Farmer-Labor Party," Edgar added.

"Who's Jimmy Carter?" Bellini asked.

"You met him. He signed like 12 books for you. But how have you had an uncle named Walter Mondale and never knew that there was a vice president named Walter Mondale? He was vice president when you were born!"

"I don't know," Bellini said. "I guess it never came up."

"Well, just tell me if you think he will do it."

"I don't know. I guess I could see."

"Please." I said. Then Bellini just stood there and stared at me. I opened my eyes wider and gave him a "go ahead" nod. He finally caught on. He called his uncle, and with much difficulty explained the situation to him. He hung up the phone.

"He doesn't want to do it."

"Why not?"

"He doesn't believe you that there was a vice president named that. He's never heard of him either."

"He voted in that election. How could he not notice that the guy who ran for, and eventually won the vice presidency had the same name as him?"

"I don't know," Bellini said. "It kind of sounds like you are making the whole thing up."

"Fine. Just go back to work," I told him.

He left.

"What's the plan now?" Edgar asked.

"I think we just need to scan the obituaries, see if we find any famous names of the recently deceased non famous, contact the family and tell them we want to honor their loved one. Surely we will have some taker."

With that we started scanning the obituaries of all the major newspapers that had free online editions. Every once in a while, we would find a name that sounded famous enough, like Tom Snyder or Kenesaw Mountain Landis, but their families would not return our calls or take our request seriously. Then we finally found it.

The family of Don Knotts, an out of work typewriter repair man from Liberal, Kansas, was more than accepting of our offer to set up a foundation in memory of their dearly departed. And the fact that his grandson, Alex Cambridge was a deputy sheriff in Dodge City made persuading them to lend the name for an award for deputy sheriffry almost effortless.

Edgar and I put a couple of hundred thousand dollars into a high interest earning account, and were able to award a twenty thousand dollar prize each year to the winner of the Don Knotts award from the money brought in by the interest alone.

The first year we decided to send out a blanket letter to all the sheriff departments in the southern and eastern United States, asking that the sheriff nominate his most valuable deputy by sending us a letter stating why he is so great, accompanied by a photo of the deputy. In all honesty, the request for a letter was just to make the thing look more legitimate, because all along Edgar and I knew we would base our decision on who would win the award solely on the deputy's looks alone. And not the prettiest either, we aren't all that gay, but the one who brought the most humor to the role of deputy sheriffry based on their appearance.

And the winner was Arthur Franklin. Either this guy had allergies the day they took the deputy sheriff pictures, or he was a real mouth breather. In addition to having his smileless mouth gaping wide in the picture, he had what would have been an excellently thick moustache, if it weren't for the quarter inch bare spot halfway in on the left side of his upper lip. His cheeks were fully blushed and drooped, and while the front of his hairline looked to be a routine uniform flattop, it was overshadowed by the bald crown of his pointed head that stuck up a good half inch above it. Yes, we couldn't have picked a better choice.

We notified the Kent County Sheriff Department in Dover, Delaware that we had chosen one of their own for the award, and they couldn't have been happier. In fact, I think Arthur was grand marshal of some parade.

We flew him down to Lubbock, and when he arrived, Edgar and I were taken aback by how nice, humble, and truly honored he was to have received this award. Kind of made me feel like a jackass for being such a jackass about the O. Henry award. But you know, Arthur needed something like this. I didn't.

The ceremony went off without a hitch. Arthur's mom flew down from Delaware to be in attendance. She cried throughout the entire ceremony. Afterward, she came up to me and thanked me for giving this award to her son. She said it meant so much to her, because Arthur had worked so hard his entire life, and had never been recognized for anything. It made me feel kind of good about what I did, and kind of jackassy for picking the guy just because he was funny looking.

No. Take that back. I am not assy. Good for me. Funny looking people need recognition, too.

Arthur

THE WILLIAM B. DOUGLAS FIASCO

When my first book was published, there was an error on Amazon.com where they listed the author as two separate people, Bernie Douglas, as I asked them to do it, and William B. Douglas, my name as the publishers gave it to the IRS. Before they got it straightened out, a few people searching for other books by me searched for William B. Douglas, and they found books by another author named William B. Douglas.

These books were law school textbooks. One of which was called *Commercial Law*. This book sold for $100. My books sold for $15, and I got less than $3 royalties for each one sold. If my books cost $100, then I could get $88 profit per book. I was under the impression that whatever I did with my own name was legal. So I wrote a book called *Advertising Law*. The Amazon profile made it look exactly like *Commercial Law*. Made it look like it could be the sequel. Charged $100. In all actuality, it was a coffee table book, and only sixteen pages, each one a screen shot of a television commercial for a small time personal injury attorney.

I only sold two. Turns out it was to William B. Douglas. Both were. Well, I wanted one for my own coffee table, and the other William B. Douglas wanted one to see who was ripping off his name. It turns out that the only people who buy legal textbooks are people who are required to buy them for class. And no law class has coffee table books as required reading. Which is why I was never a law student.

He was a professor emeritus of law at a prestigious California law school. And he knew all the legal loopholes. He wanted to take me down. So I thought, this guy writes law books, so any lawyer should know all his tricks because he gave them all away in his books, and they learned them in class. He will be easy to defeat in court. But this guy was some kind of legal genius. He made me stop publishing it, destroy all unsold copies already made, and required me to pay him all proceeds I had made from the book. But all I got was his $88. It cost me about $10,000 to publish it (I thought it would be a run away hit and printed a lot of copies). I thought that meant I owed him negative $9,982 and he would pay me the $9,982. Instead I paid all of his and my own legal fees. And then he asked me to sign his copy of *Advertising Law*.

I WILL TITLE THIS CHAPTER AFTER I FIGURE OUT WHAT IT'S ABOUT

Edgar had always been there for me. When I wanted to start the business, he jumped right on board. When I wanted to win a Grammy, he helped me. Of course we know that I could have done it completely without him, but he was by my side throughout my three arrests (or four, or five, I forgot how many I have told you about), and when I won an Oscar, he told me about it, (albeit years after it happened,) so when he failed at the only thing he ever cared about, besides goat collecting, which I never really understood, I was there for him. But it really wasn't his fault. He had a brilliant idea, but just because one Kennedy had a botched lobotomy in the forties, there was a social stigma about it. So, I did the next best thing.

Of course, Edgar also failed as an author, with the only two books he ever wrote, both about whales, and both called *Moby Dick,* failing to be picked up by any publishing house, despite the fact the he was vice president of one. But he didn't really care about that. It wasn't his passion like do it yourself home lobotomy kits were. And both books were less than a page long. Double spaced.

When Edgar and I were children, our favorite video game was Rampart, and though our parents never bought it for us, at least once a month they took us to the video store and let us rent any game we wanted, and he always rented the same game, Rampart (I always rented Kickle Cubicle, but no one cares about that). Over the years, our parents probably paid for those game twenty times over, but that's beside the point.

Edgar had always wanted to be called the best Rampart player in the world, and I thought I could make that happen for him.

After much looking, I found an actual arcade machine version of the game from an old movie theater that was going out of business. So, one Saturday when no one was there, I had it brought into the office. At the time, Bellini had the largest cubicle in the office, so I had dedicated half of the space in his cubicle to the machine, and on Sunday I had a mechanic come in and rig the coin slot to only accept rare, 18th Century Spanish eight reales, so Bellini couldn't play it at work.

I had been able to purchase about 50 of these coins, and Edgar and I would play the game at least once before lunch and once after, but as the weeks went by, our coin supply dwindled away, and it became increasingly hard to find more Spanish eight reales. Edgar really started jonesing to play the game more, and more, but eventually we ran out of coins. Sometimes it would be weeks before we could find another coin, and when we did, per the 1980's game design, within five minutes the game was over.

I could tell Edgar was getting irritated and antsy when he couldn't play his game, and I tried to keep him happy, doing my Fozzie routines, and I bought him a piano perfectly sized for Rowlf, but nothing really helped. I even read him Dicky's translation of the Rohonc Codex.

Ed note: Once again Bernie cut and pasted the entire text of *The Wind in the Willows*. I again removed it. –Bellini

One day when we came back from lunch after months of not playing Rampart, Edgar and I walked into the office to find Bellini playing the game.

"How did you get the money for a Spanish eight reales?" Edgar shouted.

"I didn't," Bellini replied.

"Then how are you playing the game?" I asked.

"The key for the coin safe is taped on the side."

"How did you see it?"

"The machine is touching my desk. I found it the first day you brought it in because it's where I used to keep my calendar."

I looked and sure enough, Bellini had put the key right back where he said it was. I opened the coin stowage and there were all of the eight reales. Later that day, Edgar and I bought a safe to keep in our office, and put the eight reales and arcade key inside. Edgar was so appreciative that he could now play Rampart all he wanted, and Bellini couldn't play it at all, despite the machine being located in his cubicle, that he pulled out Rowlf, went to the piano, and performed the entire text of Dicky Maloney's translation of the Rohonc Codex as a musical.

Ed note: No need to thank me here. But you know what happened. –Bellini coin

↑

Spanish 8
reales

I NEVER STARTED A DO IT YOURSELF LOBOTOMY BUSINESS

from *Edgar Douglas: An Autobiography of the Future Written in the Past Tense*

It was a joke. I found an old manual drill. The kind that you hold there and crank. It was in an antique store. I bought it as a gag gift for the dentist in the building. Bernie found it. I told him it was the prototype for my do it yourself lobotomy kit. Then I told him what a lobotomy was. He contacted two or three medical supply companies. They told him under no circumstances would they carry a do it yourself lobotomy kit. Bernie did his best to console me.

At the time I had my hands full with another business venture. Bernie and I had always dreamed of owning a Major League Baseball team. We had decided we would buy one when Linnaeus Hoffmann made us rich enough. We knew we would buy the Texas Rangers. We had plenty of friends in Dallas. They all told us it wouldn't be missed if we moved it. Bernie wanted to move it to Austin. He would call them the Austin Celtics. He would deny up and down it was an intentional pun. His argument was that there was another professional sports team already called the New York Rangers and no one thought that was a pun.

I figured that move wouldn't be the most financially beneficial. I wanted to move it to Puerto Rico. Call them the San Juan Saint Johns. All the good baseball players were there anyway. There would be no federal income tax. It was still in the US. It was the smartest move.

We still didn't have the money to buy the Rangers. I found out Bernie already bought a baseball team. It was called the Linnaeus Hoffmann Sloths. It was in the eight and nine year old league. As co owner of Linnaeus Hoffmann, I was co owner of the Sloths. I decided to be a very involved owner. I was like that Dallas Cowboys owner.

I immediately fired the current general manager. He was a nobody. Just some kid's parent. We needed a real baseball player. Nolan Ryan said no. Bo Jackson said no. Sammy Sosa didn't understand the question. Robin Yount said yes. To get Robin Yount to say yes I had to say we were making a movie. A documentary about Robin Yount coaching little league.

Robin Yount came to Lubbock and coached the team. He immediately expected to meet the film crew. Bellini was a communications major in college. I don't know if Bernie has already told you that. That means he has a lot of friends who think they are going to be TV stars. That means he has a lot unemployed friends with film equipment. Robin was understanding that an independent documentary would have a small film crew. Two men were all we had. Soapy and Silky. Soapy manned the camera. Silky manned the boom mic. As I said I was a very involved owner. I made sure I was always in the dugout.

I didn't go to practices though. Those are boring. And Robin took care of those. But no, the games. The games were my domain. I had a team to coach. I had a show to put on. I was in Lubbock. You know that. Bob Knight was fired in Indiana. Lubbock brought him in. Lubbock knew what they wanted in a coach. I was the coach they wanted.

In game one no. 13 on the team was first to bat. He bunted. First kid to bat. He bunted. He was thrown out at first. I went crazy. He sac bunted. To empty bases. I went crazy. Throwing bats. Cussing at parents. I pulled on the umpire's facemask. The elastic caught it. Snapped it back on his face. I was thrown out of the game. Banned for the season.

Robin stayed at my house for the summer. That made it awkward. The umpire initially filed assault charges. Bernie got him to drop it. Said he was the office tough guy. The Sloths lost every game that season. Robin said I traumatized the kids. Took the fun out of the game. I just said he sucked as a coach. Didn't understand the game like I did.

Bernie didn't care about the whole ordeal. He watched the tape of the first night. Snapping the umpire mask and the like. He started to care. He started going to every game. He decided to be "director" of the documentary. There wasn't supposed to be a documentary. It was a lie to get Robin Yount. Robin Yount thought Bernie was director. I told him that to get him here. Bernie had directed a documentary movie before. *They Really Were Nappy Headed Hoes: In Defense of Don Imus.* It had one showing at a theatre in Austin. The reels now sit in Bernie's basement. It could have been better. Bernie was under the assumption that "nappy" meant "likes to take naps" and "headed" meant "has a head." He asked what "hoes" were. He was told people that "slept around." He thought it meant took naps in lots of places. He interviewed many people who went to Rutgers with the girls. Getting testimonials about how they were nappy headed hoes. He left hours of interviews on the cutting room floor that anyone else would have put in the movie. He thought it was "dirty sex talk." His movie was an hour and a half of guys saying, "Yeah, I guess she took naps. She did have a head."

Bernie was able to sell the Robin Yount documentary. One of those channels that calls themselves a network but aren't one of the big four. Ran it as a reality show. It won him an Emmy. And another Emmy. He produced the show. It won best reality program. He got that Emmy. He hosted the show. He won best reality host. It went to his head. It was the first award he had ever won on purpose. It really went to his head.

Do it yourself
lobotomy

OK, SO DO IT YOURSELF LOBOTOMY
WAS A BAD IDEA, BUT...

This one was good. It had come to my attention that, I don't know, I had just worked too hard for the money I had made. None of it was frivolous; none of it was just from a genius million dollar idea that let it all just fall into my lap. And that was kind of what I wanted. To be the man with the genius million dollar idea. Because you hear of the guy who worked hard, built an empire, all that, and you respect him, admire him, but the guy that just had the genius idea, then did practically nothing and was rich beyond his wildest dreams, that's the man everyone envied and everyone wanted to be.

Take Bob Ross, he had an awesome idea on how to get people to paint fast, and he did little work, and he got rich, and we all envy him. Now, I know ya'll are thinking "but he did work, he painted and made a TV show." He did the TV show for free and gave his paintings away, because he was a nice person. What he made his money from was having people trained as "Bob Ross trained teachers" who went around and did work and then passed the money to him. Pretty brilliant. Little more work than I want to do, but still pretty brilliant.

I guess a better example would be Oral Roberts. The man went on TV and said that Jesus was going to murder him if the people watching TV didn't give him eight million dollars, and do it fast. And they gave him eight million dollars! Actually they gave him nine million! Genius. Well, unless you consider the eternal consequences of making such a claim. But anyway, genius idea, no work, MILLIONS!

And, of course, fearing the consequences on my eternal soul, I decided to go with the first plan of action, creating a method, teaching my method, and have the people who use my method pay me the money they make from it. Of course I didn't want to actually go around teaching my method, that would be a lot of work, but simply come up with one, have whoever happened to be around when I came up with it remember what I said and teach it in seminars in Holiday Inn conference rooms across the US, charge people to come listen, charge people to get a certificate, and then charge people a percentage of the profit they get from using my method.

So I called the staff into the conference room. I already had an idea of what I wanted to do, but hadn't bothered to write it down or anything, with the intention that the people who do write it down would be the ones to lecture. So the whole staff and Dicky, who happened to be hanging around the office, gathered in the conference room and I began.

"Acupuncture. That's a bunch of crap right?"

There was a general agreement from some, while others looked confused or shocked at such an accusation.

"And all the Eastern healings, holistic rocks, and other alternative cures that do nothing, those are crap too?"

More agreement.

"But people pay to have the procedures done to them, even though there is no evidence that they help, and there is quite a bit of evidence that they do nothing. Why? Because they are old. The methods. Not the people. They can be traced for centuries back in Asia, or to the Native Americans, or whatever group started whichever particular form of alternative medicine you are looking at. But the thing that we need to focus on is the fact that alternative medicine is a booming money making endeavor, and you can get away with practicing it, even if it doesn't work, and people like methods that are old and were used a long time ago because people don't know better."

I had lost most of the crowd, but a few were still paying attention, and those paying attention were the ones I was now speaking to.

"Me, being strongly of Anglo-Saxon heritage, I can't very well sell methods of Asian or Native American origins..."

"Unless you dress up like an Indian!" Edgar screamed.

"No, no, that's not quite what I was going after. I think there is an untapped resource, or method, if you will, of alternative medicine that the American public is just dying to bring back to popular usage, and so I give each of you the opportunity to become certified instructors of the Bernie Douglas Bloodletting Institute."

"You're starting an institute?" Bellini asked.

"Well no, but you put that word on there everyone will think this is legitimate."

"It's stupid is what it is," Hazel said.

"Well, then if you divorce me I don't have to pay you any of the millions that I make off of this, because I have a room full of witnesses saying you weren't supportive of me."

"It is really stupid, Bernie," Edgar said.

"Then you can't be an instructor."

"I'm curious. How does this work?" asked Dicky.

"I'm glad you asked. We each have four humors, blood, phlegm, black bile and yellow bile. And when you are sick it is because your humors are not in the right ratio, so you need to be cut until you bleed enough that they are in the right ratio."

"What if all you have is too much black bile?" asked Bellini.

"Well then, you need to bleed."

"Won't you still have too much black bile and then your blood level will be too low and you will be in worse shape then when you started?"

"No."

"How?"

I stared at him blankly. I didn't research this or anything. I didn't think people would ask questions. They don't ask holistic healers how a rock on their forehead cures testicular cancer do they? I don't know, they might. Holistic healers may just be better at making stuff up than I am. I am horrible at making stuff up. That's why I can't write fiction and have to stick to true, word for word accounts of the future. Luckily for me Dicky spoke up.

"Blood is the main humor of excess, so most of the time you just need a good bleeding. However if it is one of the other humors, you can easily rid yourself of excess phlegm, and we can make the person urinate, defecate or vomit to remove the bile."

"Yeah!" I said. "Wait, what's a defecate?"

With that everyone pretty much left the room, but I had all I needed. Dicky. I asked him what he knew about bloodletting. Turns out it was a lot. He wrote it all down in a diagram, which soon became the curriculum for the Bernie Douglas Bloodletting Institute.

Well, Dicky began putting out ads in the papers for job opportunities but not saying what the job is, just to meet at the Holiday Inn conference room, you know, like the door to door knife companies do to recruit salesmen.

You know what? Never mind. This story is boring. I decided not to tell it anymore. You would think writing this precognatively I would have known before I started this chapter that I wouldn't finish writing it. Oh well, it took me like twenty minutes to write it up to this point so I don't want to delete it. Long story short it, it worked for like a year.

QUEST FOR THE EGOT

I was incredibly humbled to have won an Oscar, Grammy, and two Emmys. Well, somewhat humbled for myself. But really, really humbled for Lubbock. An Oscar, Grammy, and two Emmys came out of Lubbock. No connections to Hollywood at all. All out of Lubbock. Of course it's true I could have done it anywhere, but, I did it in Lubbock.

It was shortly after the Emmys when I read an article in an entertainment magazine that said to the effect, "Is the entertainment world being taken over by an unknown?"[5] It turned out I was one award away from winning the "Showbiz Awards Grand Slam," the EGOT (**E**mmy, **G**rammy, **O**scar, **T**ony). And in history only 61 people have gotten this close, and that is out of billions of people. And all 61 of those people were famous, at least famous enough to have their own Wikipedia page. I was the only one who wasn't. The only award I hadn't been given was the Tony, which is also famous enough to have its own Wikipedia page, so I learned it is the award given to Broadway plays.

Well, this one seemingly would be hard to do from Lubbock, because the play has to be done on Broadway in NYC. So I decided to write a play in Lubbock and just have it put on in NYC. I was pleasantly surprised to learn that a lot of the plays on Broadway were musicals. I had been toying around with the idea of adapting Jonathan Swift's *A Modest Proposal* into a musical, so I thought

---

[5] It did not say that. -Edgar

121

that was our best shot. The only problem was I never sat down to write it. Whenever I thought I wanted to write it I realized how much more I wanted to watch *Law & Order,* and with just a basic satellite television package, there is rarely any time you can't find some version of *Law & Order* on TV. And even if there wasn't any *Law & Order* on TV, I had purchased all the available seasons on DVD, so that really wasn't an issue.

So I had to figure out another way to get a Tony. Luckily, for the awards won by the show as a whole, the producer gets the award. And it still totally counts toward getting an EGOT. And it turns out I actually didn't even have to do any work. You could take an old play that had already been on Broadway, just do it again, and win the award for best revival. And there are awards for best revival of play and best revival of a musical. So, what could I do? I got in touch with my musical theatre friends in NYC and told them that I was producing some shows and wanted to know if they would be interested in helping me put them on. Then we just found three musicals that had already won best musical, and three plays that won best play, and I told them that we needed to put them on and make them the best shows on Broadway. And then I gave them all my Pope comic book money and told them to get it done.

I won. What can I say? EGOTed. Thirteenth person ever. Baker's dozen. Well, really tenth. I mean, EGOTing is something so few people get to do that they add people to the list who have asterisks by their name, and you know you don't count those. Babs and Liza both didn't EGOT because they got three awards and then the fourth award was all like "We want to give you one too." And not real ones that you win, but ones that they just tell you you are going to get, like lifetime achievement things. And Whoopi got Daytime Emmys. Bleck.

Did I mention that one of my plays and one of my musicals won? They did. So put that with my two Emmys, I was pretty close to EGOTing twice. And no one has ever done that. So I made a few calls to the *Land Before Time* people. Now that I had EGOTed they were much more willing to talk to me than they were before. I asked them if they could take my best unused *LBT* script, change all names and pretend it isn't a *LBT* script, (you know, because the series had

lost all credibility) and release it as a new movie. And make me producer. And do a good job so it will win best animated movie Oscar. It
did. Score. Three quarters of the way to a second EGOT. Then I
asked them to take my third best script, make it a new *LBT* movie,
and make my second best script the liner notes. Done. Double
EGOT. First person ever.

A MAN OF THE WORLD

After I EGOTed (twice), I decided Edgar and I needed a new business venture to keep us busy, because, as you know, we have pretty much done everything there is to do with books, publishing, and entertainment in general, so I bought a resort town in China, called it Yurva, and made up post cards stating "Greetings from Yurva, China," but the plan never took off much more than me buying a resort in China and making post cards. In fact, I do not know if anyone ever stayed there, or if they did how I could get money from it, or how I could get the deed to the resort from the Chinese man I met who sold it to me, or anything like that.

What I realized was that what I wanted wasn't to open up a resort in China with a pun name, but what I really yearned for was to live in a simpler time. I mean, sure, the world is great now, with computers, cell phones, and mail that can get across the country overnight, but what happened to the days when young men walked around with canes for no reason, and beat the tar out of each other with them on the Senate floor, and countries' boundaries weren't so set in stone?

It was an Olympic year, and watching the games, Edgar and I decided that we would absolutely love to have our own Olympic team, complete with the flag to be flown when our country wins, and a national anthem to play as our flag waves. But, it is hard to start your own country, and we had nothing to go on. We thought that maybe we would be able to pick up Luxembourg, because, and this a fact that we don't often tell people, we are direct descendants of Guy de Luxembourg. We just figured that not many people would be able to trace their lineage back to 13th Century Luxembourg, and whoever was in charge over there would recognize our position, and name us Dukes. And if you don't already know, Luxembourg is the last country in the world that is a Grand Duchy, meaning, it is run by the Grand Duke.

So Edgar and I devised our plan of government for when we took over Luxembourg. First, we had to decided what song we wanted to be our national anthem, to play whenever we won an Olympic event. There wasn't much pressure here to make a good national anthem, because, being Americans, no matter what we would do, we would end up with a better national anthem than we have here.

With the exception of the UK, whose national anthem is just a plea to God not to kill the monarch, every country's national anthem makes ours look like a lactating hobo. It is a song full on nonsensical questions, raised about our flag, penned about what the flag looked like one day during a war we lost, saying nothing about the actual country, including the name. Not that hard to top.

After some discussion, we were headed in the direction of "Duke of Earl," but we realized it really wouldn't make any sense being that we were the Dukes of Luxembourg, not Earl, so we thought maybe just taking the tune of a pop song, and adding lyrics about how great the Dukes of Luxembourg were, but then Randy Newman's "Short People" came on the radio, and we knew it was our song.

The next thing to do was design our flag. I don't know if it is an urban legend or if it is true actual fact, but I had always heard that the Olympic flag contained at least one color from every flag that participated in the Olympics. To test if this was true, we decided that the one requirement for our flag was to not have any of the colors shown on the Olympic flag, so we made it a purple flag with a brown wombat on it. Nothing else. No black outline for the wombat, not even a black dot for its eye. Just purple flag, brown shape of a wombat. Having these things in order, we felt that we had enough, and caught the first flight to Luxembourg, which was actually the first flight to Houston, followed by sequential flights to Newark,

London, Paris, then Luxembourg. Once we were there, we were able to talk to absolutely no one, and apparently, no one there cared that we were descended from Guy de Luxembourg, because they all were, too. Which was actually a real disappointment to Edgar who couldn't date anyone because everyone there was his cousin.

We went back to our hotel room to think about it. Obviously, Luxembourg was a fairly large country, over half a million people, and they seemed fairly satisfied with their government. We had to think of something else. And we had to come up with a better plan for getting the country, because just showing up and asking to talk to the people in charge did not work.

So, we spent the next day sitting at a small café looking for a country to rule. The best we could find was the Isle of Man. I had been there once previously. The home of cold showers and warm beer, surely these people would love for Edgar and me to come in and show them what is going on. Plus, I kind of in the back of my mind never got over the notion of wanting to be a haberdasher, just for name, but in America, they have bastardized the word to mean anyone who sells men's clothing. And I don't want to do that. I would much rather just sell buttons and strings, and that is still considered haberdashing in the Isle of Man. Of course, I don't really want to sell strings and buttons, but I do want to call myself a haberdasher. But I would rather sell strings and buttons than menswear.

We studied up on the country, and we just couldn't figure it out. Apparently, they were kind of like an English colony, but they also have their own government, and they are ruled by the Queen, but they have their own parliament, and they are not a part of the European Union, but they issue British passports, and they issue their own money, but they take the British pound. And the UK has a Lordship over the Isle. That's all we know. But, we kind of thought it sounded like when Gandhi was pissed that the British had control of India, so we had an idea.

We went to the Isle of Man, by way of ferry from Liverpool, and arrived in Douglas, the capital. Once there we checked into a luxury hotel, and announced we were not going to eat until the Manx (people who live in the Isle of Man) were free of the British crown. We were dead set on this for about the first 30 minutes, but realized that we hadn't eaten in hours. So we decided that it wasn't cool that we were starting a hunger strike on empty stomachs, so we went out and bought a couple of baps, which were really no more than Egg McMuffins, with better eggs. So we went back to the hotel, called the local media, and told them of our hunger strike.

After the media left, we were incredibly hungry again, so we went out to a beachfront concession stand and got a couple of to-mato sandwiches. They weren't very filling, so we never broke our hunger strike, you know, because we were still hungry after eating them. And, of course we were miserable everyday when we had to take a cold shower, so I think we may have suffered even more than Gandhi did.

We set up a webpage for an independent Isle of Man, com-plete with a live streaming video of us on our hunger strike, which was on us at all times, except when one of us was in the bathroom or eating, which we only did one at a time, because, well, if we were both off camera, that would defeat the purpose, and make boring TV. Of course, I am sure if anyone watched the video, they might have wondered why two guys who didn't eat had to go number two so often.

After several weeks of this, we got absolutely no attention, no one even noticed we were there anymore. So we decided we needed to read a little bit more about Gandhi. We found out that he took a vow of chastity, then slept every night in a bed full of young naked women, to prove how awesome he was. I called Hazel and asked, and she said I could not do that, but Edgar, being the pleasantly sin-gle bachelor he is, had no problem doing this. This got us a bit of attention, with the Isle of Man having half the population of Lubbock, Edgar having a half dozen different naked girls sleep in his bed was the talk of everyone in the country.

And as soon as he started doing this, our webpage went from about three hits a day to well over 10,000 over night, and within a week, we were averaging about a half million hits a night, and you know, for a country of only 80,000, that's kind of a lot.

Soon, Edgar no longer had to go out to the streets, awk-wardly explain to the local girls that he was a rich America version of

Gandhi and was going to free the Isle of Man, and she should sleep naked in his bed so he can not have sex with her. And as horrible of a pick up line as that sounds, you have to remember, this is the Isle of Man, there is really not anything that much better to do than, you know, try to help the next Gandhi. But now, girls were lining up around the corner to sleep naked with Edgar on camera, because, and no disrespect to the Manx, but when was the last time you saw any Manx person in the spotlight? And except for my Manx readership, how many of you to still think at this point that I just made up a name and am pretending it's a real place. Well, it is a real place, and it has been overlooked long enough, and people there just want to be known, even if it is for sleeping naked in a bed with the next Gandhi.

In fact, there were so many girls willing to help with this cause, that we had to move to a different room in the hotel, one with two double beds and a twin bed (yes, they have those over there, they have a lot of rooms with weird combinations of beds, don't know why), and Edgar pushed the double beds together to get more naked women on it. And we set a strict rule that no one could sleep in the bed more than one night, and the count for the girls who had come through the room reached the hundreds. Of course this made Edgar way too distracted to sleep and made him very slæpwerigne.

We also got a lot of international support. And by international support, I mean Wales. Apparently, there is a mind set with the Welsh, at least the ones who visited our site, that if anyone has the chance to take something from England that England thinks is theirs, then that person should do it. One Welshman actually came to visit us in the hotel, and gave me a manuscript, written entirely in the Welsh language (Welsh) titled 'r Am-dro i mewn 'r Helyg and told me to publish it, and said he wanted no credit for it, and asked that Edgar and I publish it under our own names. We emailed it to Hazel and Bellini back in the States and told them to rush the publication on it immediately. Hazel told us that because of the time difference, Bellini spent almost his entire workday watching our live stream, because it had naked people in it. While we were supposed to be sleeping on the Isle, he was supposed to be working. I told her to fire him for it, and she said she wouldn't, claiming that his productivity had gone up ten fold since Edgar and I had been gone.

I think you may have seen this coming, but, Edgar and I got deported without ever having the Isle of Man given to us. When the immigration officials came to deport us, I asked if we were being deported from the Isle of Man or from the UK. He said the Isle of Man. So I asked if we could go to the UK. He said no. He had to send us back to the US. I asked if after we were back in the States if we could go back to the UK. He said no, they wouldn't grant us entry. I asked why. He said because we were banned. I said I thought we were banned from the Isle of Man, but not the UK, and he said... I am getting bored with this but I think you can see my point that I have no idea how this government is set up.

When we got back to Lubbock, there were a few loose ends to tie up in the office, a resonator guitar and ukulele to tune, a musical comedy routine to finish up for Rowlf and Fozzie, and we had to revamp our plans to form an Olympic team in case we were never given our own country.

I decided that if I wanted my own Olympic team, maybe my best bet was Puerto Rico. Because it always baffled me why they had one, since they are part of the United States, and every single one of their citizens is a US citizen, but they have one, nonetheless, and of course, I don't think they ever win anything because if I am not mistaken, all the Puerto Ricans who have athletic talent are allowed on the US Olympic team. I didn't really know how to do that, but I thought maybe if I became Puerto Rico's Resident Commissioner, that could be a start.

I had always been jealous of the Resident Commissioner's job, because it seemed so much easier and less stressful than mine. Basically, it is the United States House of Representative member from Puerto Rico who can't vote. Except in a committee, unless the vote will make a difference, you know, mean something, then he can't vote. I could so easily do that! A job for sitting there, not mattering. But getting paid the same as all the real senators and congressmen. To do nothing. And come on, that has to be a fun campaign, running for fake congressman from Puerto Rico. Because, at least in the campaigns here they say, "I am going to take a stand, vote for what matters to Texans," but for Puerto Rico? What do you say? "I would love to sit in Congress and not do anything. I can totally rock it at attending meetings, where I can just sit there and not be expected to do anything. And get paid the same as real congressmen. Seriously. I can do that. I can show up to meetings on time and sit there until the meeting is over." I don't know, if I saw me on that commercial, I would vote for me. Unless I was running as a Tea Party candidate. Don't want to have to explain that one to Jesus on Judgment Day, you know, why I voted Tea Party. Unless I die the same day as Edgar. Then I wouldn't mind explaining it. I would just slip it in when Edgar is explaining the hundreds of naked Manx girls. Just a little "Sorry for voting Tea Party" before Edgar gets to the part where he pushed the beds together, and I should be good.

But, fortunately, I didn't have to figure out how to become the Resident Commissioner long, because we were contacted by the UK. I don't know who, because I couldn't understand through the accent, and it was some title I was not familiar with anyway, but he asked if Edgar and I were still interested in taking over the Isle of Man. Of course I said yes, and asked if this meant our ban was lifted. The accented man explained to me that since Edgar and I left, there was great unrest in the Isle of Man, since we were kind of the most exciting thing to happen to them for a while. And, there was kind of the sentiment that, yes, even though Edgar and I would probably be the most horrible rulers a country could possibly have, as of now they were just dealing with a very confusing government that the British held over them. They liked the idea of a government of their own, completely free from the influence of any other country.

Edgar and I were given three months to come up with a plan of government and to actually take over a country. And, as you probably know, all we had was a flag and a song. And, I was starting to have doubts about the flag. I mean, sure, it was awesome, but we designed it when we were planning on taking over Luxembourg, and the Manx flag is *really* awesome. The best I can describe it is as a three legged leg. And I have no idea what it is supposed to mean, but Edgar and I decided to keep it, and had two official national flags. But the wombat flag was definitely the Olympic Manx flag, because of the color thing.

That day, Edgar and I took a long lunch at Home Plate Diner to try to figure out how this government would work.

"Well, I think we should stick with what we were planning on with Luxembourg and make it a Grand Duchy," I suggested.

"Douchy?"

"No, Duchy."

"What?"

"Duchy. A dukedom," I explained.

"What?"

"Like, a kingdom is presided over by a king, the dukedom is presided over by the duke."

"When did we decide that?" Edgar asked.

"With Luxembourg. It is a Grand Duchy, we were just going to keep it the same."

"So, what you are wanting to do is make basically a new Luxembourg?" asked Edgar.

"Yes."

"So, do we call it New Luxembourg."

"I think we can. Saying Isle of Man out loud always makes me feel kind of gay. I feel like after I say it I should specify that in reality I love women."

"So, it's New Luxembourg then?"

"Yeah, well, I think a more proper title would be The Grand Dukedom of New Luxembourg," I suggested.

"And which one of us would be the duke?"

"Me."

"Why you?" Edgar asked.

"Well, it was my idea, and you are the elder brother, you would be the king, and as the younger brother, I would be the duke. Bernie Douglas."

"So, if I am king, then I out rank you?"

"No, it's a dukedom. There is no king."

"Well, if neither of us are kings, wouldn't we both be dukes?"

"Well, yeah, I guess, but these people are fresh off of being British, and they will get confused."

"What do you mean?" asked Edgar.

"Ok, when Queen Elizabeth's husband died, and her daughter became queen, they thought it would be too confusing for British people if they were both called queen, so they called the old Queen Elizabeth the Queen Mother, and her daughter the young Queen Elizabeth just Queen."

"What are you getting at?"

"I could be the duke, and you could be the duke brother."

"Alright, I'll take that if we change the name to the Grand Dukedom and Duke Brotherdom of New Luxembourg."

"That sounds good to me," I said.

"So are we just going to leave it at that? We are in charge of the government, and no one else is?"

"Well, no, they have a parliament, and I kind of like that."

"But we hardly know anyone in this country. We know nothing about them, how they think, what directions they lean politically, do we really want to leave our country in their hands?"

"No, but, if we are the duke and duke brother, than we could appoint the parliament."

"We have three months to do this, how are we going to appoint and entire parliament?"

"Well, there doesn't have to be a set number of people in parliament, it can change every year, but this first time, it could be just you and me."

"How are we going to get any respect if we do this?"

"You know as well as I do who we are descended from, and I'm not talking about Guy de Luxembourg."

"Bernie, we don't talk about that."

"You know, these days, there is hardly anyone without French blood in him."

"But you don't go around flaunting it."

"Look Edgar, he wasn't just King of the Franks, he was the Holy Roman Emperor."

"I don't know."

"Look, we can reclaim the family throne, and you are the oldest so you would get to be the Holy Roman Emperor, you'd add it to the duke brother title, we'd get some more respect."

"I guess."

"Grandpappy Charlemagne would be proud."

"Would we need to add something to the name of the country then?"

"I think we should. Maybe The Grand Dukedom and Duke Brotherdom of New Luxembourg of the New Holy Roman Empire?"

"Yeah, but I think we should keep the Isle of Man in there, for old time's sake," suggest Edgar.

"Alright, so, what if we make it The Grand Dukedom and Duke Brotherdom of New Luxembourg of the New Holy Roman Empire at the Isle of Man?"

"I think that will work. But won't we need the Vatican's blessing to be the New Holy Roman Empire?"

"I don't think that will be a problem."

"I think it might be difficult to get the Vatican to take us seriously in our request."

"I think you are forgetting that I am the sole owner of the world's largest *The Life of Pope John Paul II* comic book collection in the world. I'm kind of in tune with the Vatican."

"Well, I guess we should wire someone over in The Grand Dukedom and Duke Brotherdom of New Luxembourg of the New Holy Roman Empire at the Isle of Man, to tell them to change the names on the maps."

Edgar in bed with all those nekkid lady people.

IT'S REALLY HAPPENING

With about three weeks until the scheduled take over, Edgar, Hazel and I moved to the Isle, bought a beachfront condo in Douglas (Bernie Douglas!), ordered a couple of hot water heaters to be shipped in from the United States, and tried to settle in. We had temporarily left Linnaeus Hoffmann in the obviously incapable hands of Bellini, and had given him our office. Edgar and I kept our Rowlf and Fozzie and ukulele and resonator guitar, but we bought Bellini a pair of congas and Rizzo the Rat in hopes that he would keep running the company along the same lines we did. I also sent a weekly meal stipend to Home Plate Diner for him, and left him twelve unfinished *Land Before Time* manuscripts to work on in his spare time. And, probably the most generous thing we did for him was give him the key to the Rampart arcade machine, and changed the currency acceptance from Spanish eight reales to Manx five pence pieces.

In the GaDaDBoNLotNHREatIoM (The Grand Dukedom and Duke Brotherdom of New Luxembourg of the New Holy Roman Empire at the Isle of Man) we were slowly adjusting to island life, eating baps every morning, long horn sheep every other meal, wearing sweaters, watching some TT race, introducing scores of wombats into the ecosystem, just the normal Manx stuff.

Not long after we arrived, we were greeted by the Welshman who had given us the manuscript that I can't pronounce or remember the name of, congratulating us on our acquisition of the nation, and informing us that he was a dean of the University of Wales, asking us to join in their commencement ceremonies, where we would be given our honorary doctorates in Welsh. Edgar and I were absolutely dumbstruck, asking why we would even be considered for such an honor.

"Honestly, you took something from the English, and for that we are eternally grateful, but officially, it is for translating the Rohonc Codex into Welsh."

"We didn't even translate it into English," Edgar protested.

"Yes, we understand the joke. We Britons are very keen on subtle humor, but the manuscript I gave you was a perfect Welsh translation of *The Wind in the Willows,* the best in all of Cymru."

"But we didn't write that."

"The bloody wonder do you think I had you publish it under your names for?"

"Oh I get."

Edgar still stared blankly at me.

"So they would have a real excuse to give us the doctorate."

"Ohhh."

And then we had tea and crumpets, and he left.

Later on, we actually got to meet with the Prime Minister of the United Kingdom, which, at first I was incredibly excited and nervous about, until, I realized I was about to be the crown Duke of the second oldest Grand Duchy in the world, and he should be excited and nervous to meet me. He explained to me that after reading the Wikipedia entry on the Isle of Man, he honestly didn't think he had the authority to give it to us, because he couldn't find anywhere where he had any authority over the Isle at all. I was quite disappointed, but he said that that King Henry IX is the head of state, so he asked King Henry if he would mind giving authority of the Isle to us. Henry said he had never heard of such a place. And then, Henry too read the Wikipedia article on the Isle and discovered that he had a Lieutenant Governor acting as his liaison in all matters dealing with the Isle. (It occurs to me, that as you are reading this you may not know how Henry IX became king, because with me writing this precognitively, chances are you are could be reading it before the historic events that I know have come to fruition. Ok, Queen Elizabeth lived to be 103 years old, and held onto her reign until the day she died. This left her son Charles to become king at the age of 81. He lasted about three months and then he died. So, his son William became king at age 47. And then he converted to Hinduism. And of course his subjects didn't like this, him being the head of the Church of England and all. And plus he had moved to India, and started hating England, grew his hair out all long, grew a beard, and really didn't want to be King of England anyway. So he resigned the role of king and gave it to his brother Harry. Who is really named Henry.)

Of course, he had no idea who this liaison was, so he asked around the palace for a couple of days and finally found this Lieutenant Governor, and he asked him very politely if he minded if the King gave all control and power in the Isle of Man to a couple of brothers from Texas wanting to set up a Dukedom and Duke Brotherdom. The Lieutenant Governor admitted that he hadn't done anything in literally years, and as long as he kept getting paid, he didn't really care what happened, so it looked like we were getting ourselves a country, officially now, from the King of England.

I decided it was about time that I appointed the Prime Minister of The Grand Dukedom and Duke Brotherdom of New Luxembourg of the New Holy Roman Empire at the Isle of Man, so after hours of talk with his agent and publicist, I finally got a hold of George Wendt and told him the great news, that he was appointed Prime Minister of The Grand Dukedom and Duke Brotherdom of New Luxembourg of the New Holy Roman Empire at the Isle of Man. He told me he'd never heard of the place. I told him that as of right now it is just the Isle of Man, and next week it would be The Grand Dukedom and Duke Brotherdom of New Luxembourg of the New Holy Roman Empire at the Isle of Man. He said he'd still never heard of it. I told him it was smack dab in the center of the British Isles in the middle of the Irish Sea. He said he had heard of the British Isles, so I told him that it was a nation in the middle of them, and he was now the Prime Minister of it.

He turned it down.

I said it really wasn't up to him. He disagreed and hung up.

I left a message with his agent explaining that the newly penned constitution of The Grand Dukedom and Duke Brotherdom of New Luxembourg of the New Holy Roman Empire at the Isle of Man did not allow for the Prime Minister to turn down the position, and whether he liked it or not, George Wendt was the Prime Minister of The Grand Dukedom and Duke Brotherdom of New Luxembourg of the New Holy Roman Empire at the Isle of Man. She thanked me for the message, and that was the last I heard from either of them for a long time.

Before we acquired the country, King Henry wanted to meet with us, Edgar and me, to make sure our intentions were pure, or something like that. I think it was really just a formality. He really didn't seem to care who got the country.

Then a lot of other stuff happened, which I am sure that if you want to read it you can read it in a history book, or maybe Edgar's book. But, let's just skip to the good parts. Edgar and I bought suits that look straight out of a Charles Dickens novel, or at least the movie adaptation of one, Hazel dressed in her best glad rags and hat, and I got to give my inaugural address, (which I realize might be the wrong word to use for becoming a Duke from total obscurity, but I really don't know the proper word.)

I stood in front of what very possibly could have been the entire Manx population and gave my address:

"I would like to thank King Henry IX, the King of England and Canada, not just for giving me and my brother this great nation of The Grand Dukedom and Duke Brotherdom of New Luxembourg of the New Holy Roman Empire at the Isle of Man, but also for being a truly a great man. Let me tell you a story. The first day everyone got together to discuss this acquisition, I was completely nervous, surround by such powerful men as the King himself, his sons, the Princes of Wales, American President Gabe Kaplan and for some reason that has still not been explained to me, Bono, that I farted. And it was a rank, noxious fart that made everyone at the table a little queasy. It was very sulfuric, and was most likely caused by the blood sausage that I loaded up on at breakfast that morning. Already feeling like an outsider, this just made me want to crawl into a corner and die, but Hank, that's what he let's me call him, stood up and said, 'It was me who farted.' He did that for me! He took the blame for my fart. And he would take credit for a fart emitted by any one of you as well. And that's not just because he has a critical bowel ailment that makes it impossible for him to flatulate, and he doesn't want anyone to know about his clinched sphincter, so he acts like he farts when he really doesn't so people don't get suspicious as to the reasons he never toots, but he would want to save you from embarrassment. Sure, it will also save him the embarrassment of being a freak of nature with no natural way of releasing gas pressure anally, but that's not why he does it. So Hankie, thank you.

"I also want to speak directly to the Manx people, and thank you for your overwhelming support. I have read the recent polls, and I am truly touched that only 1% of you disapprove of our new plan of government. And although we only have a 4% approval rating, 95% of you said that you really don't care. And those are numbers we can work with. It is that common attitude that the Duke Brother and I will adopt, and bring to you, and share with you. And in lieu of Edgar, your new Duke Brother, giving an acceptance speech, we would like to do a routine that we worked up with Fozzie and Rowlf."

And, not surprisingly, 4% of Manx approved of my inaugural address, 1% disapproved, and 95% just plain didn't care.

SETTLING IN

We built a large manor in Douglas (the city, not one of us).
But going back to that previous parenthetical, you would not believe
the disappointment that some tourists experience when they are
told they will be getting to explore the sites of Douglas, and it is only
the city and not my named body (or the body of my brother or wife).
We had a large mansion on the manor, for me and Hazel, and an
equally large guesthouse to be the permanent home of the Duke
Brother. Connecting the two houses were walkways leading to our
official state offices, also on the estate.

To show support, many heads of state of nations that sup-
ported us gave us ornate gifts for the estate, but none more than Ireland, who as you know, was able to completely break free from England's grip as well. Ireland, having heard of my charitable efforts in
Lubbock, and realizing I had quite a fondness for statues, donated a
very large one to sit right at the entrance to the estate. They had a
large unveiling ceremony, similar to the one I had for the first Meat
Loaf statue, complete with the purple cloth, draping the statue,
completely concealing any idea of what might lie beneath it.

Edgar and I came to the unveiling ceremony wearing our
first suits custom tailored by an actual European, so the shoulders
were more rounded and naturally shaped. We looked very handsome. Which, wasn't anything new. I think most of our popularity
and success in life has come to us because we are both ridiculously
handsome. Me more than Edgar, because I have more pleasing facial
features. And to top off our outfits, we donned our nicest top hats,

reminiscent of the Kennedy inauguration. Not to be out done, Hazel wore an even taller hat. And some kind of dress thing. She had a look she needed to maintain, after all, not only was she the Duchess of the Isle of Man, she was Duchess Brother Sister in Law. That was probably the title that took us the longest to figure out, because as the sister in law of the Duke Brother, it wouldn't fit to call her the Duchess Sister in Law, because you would think then that she was the Duke's sister in law, but she wasn't, she was my wife, and plus, the title Duchess Sister in Law was reserved for the wife of the Duke Brother, whenever he finally gets one. So we wanted a title like Duke Sister in Law, but she can't be called a Duke, because she is a woman, and that would be gross. So we had to reference the Duke Brother, and her being a woman, and his sister in law all in one title, so that's what we came up with.

Some Irish guy was at the podium, I think presenting the statue to us, but I honestly have no idea what he was saying. I have a hard enough time understanding what the Manx are saying because they just don't sound like people in Lubbock, TX, all talking faster, putting weird emphasis on words, but finally, he pulled off the cloth and there were three men in the statue, all of them with long hair, two bearded, and each wearing a ridiculously collared shirt unbutton down past the bottom of the sternum with a massive amount of chest hair.

I leaned over to Edgar, "What is this."

"I think it is some kind of joke."

"Why?"

"It's like the college fraternities that like to prank each other, I think they are starting a rivalry."

Hazel poked her head in between us. "What are you two whispering about?"

"Trying to figure out what this statue is. Edgar thinks they are pranking us."

"It's the Bee Gees," she said.

"Well FDR on a tuna, Eddie, you were right. They got us good."

"It's not a prank guys, they picked the Bee Gees because they were born here, and maybe the most recognizable Manx people in the world right now."

"No, I think I am right. They pranked us good. We need to get them back."

I smiled. "I got an idea. I will tell you tonight."

"Good. While we are here, I have a question."

"What is it?"

"While we were in Lubbock you kept putting up statues of Meat Loaf everywhere."

"Yes, but that's not a question."

"I know, but I was just wondering, why Meat Loaf and not John Denver."

"Because Meat Loaf briefly attended college in Lubbock and then dropped out."

"So did John Denver," Edgar asked.

"Are you lying?"

"No, he went to Tech and dropped out."

"Why didn't you tell me this earlier!" With that line I forgot we were whispering. The ceremony speaker stopped and everyone was looking at me. I started whispering again.

"I, I, don't even know what to say, Edgar. This, this, I thought I had my life in order, thought it made sense."

"Don't worry about it, Bernie. Your life still makes sense. If I know you, you will forget about this tomorrow."

"No, I can't. I made it my mission to give Lubbock the statues it deserved and I failed them."

"Bernie, your mission was to entertain yourself where you were at any cost and without regard to other people, and you did that. You did it beautifully. And now you are somewhere new, I am sure you are going to forget Lubbock and do whatever you want to this place just for your entertainment as well."

"Thanks, Edgar. That means a lot."

"I wasn't trying to help."

That night we went back to our office, where looking out the wall length windows we could see the Bee Gees in all their "glory."

"Alright Edgar, I got the perfect prank."

Then the phone rang. I answered it. It was Bellini.

"What do you want?"

"The business is out of control. I need help."

"Look Chris, we put you in charge because you have been with Linnaeus Hoffmann longer than anyone, and we gave you all the tools that we had to make this company work."

"Bernie, you left me with a puppet and a personal assistant who is not allowed to do anything but play piano."

"And a pair of congas."

"Oh yeah, those were very nice, thank you."

"So, are you just not getting new authors, or are the existing ones not putting out, or what?"

"No, we have plenty of new authors, and the numbers of repeats from the existing authors is unprecedented."

"So are they not selling or what?"

"No, sales have doubled."

"What's the problem?"

"We are overloaded. Proofreaders are working day and night, with Hazel gone it takes twice as long to format the books now, and then it's almost impossible to get a galley in by the deadline..."

I interrupted. "What have you been ordering at the Home Plate Diner lately?"

"I've been working through lunch."

I was speechless and exasperated. It was apparent to me that the YEARS Edgar and I had spent in Lubbock, giving Bellini the perfect example of an exquisite business model had been wasted, so I just quickly gave him something that I knew wouldn't work but would get him off the phone. "Take the people working on new author acquisitions, and the people who are working on getting new novels from our existing clients, reassign them to the jobs that we are backed up on, like proofing and design, halt all acquisitions until we have the books in production under control, and have marketing switch focus from the books that already show signs of a following to the lesser known and anticipated titles, so we will have a better overall sales, and our money will be focused on improving overall sales and won't waste money just patting ourselves on the back. Got it?"

"Sounds good."

"Bye."

Now I turned to Edgar. "Have you been thinking of any good pranks?"

"What if we tell them that Northern Island, inspired by us, wants to leave the UK as well, and tell them that we have worked up a peace treaty, have them show up to sign it, and then they will just feel silly when there isn't one."

"That's pretty good," I agreed. "I was thinking that we go on a tour Ireland, and every time we attract large enough crowd, we duck into a bathroom, making sure the crowd follows us in, then go to the urinal, drop our trousers and our underpants to our ankles, stand there urinating bare buttocksed, then we look around and notice that no one else has their bare buttocks hanging out, probably looking confusedly at us, and we ask why they don't have their pants at their ankles, and act disgusted at how uncivilized and uncultured they are, until the whole country thinks the proper way to urinate in public is with your trousers and undergarments at you ankles."

"Not bad," Edgar comments, "but what if we eat babies."

"I don't see how that would be pranking Ireland."

"We could tell them that the *Modest Proposal* they submitted in the 17th Century was a really good idea, and we could enact it into law, and force them to admit it was a bad idea."

"What if," I suggested, "we infiltrate the Guinness factory, and make it taste really bad and bitter, so they will no longer want to drink it."

"Have you ever had Guinness?" Edgar asked.

"No."

"Just trust me that that one won't work. But thinking along those lines, we could switch their potato seeds next season with rhubarb, and then they will be really surprised the next year when they have the world's biggest rhubarb crop."

"I think that one is way over the line, Edgar."

"What do you mean?"

"These are the same people who starved to death by the thousands because they were such picky eaters they refused to eat anything besides potatoes. We could be charged with genocide. What if we took a snake to Ireland."

"What do you mean?"

"They don't have any snakes there. According to Irish lore, they were driven out by St. Patrick, and according to reality, there have never been any there, ever."

"Even better," Edgar said, "as the New Holy Roman Empire, we are kind of the authority on Catholicism and such, why don't we just change the official documents to show that St. Patrick never made it to Ireland, but instead is the patron saint of Iceland, then report our recent 'finds' and then we put the snakes in Ireland and act like they had been lying about not having them this whole time."

So, we decided to go with the snake and St. Patrick prank, with the only change being that we would drop the snakes in Ireland first, then when Ireland was all "What the pants just happened?" we would pop up with our latest Vatican findings, and claim St. Patrick never delivered snakes out of Ireland, and that they had been lying this whole time, and now that the snakes were so overabundant, they could no longer lie about it, and it is pretty obvious that they were being deceitful this whole time. We were even thinking about formally asking Ireland to give the symbol of the shamrock to Ireland, since it was Iceland's patron saint and not theirs that used it as a symbol of the Trinity, with the mention that we are sure if they give the shamrock to Iceland, Iceland would be more than happy to give Ireland the use of Saint Thorlac Thorhallsson, the patron saint of Iceland, since now they are aware of their more prestigious saint, they will find they have little use for Thorlac. And, the loss of the shamrock, in my opinion, can be replaced by the symbol of the skate. And not the wheeled footwear, but the stingray. It is the traditional meat for the meal for the feast of Saint Thorlac Thorhallsson, observed on December 23. When viewed flat and from above, with the tail at the bottom, it looks enough like a shamrock to me to replace it in pictures, or statues, or wherever they put them, and it really shouldn't be that big of a deal to the Irish, since, as we know, the shamrock is not the national symbol of Ireland, but the harp is.

So, in a top secret mission, Edgar and I called up some aviation buffs we knew in Lubbock, told them our plans, and they were up for it. Of course they didn't have a plane that would get to the Isle of Man, so they took a commercial flight to London, and then another one to Liverpool, and then a ferry to Douglas, but they arrived here safely. Then we contacted dozens of reptile suppliers, posing as pet store owners, and bought the lot. Literally over a thousand. Then we loaded them up on a couple of old British bombers that surprisingly we just had laying around, and our friends both went up, flying high enough that they weren't really visible from the ground, and they dumped all of the snakes.

The original plan was to evenly disperse them all over the Irish countryside, but the guys were kind of nervous, afraid of getting caught or what not, so as soon as they were over land they dumped their entire load, right over Dublin. But that's okay, because can you imagine the look on all those drunken patties' faces when they were sitting in their living rooms, drinking whiskey and hitting their wives, when all of a sudden snakes slithered down their chimney, and maybe ate a baby or two?

We were about to call up Ireland and tell them when we pranked them good, when one of my advisors came in and told me that Ireland had just been attacked by international terrorists, and the Irish Army was preparing for retaliation. I asked him if we had an army, and he wasn't sure, but I told him to let Ireland know that if we did have an army, we would help in any way possible.

I decided not to call Ireland immediately, since they were just attacked by terrorists, but I'd give it a few days. Later that day, while watching the British news (we didn't have any national Manx networks at the time), I heard of the terrorist acts in Ireland. Apparently, what the terrorist acts were, were people dropping snakes over the city of Dublin. However, since they were so high when they dropped the snakes, combined with the fact that most of them landed on hard streets and rooftops, every single snake died on impact. Which, I guess is not a bad thing. I mean, we still got our prank off, and we didn't leave any lasting ecological damage, like it was becoming increasingly more apparent that we did here in the Dukedom with our wombat introduction.

Well, it wasn't hard for them to trace the snakes back to us, I mean, every single reptile dealer in northern Europe sold us snakes, and Edgar and I had to figure this out.

"I have an idea," Edgar said. "I know they can trace the snakes to us, but what if we pawn it off on Linnaeus Hoffmann, say they were for Bellini, he came and picked them up and we have no idea what happened after they left."

"No, that's no good. Bellini is the only person we have that can keep Linnaeus Hoffmann from going down the crapper, and plus, as far as I know, I am the only LH staffer who has been to prison, I still like being the tough guy."

"But I don't think you realize how hilarious this would be, he would be sent to the Irish version of Guantanamo Bay, with all that, well, I don't know what they do there, but trust me it is going to be funny."

"Why would the Irish even have a Guantanamo Bay?"

"I don't know," Edgar said. "To keep the Protestants in. Or the Catholics. I forget which one is bad."

"What if we say it was an accident," I suggested. 'We could say that it wasn't a terrorist act, we were just trying to bring our snakes home, a latch broke, and every single one of our snakes fell out and died. And we are heartbroken, because we were hoping to start a children's reptile museum in Peel."

"Why was the plane over Dublin then?"

"Because it was coming from Canada."

"A single engine bomber?"

"They don't know it was a single engine bomber. They could think it was one large commercial size plane."

"Do you think they will give us the snakes back?"

"I hope so. You could make some really nice boots."

"I was thinking a belt myself."

"Oh, that would be nice."

After that, we had a press conference talking about our tragic loss of our beloved snakes on a routine flight from Canada to the Dukedom, and we offered our most sincere and heartfelt apologies to anyone who had been affected by this tragedy, as it greatly affected us as well. And just for good measure, we said the whole thing could have been avoided if it were not for Christopher Dale Bellini of Lubbock, TX, USA.

OLYMPICS

As you may or may not remember, Edgar and I decided to get our own country simply to have our wombat flag fly over the Olympic stadium while our national anthem, "Short People" is played over the audience, and we have been trying our hardest to was find gold medal quality athletes in the Dukedom. And that's nothing against the people who live here, they are immensely talented, its just a very small number of people to choose from. Think about it, to find one Olympic champion in the Isle of Man would be like cutting Lubbock in half and saying, "find someone who's an Olympic champion at something." Just not a big enough pot to choose from.

I am sure that I don't have to mention this, because I am sure that you all remember the last winter Olympics, that we actually hosted in Douglas. Which, was a challenge since we don't even have a single ski resort in the Dukedom, but we wooed the International Olympic Committee, promised to build the world's largest, most state of the art, indoor ski resort. Which would have been awesome. It was being touted as the Olympics of the future. You know, because the future wouldn't have any winters at all. Global warming. The reason we were pushing so hard for it is because whoever is the host country can put all of their teams in the Olympics, even if they don't qualify. And Edgar and I seriously couldn't qualify, but if we could get in anyway, well, we'd go for it.

I have always felt that probably everyone has enormous talent that they just don't know about. They never had the opportunity to discover it. Take the luge for instance. You see the winner each Olympic year, and know he is the best in the world, but, how many people have actually tried luge before? Not many. What if the luge champion had been born in Nigeria? He would still have that inner luge talent, but never know it because he would never luge. That's probably why champion runners deserve the most respect, because everyone in the world has tried to run before, so there are no people out there with running talent who haven't discovered it yet, so the guy with the gold around his neck for running is literally the best runner in the world. It is very likely, maybe even probable, that as I am sitting here writing this, that I am the best, most talented accountant in the world, but, because I have never dabbled in accountancy, no one will ever know it. Not even me, because it sounds really boring.

That last paragraph had very little to do with anything in this book, except for the fact that growing up, watching the Olympics, I always felt like I would do really well as one of the middle guys in the four man bobsled who just sit there, and I thought Edgar could do equally well as the other middle guy who sits there, so we went into the Olympic selection process with the feeling that if we get the Olympics, then we could be the middle men on the bobsled team, have a guaranteed spot in the games, and probably win a gold medal.

Of course, once we were awarded the games, we started to crunch numbers and realized that it would cost about $800 million to build this indoor skiing facility. And, if you remember our population, you would realize to get this money, we would have to tax each person in the entire Dukedom $10 million just to build it,[6] and with the average household income being right at $35,000, it would be a hard sell to enforce that tax. So we had to come up with another strategy. It's not unheard of in an Olympic game to have some of the events, such as the kayaking or cross-country skiing held in differ-

---

[6] Quite obvious now that Bernie isn't the most talented accountant in the world, right?- Bellini.

ent, nearby cities, and we knew this is what we had to do. We had to find a nearby place with a mountain to host the skiing events.

Luckily, we had Poland. Warsaw was the last city still battling it out with Douglas to host the games, and we felt like they would probably enjoy still hosting at least part of the games, and they already had all the facilities, so we called them up, asked them politely and they agreed. So we built an ice skating rink for the figure skating, and ice skating rink for the hockey, decided that that was probably too many ice skating rinks, then changed one of the ice skating rinks to a shopping mall and called it good. We also bought a flother machine but that was really just for our own personal use. We had the opening ceremony in Douglas, followed by hockey, figure skating and speed skating, and then we went straight to Poland for everything else, including Edgar and me as the middle two guys in the bobsled. We didn't make it to the next day. In fact, there was only one medal earned by the Manx in the entire games, a silver in men's curling. So although our wombat flag with no colors correlating with the Olympic flag did fly in the ceremonies, we didn't get to hear Randy Newman's "Short People."

But the summer Olympics, the summer Olympics was when the Manx shined. The Olympiad following ours was in Cuba, which was fiercely protested and boycotted by the United States, so, there were some of the best athletes in the world that could not take place in the Olympic games. But thanks to our laxed national policies, anyone could be on the Manx Olympic team, as long as they had at least a one-week residency in the Dukedom. And of course, the Dukedom paid completely for the athletes' airfare to the island and boarding, so they had no reason not to come here. Plus, we let them keep their own trainers, paid their trainers, all that stuff. And with the US out of the games, we had no real competition, and won 40 gold medals. It wasn't until that time that Randy Newman learned that we were using his song without his permission as our national anthem. He sued Cuba for royalties for playing the song without permission, but then surprisingly enough, gave us complete permission to use the song in any capacity we wanted.

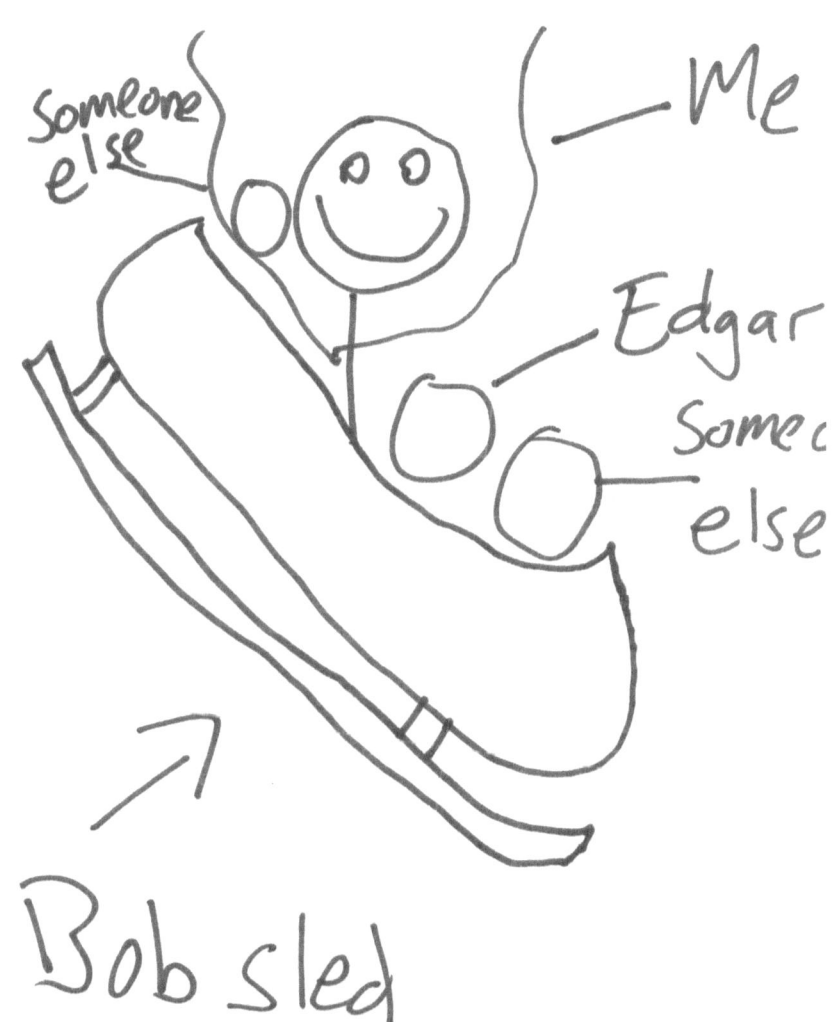

THE END OF IT ALL

I guess I didn't really realize that George Wendt was not acting as the Prime Minister until I got a cease and desist letter from his attorney while building a statue of him along the Manx coastline. And it wasn't the statue he objected to, because the first two dozen he seemed to enjoy quite well, but as you know, I like my statues to be as realistic as possible, and I wanted his measurements to be exact, up to date you know, but the man never would sit down for a proper measuring, so I would have to hire people to track him down on the streets and run up and do surprise measurements one at a time. Assuming all of the measurements went as planned, it usually took about 14 separate occasions to get all the measurements I needed. And twice the guys getting the inseam were punched in the face.

And our approval rating went down. Not our personal ones. Actually, for Edgar and me personally, we had a 35% approval rating, and a 64% not caring either way. But as for us running the government, our disapproval was an overwhelming 7%, and approval was on 1%. But not the Dukedom concept. The Manx loved being the world's second oldest Grand Duchy, but, they wanted more serious leadership, and that is something that I was unable and unwilling to give them. I offered to resign my post, but they wouldn't hear of it, and Edgar was not willing to give up his title of Duke Brother, so we decided to go with a democratically elected parliament, representing the people, and not just Edgar and me appointing ourselves, and we brought back the Lieutenant Governor, and Edgar and I kept our titles, and positions, just resigned all of our power. I was still living off of the Broadway money, which more than tripled my comic book money, and Edgar and I both still had a steady income being co owners of Linnaeus Hoffmann Publishing, but we were ready to cut the strings and just live out the rest of our lives in the peaceful serenity the Isle.

So we decided to take Linnaeus Hoffmann public and sell all our shares, invest the money, and live off the interest, and maybe blow a lot of it building statues. First thing we did was fire Bellini, because we thought that would make the business look more attractive for potential shareholders, and then we went public and sold out. We both ended up wealthy beyond our wildest dreams, well I already was, but now Edgar was satisfied, and Bellini had apparently put no money back, his wife left him, and he died penniless by pulling his own head off.

The End.

AFTERWARD
by Edgar Mls. Douglas

Bernie was well known for the job he did. His career path in life. But he was extremely bad at his job. This is not unusual. Today we still remember people like Amelia Earhart and Oral Roberts. Both famous for their professions. Both extremely bad at them. Bernie was unique though. He took more pride in his failures in life than accomplishments. I feel it is because he knew them all to be accidental. (The accomplishments). Bernie was a good man at heart. He was arrested several times. Each time was because he was trying to be innovative. Do something in a new, better way. He didn't know they were illegal. He didn't mean to break the law. Never dreamed he was breaking the law. That is why he could take pride in them. Fighting the system. Going against the norm.

He did brag about his accomplishments. But all the talk was to cover what he didn't do. He wanted to win an Oscar for best screenplay. He wrote hundreds just for that purpose. He never did. He wanted to win a spoken word comedy Grammy for either his stand up work or reading one of his books on tape. Instead he won for someone else turning his screenplays into liner notes. If he would have gotten his Grammy and Oscar for these he would have never wanted to EGOT. He would have been a lot happier.

Bernie ended the story in the middle. It's not his fault. He didn't know any better. Soon after he finished penning these last words on his department store brand typewriter, he was dead. Figuratively speaking. He lived a long time after he wrote it. He wrote it precognitively. You know that. He died soon after the events of the narrative transpired. He will die then. I will admit I am not sure how the tone should be in the afterward of a precognitive memoir. I will just tell you what happened.

Bellini killed himself. Bernie said that. Bellini had to be demented. He had planned this out for a long time. He even had set a pre need arrangement with the funeral home to be buried in a casket made for a seven foot man even though he was barely five six. He requested to be laid to rest with his arms outstretched straight above him. He wanted to be holding his detached head in place on the pillow in the casket. The rest of his body would be laying a foot lower.

Bernie was kind of correct when he stated Bellini died by pulling his own head off. What Bellini did was construct a noose out of piano wire. He put it around his neck. He sat in a chair. He slathered his hands with super glue. He glued his hands to the sides of his head. He leaned back in the chair. He fell back. He decapitated himself. He still had his head firmly grasped and glued in his hands.

It messed with the medical examiner. Really messed with him.

Later Bernie died. Bernie took up hot air ballooning when he retired. It is not that strange of a hobby for a bored, rich retiree. Bernie took it to an extreme, though. Bernie took up ballooning to the exclusion of all other means of transportation. Bernie would get in his balloon to get a sandwich. He fired up the hot air balloon to fly it a couple blocks to the pub. It would take forever. Just to unfold the envelope and inflate it would take a long time. Then he was at the mercy of the wind. He would hover low trying to see an open spot. The he would throw down his anchor and try to snag a landing. Often times the spot he would land would be further from the pub then his starting position was. He packed sandwiches to take on the trip to tide him over. It was a mess. But Manx people had come to love their eccentric duke. They were always happy to have their road blocked off by a ridiculous balloon.

Bernie had bought another balloon. This one for racing purposes. He had moved Dicky to the Dukedom and Duke Brotherdom. He gave his second balloon to Dicky. Bernie had equipped both balloons with harpoon guns he had taken from the whaling museum he set up in West Jurby. I don't know why he did this. Bernie and Dicky both sailed their balloons to their maximum sailing altitude. Then they started dueling. Bernie had a video camera aboard his balloon. It captured his last words. As Dicky's harpoon severed the ropes and Bernie realized he would soon fall to his death, he mumbled "Worth it."

After Bernie died I found his old journals. He had dozens of them. Each one with only one entry. Most of them years apart. He had a short attention span. Most of them made no sense. All but one were titled "my next million dollar business idea." Several had to do with building a resort and casino based around a duck pond in Las Vegas. Another few focused on trying to get Maury Povich to retire and let him host the show. This was the one not titled "my next million dollar business idea."

Wednesday 23 May 2018

I sold all my Pope John Paul II comic books. Getting them all, or at least all available ones, proved a lot less satisfying than I had imagined. There was a thrill in getting them, but once I got to the point where I couldn't get anymore, there wasn't a feeling of accomplishment. Just an empty feeling of what do I do now. So I decided to collect other things that would be harder to obtain the full set, like Barber dimes. So, I got to all of them except the 1894 S. But that was equally unsatisfying, because I still want the 1894 S dime, but there were only 24 made, so I still had the empty feeling, but it also led to a feeling of frustration, having an incomplete set and all, so I decided what I needed to collect were the things that money couldn't buy, and not like love and friendship and stuff, but the things that I have to work towards getting, not just shell out money for. Like the keys to cities. I would love to have some of those. And do something to deserve those keys, see how many of those I can get, because there are an endless amount, I could work my whole life and get those, and still have more to get. And any town would be fine with me. West Bend, Iowa; Bangor, Maine; any city. Or maybe honorary doctorates. Bill Cosby's got like a dozen or so, and he has a real doctorate so he doesn't even need one. At least, you know, if I get a couple of them I would have something to show for my work. I could write 500 *Land Before Time* scripts, but if none of them are made, I got nothing. But if I cure leprosy, and three cities in India give me their keys, well that's pretty cool.

PART 2: THE SHORT WORKS

For as long as I have been a writer, I have written sketch comedy. There was a time where I would do nothing but write countless sketches so if I ever got hired on as a staff writer for Saturday Night Live I would have some in the bag already (I knew at the time it wasn't a possibility, but a kid can dream). While doing that, this next bit was born. It was apparent that the target audience for this piece would not be the same as the rest of my sketch comedy, so I took it out of my sketch comedy folder and created a new folder, titled "Children's Show."

CHILDREN'S SHOW

Pilot Episode

Bernie: Well, hey there! My brother Edgar and I were just about to write a book. Now, so far, we have divided the book up and decided what each one of us would write. So I am going to write all the words that are nouns, pronouns, conjunctions, adjectives, adverbs, verbs, prepositions and indefinite articles.

Edgar: And I am going to write all of the definite articles and partitive articles!

Bernie: Good. So, first things first, let's come up with a name for the book. (Writing on chalk bored while saying) Jimmy Gets ____ Tree Stuck on His Face. (Stops writing.)

Edgar: You left a word out. Does that mean it needs a definite article?

Bernie: Well, I don't know yet. We do need an article, but we have to see what kind of article we think will go in there best.

Edgar: Well, we could put a direct article in there if we are talking about one particularly important tree, or if we don't know which tree it is yet, we could put an indefinite article there.

Bernie: Since it doesn't matter which tree he gets stuck on his face, and we haven't talked about any special trees yet, we should probably put an indefinite article there.

Edgar: That's a great idea, Bernie! Now, which indefinite article are you going to use?

Bernie: That is a great question, Edgar, let's look at our indefinite articles. (Pulls down screen from that thing above boards that you pull maps out of. It says "Indefinite articles: A, An.")

Edgar: A and An. Both of those are awesome words! Which one are you going to use?

Bernie: I don't know! It all depends on the noun after the article. Now which noun is it?

Edgar: Tree!

Bernie: Oh, I love the word tree! It just sounds so strong and woody!

Edgar: So do we need a strong and woody indefinite article?

Bernie: Not necessarily. We have to say the noun out loud to know what indefinite article we use.

Edgar: Tree. Tree. Tree. Tree. TREEEEE! TREEEEEEE!

Bernie: And when you say tree out loud, what is the first letter you hear?

Edgar: Tree. Tree. T-ree. Tuh- ree. Tuh. It is a "T" sound.

Bernie: That is right, and T is a consonant, and when an indefinite article is right before a word that starts with a consonant sound, we use the indefinite article "a." (Writes "A" in the blank on the board.)

Edgar: Jimmy gets a tree stuck on his face! This is starting to be a great story! Let's write some more!

Bernie: Ok. (Writes on board while speaking.) ____ tree looks silly on his face.

Edgar: OOO!! The blank is before the word tuh-ree. Are you going to use "A" again?

Bernie: No, not this time. Since we have already said which tree we are talking about, and everyone knows we are talking about the tree stuck on Jimmy's face, I think we should use a definite article!

Edgar: Awesome! Those are the words I get to write!

Bernie: That is correct. Now let's look at our list of definite articles. (Pulls down screen, which says "Definite articles: The.") Well, here are all the definite articles, "the." So what word do you want to put in there?

Edgar: I think I am going to write "the." (Writes the.)

Bernie: Alright. "Jimmy gets a tree stuck on his face. The tree looks silly on his face." That is a really good book right there. I think we are done!

Edgar: But wait! You said I get to write all the definite articles and partitive articles! All I have written so far is a definite article.

Bernie: That is true, but we wrote this book in English, and in English there are no partitive articles.

Edgar: But I want to write one so bad!

Bernie: But our book is already finished! And it's all in English. How will we ever get a partitive article?

Edgar: Well, let's write one more sentence, and let's write it in French.

Bernie: Okay, but what will we right the sentence about?

Edgar: Maybe Jimmy can get something else stuck on his face.

Bernie: That sounds great! Maybe Jimmy can get some coffee stuck on his face! In French that would be "Jimmy a ___ café a tenu à son visage."

Edgar: That is wonderful! Now I can write a partitive article. But I don't know any.

Bernie: Well, let us look at our list of French partitive articles. (Pulls down screen saying "French Partitive Articles: Du.") Well Edgar, you have a lot of words to choose from, which one are you going to write?

Edgar: I think I am going to write du. (Writes du in the blank.)

Bernie: Well, now our book is complete. Let's read it. "Jimmy gets a tree stuck on his face. The tree looks silly on his face. Jimmy a du café a tenu à son visage."

Edgar: Now, I am not going to lie, this is probably the best book I have ever read.

Bernie: It is at least the best one we have ever written.

Edgar: We need to print this up and get it in the library right away!

Bernie: I am on it!

After writing the children's show, I realized that Jimmy Gets a Tree Stuck on his Face *was a really good title, and there should be a children's book called that. So the next night I sat down and wrote this.*

JIMMY GETS A TREE STUCK ON HIS FACE
A Children's Book

One morning Jimmy was waiting on the sidewalk in front of his house, hoping the bus would come soon to pick him up for school.

Little did he know, he had a tree stuck to his face. He didn't even notice. If you had seen him standing there on the sidewalk, you probably wouldn't have noticed it, either.

The bus finally arrived. Jimmy boarded the bus, happy, smiling and full from the breakfast his mother had made for him.

He noticed all the other kids looking at him. He wasn't sure if something was wrong, or if this is how they always looked.

Just then, Toby, a boy in his class, shouted, "Hey Jimmy, are you a wood chuck?"

"No," Jimmy replied. "I am not a wood chuck at all!"

"Well, then," Toby taunted, "if you aren't a wood chuck, why do you have a green tree stuck on your face?"

Jimmy took his seat on the back of the bus. Now he knew why the kids were staring at him. He realized he had a giant tree stuck to his face.

The bus made it to Jimmy's school, and Jimmy got off, trying hard to hide the tree from all of his friends. Claire and Callie ran up to Jimmy to say hello, but Jimmy just turned his head the other way. He didn't want them to see the giant tree stuck to his face.

When Jimmy got to his classroom, he sat in the very last row. Maybe the other kids wouldn't notice him if he sat in the back. He tried to hide his head in his arms. He peeked through his fingers as the other kids entered the classroom. They all looked at him. He knew why they were looking. It was because he had a giant tree stuck to his face.

His teacher, Miss Fisher, started class. The lesson was about dinosaurs. Dinosaurs were Jimmy's favorite thing to talk about. Usually whenever Miss Fisher talked about dinosaurs, Jimmy would raise his hand and answer every question. He probably knew more about dinosaurs than any other kid in his class. But today he didn't raise his hand. If he raised his hand the other kids would look at him, and they would see the giant tree stuck to his face. It was very embarrassing.

The bell rang for lunch. Jimmy's heart sank. All of the kids in his grade would be in the lunch room, and they would all see the giant tree stuck to his face. He couldn't let that happen. His mom had made him a sandwich, so he didn't have to wait in the lunch line. When he entered the lunch room, he went straight to the table in the back corner and sat facing the wall. No one ever sat at that table. At least he could eat his sandwich without anyone seeing the giant tree stuck to his face.

"How did I get a tree stuck on my face?" he wondered. He had never seen anyone else with a tree stuck to their face, and he certainly didn't remember getting a tree stuck to his face. Where did this tree come from? And why, oh why, did it have to be stuck to his face?

Lunch was over, and it was time to go to recess. Jimmy loved recess. Well, most days he loved recess, but most days he didn't have a giant tree stuck to his face. Jimmy went to the swing set and sat down on a swing, facing away from the school. He wished recess wasn't so long. He wished school was over. He just wanted to be home, alone in his room, where no one could see the giant tree stuck to his face.

Just then, he felt a tap on his shoulder. He turned around. It was Miss Fisher.

"What's wrong?" Miss Fisher asked. "You don't seem like yourself today."

Jimmy didn't say anything. He just looked down at his feet dangling above the ground. Why did she have to ask that? Couldn't she see the giant tree stuck to his face?

"Let's go inside," Miss Fisher suggested.

Jimmy didn't say anything, but he stood up and followed Miss Fisher into the school.

Jimmy sat down in his desk at the back of the room. Miss Fisher sat down at the desk next to him.

"Jimmy, what's wrong today?" Miss Fisher asked. "You don't seem like your usual happy self."

"Don't you see it?" asked Jimmy.

"See what?"

"The giant tree stuck on my face!" cried Jimmy.

"Let me see," said Miss Fisher.

She looked at Jimmy's face.

"Why do you think there is a tree on your face?" Miss Fisher asked.

"This morning on the bus, Toby said there was," Jimmy replied.

"Oh, I see," Miss Fisher said. She got up and walked to her desk. She pulled something out of her drawer and came back to sit next to Jimmy.

"What did you eat for breakfast this morning?" Miss Fisher asked Jimmy.

"My mom made me an omelet. It was really good," said Jimmy.

"Did your mom put any spinach in your omelet?" Miss Fisher asked.

"Yes, she always does. She said it will make my muscles strong."

Then Miss Fisher held up a mirror. This must have been what she got out of her drawer. As Jimmy looked into the mirror, he saw there wasn't a tree on his face at all! There was a piece of spinach stuck between his two front teeth. He pulled it out with his fingernails and wiped it on his jeans.

"See?" said Miss Fisher. "There is nothing to be embarrassed about. Just a little spinach. Toby was probably just jealous that your mom made you such a great breakfast."

"I bet you're right," said Jimmy. "It was a really good breakfast."

Jimmy moved to a desk closer to the front of the room, smiling and knowing that there was not a tree stuck to his face.

Miss Fisher went back to her desk and put on some more lipstick before class began again. Little did she know, she got some of the lipstick on her teeth.

The bell rang and class began again. Miss Fisher walked to the front of the room and smiled.

Toby raised his hand.

"Yes Toby," Miss Fisher said.

"Are you a pelican?" Toby asked.

"No," Miss Fisher said. "I am not a pelican at all."

"Then why," Toby asked, "do you have a red snapper on your face?"

I am sure Harper Lee considers herself a novelist. And why not? She did write what I consider to be, for it's time, the Great American Novel, To Kill a Mockingbird. *And just because she only wrote one novel, no one can dare say she is not a novelist. By the same token, I have to call myself a poet. I have, however, only written one poem that I will take credit for, and I am determined to let it stand alone, forever, as the only poem ever written by Bernie Douglas. But it is a poem, written by me, so, I have to be a poet, right? (I tried to write a haiku about the humuhumunukunukuapua'a, but it didn't work out.)*

I was on a trip with the English department of my university the summer after my junior year to the British Isles. Being a lot of English majors on the trip, you can imagine there was a lot of amateur poetry being written. At the time I was putting the finishing touches on How to Die, *but EVERYONE else was writing poems. Not to be out done, on a ferry from the Isle of Man to Dublin, I wrote this next little number. Now, I must say, for the most part I absolutely hate amateur poetry, but this poem is absolutely amazing.*

THE WAVES OF IRELAND

As I look out my window,
The crashing waves catch my eye.
They remind me of what I am eating,
Which is a pie.

So one day I was thinking I needed a back up plan incase this writing thing didn't work out, which, as it is pretty clear, it won't. So I thought, the one thing I like more than writing was sandwiches. I mean, I really like sandwiches. But I thought, I really like hot dogs and hamburgers, too. Could I like these more than I like sandwiches? Yes, but there was one thing missing, the toppings. If there could be burgers and hot dogs with the toppings of a sandwich, I would love it. So I made a menu for a restaurant, that made hamburgers and hot dogs as good as sandwiches. Each menu item you could get either as the hamburger or the hot dog, and they would be priced accordingly. And somehow I am going to contaminate every single menu item with peanut oil, because it is only human nature to want to discriminate against a group of people, and since I have no problems with people of other races, creeds, religions or sexual orientation, I choose to discriminate against people with peanut allergies. Oh, and the restaurant will be called Taffy's. (And once I read a memoir by a celebrity, and every once in a while, for no other reason than just to make the book thicker, he would put a recipe, and I thought it was the most hilarious thing ever, and I just had to do it.)

TAFFY'S

The Kissenger
Half pound beef patty or third pound all beef frank
Sauerkraut, Dijon mustard, sliced wurst, German cheese.

The Gentile
Half pound beef patty or third pound all beef frank
Pulled pork, bacon, mayonnaise, cheddar.

The Real American
Half pound beef patty or third pound all beef frank
Creamed corn, green chilies, diced tomatoes, jalapenos.

The Dolphin
Half pound beef patty or third pound all beef frank
Tuna salad, red onion, sprouts, mayonnaise.

The Python
Half pound beef patty or third pound all beef frank
Egg, bacon, Spam, sausage. (Baked beans and tomato on request.)

The Bishop
Half pound beef patty or third pound all beef frank
Lean corned beef, dill slices, mustard.

The Irishman
Half pound beef patty or third pound all beef frank
Mashed potatoes, potato chips, hash browns, gravy.

The Famished Irishman
Half pound beef patty or third pound all beef frank
Corned beef, cabbage.

The Welshman
Half pound beef patty or third pound all beef frank
Leeks, cabbage, lamb, caerthilly.

The Scotsman
Half pound beef patty or third pound all beef frank
Haggis.

The Breakfast
Half pound beef patty or third pound all beef frank
Bacon, egg, cheddar.

The Lemming's Breakfast
Half pound beef patty or third pound all beef frank
Canadian bacon, egg, cheddar.

The Limey's Breakfast
Half pound beef patty or third pound all beef frank
Blood sausage, egg, cheddar.

The Montezuma's Breakfast
Half pound beef patty or third pound all beef frank
Chorizo, egg, refried beans, cheddar.

The Nostalgic
Half pound beef patty or third pound all beef frank
Macaroni and cheese, bologna.

The Babe (The Big Blue Ox one, not the baseball player or pig one.)
Half pound beef patty or third pound all beef frank
Bacon, mushroom, bleu cheese crumbles.

The Playground
Half pound beef patty or third pound all beef frank
Peanut butter, bananas.

The Dairy
Half pound beef patty or third pound all beef frank
Cheddar, provolone, fried cheese wheel, mayonnaise

The Bore (With an "E")
Half pound beef patty or third pound all beef frank
Lettuce, tomato, pickle, onion, mustard, mayonnaise, cheddar.

The Boar (With an "A")
Half pound beef patty or third pound all beef frank
Bacon, lettuce, tomato, pickle, onion, mustard, mayonnaise, cheddar.

As anyone knows, all good restaurants have an eating contest, where there is a ridiculous menu item that individuals try their hardest to eat, and then fail, and the free meal costs about fifty dollars. But if they win they get the meal free and their name on the wall. This is my eating contest.

The Vegan
Half pound beef patty AND third pound all beef frank
Bacon, pulled pork, Spam, bologna, Canadian bacon, chorizo, blood sausage, sausage, haggis, wurst, corned beef, egg, cheddar, provolone, fried cheese wheel, mayonnaise.

THOMAS EDISON

Seriously, the guy was kind of dumb. Ok, I know hindsight is 20/20, but it took the man 10,000 tries to find something that would work as a filament in the light bulb. 10,000. What the heck? First off, there are only so many metals that you could possibly use. Even if he skipped the "only use metal" mentality and went with all the elements, there are only like, what, 120 of them? Give or take a few, because I am too lazy to look it up. And even if he used elements not in the table, like the elements according to Buddhism, that's only 6 more, but I think he probably had a really hard time when he tried to use consciousness as a filament. Now, I am going to take this opportunity to say I don't know that much physical science. Didn't learn much in high school and college, and really, I never cared about it, so take this entry however you want, but, I'll get back to the point.

10,000 tries.

It took him 10,000 tries. If I was Edison, this is how I see the whole thing going out: "Hmm, I need something tangible, so for now I am going to skip the noble gases. I'll start with carbon, the basis of life. Whoops, no that burned up too fast. Let's go to a metal. Gold, hmm, that was good, but it melted and went out. I'll try tungsten, since it has the highest melting point of all metals. Well holy crap, that worked. Third time is the charm."

There, did you count that? It took three. Was that really so hard? Even if he didn't just use elements, say he started with steel, or something else, once he realized that he needed something that burned longer, why did it take him 9,999 tries to pick the metal with the highest melting point? I bet if he were alive today, he would have been that one person in the theatre who was surprised when he found out that Bruce Willis was dead in *The Sixth Sense*. That movie, with me, really, really missed the mark, because I didn't know I wasn't supposed to know he was dead. The guy dies in the first scene, then the whole movie the only person who sees him is the kid who sees dead people, I didn't know that was a big surprise. Then at the end when he figured out he was dead, I was thinking "about time you figured that out, we've all know for the past hour and a half," and then there was a collective gasp, and I'm thinking, "you mean, you didn't get that? Are you serious, because, he died in the first scene?" I knew there was supposed to be a surprise ending, I just thought it would be a surprise, like maybe Bruce Willis came back to life. I don't know, at least something surprising. But I really would like to find Edison's experiment journal in a museum somewhere and see what it says:

5,547- Wool- Burned up.

5,548- A grasshopper- Pissed off the grasshopper.

5,549- Jello- Didn't really do anything.

5,550- A different color of Jello- Nothing.

5,551- Tried consciousness again- Still couldn't pull it off. Those Buddhists are weird.

5,552- Urine- This one wasn't serious, but I got bored and the opportunity presented itself, so I thought, "Why not?"

5,553- A third color of Jello- I think I'm on the right track here.

Going back to the earlier mention of my file of sketch comedy, most of it was lost when my house was broken into in January 2009. However, the following is one of the few sketches to survive. (By the way, if you don't know who RUN DMC is, skip this whole sketch and continue on to How to Die. *It's newly revised!)*

WHITE DMC

V.O.: (With graphics displaying events being spoken of) Through out the ages, one question has always been on the mind of mankind: "What if." What if Moses didn't lead the Israelites out of Egypt? What if Napoleon had won the Battle of Waterlou? What if Run DMC had been a couple of white guys from the suburbs?

(White and DMC in recording studio)

White and DMC: (Rapping) It's complicated to rock a rhyme to rock a rhyme that's right on time, it's complicated.

White: Complicated.

DMC: Complicated.

White: Complicated.

DMC: Complicated.

(Producer enters)

Producer: Alright before we go on, just a little note, that last part seems to get jumbled.

DMC: Which one?

Producer: When you keep saying complicated.

White: Oh yeah that part is kind of tricky.

Producer: Just try to make it easier to say, maybe a word with less syllables than complicated would be better.

White: Alright.

DMC: No problem.

Producer: Oh, and before we get to it, I was reading over the lyrics for this song, and there is one that I don't understand.

White: Which one?

Producer: We are not thugs, we don't spin mugs.

DMC: Yeah that was my line.

Producer: What does it mean?

DMC: When I was in junior college I took a ceramics class, and they made me make mugs on a spinning wheel, and that stuff was just stupid and I'm not gonna do any of that.

Producer: I just don't really think that line will connect with the audience.

White: It will if they have ever tried to spin a mug.

DMC: Do you know how hard it is to stick a handle on a spinning object.

Producer: Why didn't you wait until it stopped to put the handle on it.

DMC: I did. That is why I said I don't spin mugs. I can spin vases, but to make a mug, I have to put a handle on it when it's not spinning.

Producer: So, you still spun a mug, you just put the handle on it when it was not spinning.

DMC: No, I spun a cup. It was not a mug until it stopped spinning.

White: Yeah, what kind of messed up junk you thinking?

Producer: I just don't see how your fans will be able to connect with that line.

DMC: Well, I hope that our fans don't spin mugs either.

Producer: Look, I'm paying $100 an hour for this studio space, I don't have time to discuss the technicalities of spinning mugs.

DMC: Now when you start spinning it is just a lump of clay, and I don't think anyone would call a lump of clay a mug, because it is not completed. By the same token, when I am spinning this lump of clay, I am spinning it into a cup. At no point when it is spinning does it have a handle, so there is no reason to say it is a mug. Now, after I spin, I put the handle on it, but that is an after thought. If you want to say that I spin lumps of clay, more power to you, you could even say that I spin cups, but I'll be whacked if people are going to say I spin mugs.

White: I've seen him cap a cracka for less than that.

Producer: Let's just do this song, and if you can't get complicated out, just think of shorter words you can use.

White: But it's tricky.

DMC: Tricky.

White: Tricky.

DMC: Tricky.

Producer: Let's just see what we can do.

(Producer exits.)

White: I think I got this one.

DMC: Ok.

White: (rapping) It's more than a little difficult to rock a rhyme to rock a rhyme that's right one time, more than a little difficult.

DMC: More than a little difficult.

White: More than a little difficult.

(Producer running in)

Producer: What are you doing?

DMC: Yeah, we did what you told us to, and it kinda sucks.

Producer: I told you to shorten it.

White: No you said to use shorter words.

Producer: I mean just one. Use just one word, shorter than complicated.

DMC: Oh, I thought you didn't want us to say complicated, because it was a big word and you didn't know how to spell it for the lyric sheet.

White: Yeah, that was actually my biggest concern.

Producer: Spelling is not my concern here, now, I think you know what I am asking for, let's just get this done.

DMC: What if instead of I don't spin mugs, I say I DO put handles on cups, do you think that would be easier to understand?

Producer: No, just leave that part alone, and let's try this again.

(Producer leaves)

White: Alright, I think I got it this time.

(rapping) It's not as easy as it looks to rock a rhyme to rock a rhyme that's right on time not as easy as it looks.

DMC: Not as easy as it looks.

White: Not as easy...

Producer (running in): What are you doing? That was worse than last time.

White: But I thought it was all pretty easy to spell.

DMC: The longest word was looks, and really, if you count both "o"s as one letter it is only four letters.

Producer: I don't care about how easy each word is to spell, I just think we need to shorten it down to something easier to say.

DMC: Did you know I comes before E except after C.

Producer: Just change it.

White: Except when sounding as A as in neighbor or weigh.

Producer: Just give me a word that means the same as complicated but is shorter.

White: That's tricky.

Producer: Perfect.

White: What?

Producer: That's perfect, use tricky instead of complicated.

DMC: You mean say it's tricky to rock a rhyme?

Producer: Yes.

White: No, it's not tricky to rock a rhyme..

DMC: To rock a rhyme that's right on time.

White: It's tricky to come up with a shorter word to put in there.

Producer: But I think what we have here is fine, let's just work with it.

DMC: So we aren't concerned with the spelling any more.

Producer: No.

DMC: Ok I think I got it. Let's lay this track down.

Producer: Ok. (leaves)

DMC: (rapping) On a scale of one to 10, 10 being extremely difficult and one being the easiest I would probably rate rocking a rhyme at a 7 because hey it's not as difficult as solving the 4th order differential equation, but it's not like tying your shoe either, even though tying your shoe...

V.O.: After the failure of their album, *Harder to Tear or Puncture than Tanned Cow Hide*, White DMC split and parted ways. Years later, they would reform under the name Nickelback, and though their song writing and lyrical ability had waned since their White DMC days, their popularity inexplicably rose.

HOW TO DIE: OR THE GOOD GATSBY
The Bernie Douglas Revision
(Bernie Douglas!)

DISCLAIMER

This book is entirely fictional. Nothing in here is based on real people or events. If you were with me when something happened and you think it looks like a scene in this book, it isn't. If you think something in this book seems like a satire of a real event, you are mistaken. If you think a character in here reminds you of yourself, you are wrong. If you say, "I did those things and said those words in the story," you are lying.

Also, if any names in this story resemble celebrity names, that is purely coincidental. Honestly, it happens all the time, and some names are very common. I know a guy named Jimmy Rogers, but I don't claim that his parents named him after the Mississippi Blue Yodeler Jimmie Rodgers, it just happens, that is understandable, but it goes to prove that just because someone thinks a name resembles a celebrity's name, doesn't mean it really does.

PRELUDE

I really hate F. Scott Fitzgerald. Not his writing, no, I love that. It is the fact that Fitzgerald selfishly stole *The Great Gatsby* for himself. Now even if I wanted to write *The Great Gatsby* and came up with the idea on my own, word for word, I couldn't write it, because F. Scott Fitzgerald ruined it for everyone. Frankly, I don't even know what the heck a Gatsby is, and then F. Scott Fitzgerald had to go and make his book the *great* one. He couldn't have even settled for a *good* Gatsby, no he had to one up everybody.

And to add insult to injury, a young Robert Redford was in the film version of Fitzgerald's little Gatsby book. How can I compete with that? There hasn't been a young Robert Redford since 1987, and even then he was starting to get saggy.

Despite the difficult hand I have been dealt, there are two things that help me get through my days. One—the editor of *The Great Gatsby* changed up the book to the extent that it completely ruined the meaning, and F. Scott Fitzgerald never lived to see his book published as it should be. Two—even though a young Robert Redford is a thing of the past, living on only in memories and VHS, there still is a young Tracy Morgan, and if I thought anyone deserved to be in a good Gatsby movie, it is Tracy Morgan.

INTRODUCTION

Why is it that anytime someone dies peacefully in his sleep, someone is always there to say "that's how he would have wanted to go" or "he couldn't have written it any better." I take personal offense at these statements on the behalf of the deceased. Are they saying the guy was boring, that he just didn't have a creative bone in his body, or what?

I have decided I do not want any such talk at my funeral, so here it is: how I would die if I wrote it (not really *if* as much as *when* I wrote it). Make sure you read it, so if by the off chance I die another way you can scold the geriatrics at my funeral who claim they think they know how I wanted to go. And while you are at the funeral home, check and make sure there are no Thomas Kinkade prints hanging in the viewing room. If there are, I must kindly request that you remove them. Better yet, make your own drawing and tape it over the Kinkade. Maybe a nice mallard. Yeah, that would be nice. At least it would be real art. And the Kinkade should have a really nice frame that would compliment the mallard, because that's all the Kinkade print is worth, the frame.

Back on subject, just writing the means of my demise does not mean I intend on dying in one of these manners, or any way at all. Actually, I plan on living forever. So far, so good.

TIJUANA

I am with Jesus Jones: right here, right now. But back then I was on a plane, a plane heading back to Lubbock from Seattle. Every once in a while it's important to just go somewhere to get away from it all. I go to Ivar's. Ivar's is a seafood bar in Seattle, and despite the high price of plane tickets, a roundtrip flight to Seattle to pick up a lunch at Ivar's is well worth any monetary cost.

I arrived at the airport in Salt Lake City, where I had to change planes. I went into the bathroom to check myself in the mirror when a man walked in and looked me straight in the eyes. It was obvious that this man was wearing a fake beard and wig, and, not being able to think of any legal reason why someone would want to hide their identity, I was pretty sure he was a terrorist, so I ran out of that bathroom as fast as I could and sat by the gate for my next flight, making sure I was in plain view of a countless number of witnesses at all times.

Soon enough, it was time to board. While sitting on the plane, I began to chat with the man next to me about the terrorist I saw in the bathroom. However, all he wanted to talk about was the fact that Terry Bradshaw was on his last flight. Like I really cared that he saw a long distance phone company's spokesman. Apparently, according to this man, before Terry Bradshaw became a long distance phone company's spokesman, he was a football player. I didn't believe him, though. It was like the time my grandmother tried to tell me that Paul Newman was an actor before he invented salad dressing; it's just one of those things old people say to try to make me look dumb in conversation by saying something like "Hey, did you hear that guy who played The Gipper in <u>Knute Rockne All American</u> became president," and then everyone just laughs at me for being so gullible.

However, in the course of this conversation, I found something very queer. Terry Bradshaw and the terrorist I saw were both wearing black Hawaiian shirts, cut off khakis and leather thongs. It oc-

186

curred to me that maybe these two guys were one in the same, because honestly, how often do two straight men in the same airport have identical shirts, pants and footwear? But the thing that let me know the man I saw wasn't Terry Bradshaw was the fake beard. It was on too perfectly. And to put a beard on that perfectly, one would have to be a lot more sober than Terry Bradshaw after a three-hour flight.

Soon, I arrived in Lubbock and was greeted by my cousin Todd, who would accompany me on the rest of my journey to Tijuana. We boarded yet another plane, and I sat semi-comfortably back in my seat. Before takeoff, I looked around at the other passengers and sat back feeling fairly safe. (Come on, admit it, you do it, too.) The closest-looking thing to a terrorist I saw was Todd, who for some reason had inexplicably developed rather Eastern European-looking features, which weren't at all hindered by his thick, black beard.

With only slight turbulence and the annoyance of a toddler, Todd and I arrived safely in Tijuana. Stepping off the plane into Mexico, we were greeted by the sight of a man holding a sign with our names spelled phonetically (Tod e burny). This man was Eduardo. He was a bookie of sorts. I had made what I thought would be a lucrative business deal with the man a few years earlier, and now I was here to settle the score. Todd had come along, not so much for the company, but so I could write that terrorist bit and make fun of his beard in the previous paragraph.

After retrieving our luggage, we followed Eduardo outside, where he hailed us a cab. I had heard horror stories of Mexican cab drivers dropping tourists off in dark alleys, telling them it was the location they requested, where they would promptly be robbed at knife point and killed: a fact that made me wish Eduardo had come with us in the cab, especially when the driver pulled up into a dark alley and assured us this was our destination. Trying to look brave, (and wishing airport security hadn't stolen my knife) I handed the driver his pesos and stepped out of the cab. Todd was a bit more hesitant, but he followed my lead. I saw light from an open door at the other end of the alley, with the silhouette of a man standing in the doorway.

I took a deep breath and started walking toward the man. My fingertips started to feel sweaty, while my palms remained cold and dry. Light shone on the man's mustachioed face. To my relief, it was Eduardo. I followed him inside the building, which appeared to be the back of a hot dog stand. Apparently, to a Mexican, crappy American food venues are the equivalent of our Taco Villas.

Then, in the middle of the room, I saw my prized investment. Barely a foot high, with spiked spurs on his beak, this "prized fighting cock" hardly seemed worth the cost of the plane ticket down here. Then, some guy with a rather impressive skulletino rang the bell, causing a man with thick leather gloves to throw my rooster into the center of the ring, while another man threw his bird in as well.

As the cocks began their fatal dance, Eduardo walked up and handed me a hot dog purchased from the storefront. I ate it, but quickly realized why Mexicans loathe fast food Tex-Mex so much. A pain started in my chest and crept up my throat. Thinking back, I didn't remember taking my Prilosec this morning. But then again, I don't remember ever taking Prilosec, so this morning shouldn't have been any different. I was reaching for the Tums in my pocket, but the burning inside my chest was something more.

For some strange reason, I was reminded of a book I once read on spontaneous human combustion, which, by the way, isn't an appropriate source for a paper on "The Canticles." While searching my pockets for the Tums, I felt a tiny container of nitroglycerin pills my doctor gave me to take in case I ever had a heart attack. I had never had one before, but if I had to sit around one day trying to think of what a heart attack felt like, there is a good chance I would imagine it just like this. As I lay contorted on the ground, I manage to remove one of the pills from its container and put it in my mouth. Just as I swallowed the pi...

THE BANK ROBBERY

I once heard that Ben Franklin had several beds in his house, so if one became too warm in the middle of the night, he could go to the next room where there was nice, cool bed waiting for him. That's a really good idea. I haven't heard much else about this Ben Franklin character, but with the genius and ingenuity to come up with a plan like that, there is no telling what he could have done if he really put his mind to it.

I hate warm beds. They are hot, stuffy and uncomfortable. Some people say that they are "warm and toasty," and while I don't disagree, I'm just wondering why they would say it like it was a good thing. (It's like the prescription drug commercials where the actor says "and I am glad there is a low risk of sexual side effects," or the fake mayonnaise commercials that brag about their tangy zip. No one is glad to have sexual side effects or wants their fake mayonnaise to taste tangy, but even the most horrid of things can sound delightful with the right advertising campaign.) Personally, I have never been in a toaster, never found one I would fit into really, but a toaster isn't the kind of place where I would want to spend an evening sleeping. If it does that to bread, imagine what it could do to people.

That morning, I stepped out of my sweltering bed and decided to start a new day. I had to go to the bank. I didn't want to, but I had to. Last time I went to the bank the teller called the cops on me for "disturbing the peace." I think it was the bank that was disturbing the peace, because I would have felt quite at peace if the bank wasn't so, I don't know, how should I say this . . . stupid.

Alright, here's the deal:

A couple of months ago, I wrote a check for $30. The bank ran it through like it was for $300. I had plenty of money in my account to cover a $30 check, but not so much for $300. Luckily, that check didn't bounce. Unfortunately, the next seven I wrote did.

189

Obviously, it wasn't my fault. I wrote checks totaling $210, and I had plenty of money in my account to cover all of the checks if they hadn't have screwed up with the $30 check, but they didn't see how it was a problem. They said since the check that they messed up on did not bounce, then it was my fault I had seven bounced checks. I saw that it was their fault, the rest of the people in line behind me saw it was their fault, but for some reason the logic of the situation failed the tellers.

In hindsight, yelling and throwing things was not the best way to get my point across, but I had tried everything else, and that all failed, so what was I supposed to do?

Back to today: I walked to the bank and was standing in line with a laundry bag full of coins to deposit. The Jews[7] at the bank charge an outrageous rate (about 2%) if they have to actually do their job and roll your coins for you, so I had spent the previous day rolling them myself, knowing that as soon as I came in they would have to unroll all the coins and recount them to make sure I wasn't lying about how much I had.

I was in line behind a little old lady who was writing a check for cash, and had been for the past 15 minutes. I had picked up a sucker from the bowl on the deposit slip counter and was very curious as to whether or not I could get it to stick to the backcombed ball of poof in front of me. I made sure that the sucker was sufficiently wet, to the extent that it was surrounded by a thick sticky coat, so when it mixed with the AquaNet it would make a knotted dread of syrupy delight.

I gave the sucker one last twirl in my mouth and started to tangle it in with the blue helmet in front of me when I heard someone yell "FREEZE!" When I turned around to tell the man it was just a joke, I noticed he wasn't talking to me at all. I was momentarily relieved that even though there were armed gunmen a mere five yards away, they were pointing their weapons at someone else. My relief, however, was abruptly ended by what felt like a brick across my face. I had always been taught as a child to "turn the other cheek," but I was more of an "eye for an eye, tooth for a tooth" kind of guy. I turned to smack this guy in the face when I realized it was the little old woman with my green sucker stuck to her bosom. (When the woman is over 60, they are called bosoms. My editor advised me not

---

[7] That Jew remark wasn't racist. Simply, the tellers at the bank happen to be a nice Jewish couple named Meron and Laila Morganstein. If anyone is to blame it is the lousy French man who owns the bank who set up the ridiculous stipulations. Stupid Gentiles.

to go into the details of why they must be called bosoms, so just trust me on this.)

I could not fathom what that woman must have stuffed in her purse to make it have that kind of impact, because I was under the assumption that Depends were fairly soft and padded. While the initial numbness and shock from the blow wore off, I lay on the ground staring up at the old woman, dumbfounded, as she pulled an antique (but surprisingly shiny) Colt .45 (the gun, not the malt liquor) out of her purse.

Luckily, a blow upside the head was all that I was getting from her. As the masked men saw this woman with the gun, I could tell that they had an instinctive fear flow over them, but this was soon replaced by absolute hysteria; not the kind of hysteria where people go out and buy crates of bottled water because they think the computers are going to take away their birthdays, but more like the kind of hysteria where you take the "cal" off of hysterical and put the "a" back.

The bank robbers' profuse giggling would have ended abruptly if old women had the finger strength to pull the trigger on a Colt .45, but they don't. At least this old woman didn't, and luckily she hadn't been exercising that finger very much. As the bank robbers kept laughing, I grabbed my coins and fled the scene.

I could have been two blocks away before the robbers left the bank, but I saw a street vender drawing caricatures for $5.00, and no one can pass up a deal like that.

I was in the middle of having my face painted on Al Rocher's body (the skinny Al Rocher, not when he was fat. I have self esteem issues.) when the robbers passed. Luckily they didn't recognize me as the crying man lying on the floor in the bank only moments earlier.

The man finished the drawing, so I gave him a roll of dimes, grabbed my new purchase and left. I caught a cab home, went inside and decided to make a sandwich. I wanted pastrami on rye, but all I had was corned beef and sour kraut. Though I do love the Reuben (I have this thing for sour kraut, like Henry Kissinger; I just love it. And puns. I absolutely adore puns.), I didn't want one. I wanted pastrami on rye. I decided that instead of walking *all the way* to the store around the corner and *all the way back*, I would just drive to the delicatessen across town, where they would make one for me.

I hopped into my car, forgetting that last night I was practicing making mafia-style car bombs on my ignition. I adjusted my mirror, put the new CAKE album in the CD player, slid my key into the ignition...

WOLF

As many people know, there is a big problem with people being eaten by wolves. This problem came to light in recent years when former President Gerald Ford was eaten to death by wolves in 2006 at the senseless age of 93.[8] However, this was not the first case of a president being eaten by wolves, as the death certificates for both William Taft and Grover Cleveland list cause of death as "death by wolves."

Everyone knows the story of how Rome was founded. Rome's founders, twin brothers Romulus and Remus, were orphaned at a young age and raised by a she-wolf who let them nurse on her teat. However, very few people know the true story.

Rome was originally founded by two brothers, Clyde and Lloyd. They built the city from the ground up. They poured a lot of hard work and dedication into the city. Due to the intense heat, the brothers gave up summer work completely. They were just about ready to start work up again in the fall in the new city of Clloyd when the she-wolf came and ate them, so the twins she was nursing could start the city.

Not long after that, the Greek philosopher Aristotle was eaten to death by wolves, only he was too drunk to notice. His students then made up some complex story about how he wasn't eaten by wolves, but really, that's too boring to get into right now, and, quite frankly, no one cares.

Some people also got eaten to death by wolves in ancient Lithuania. However, no one knows the names of any ancient Lithuanians. Chances are, however, that there was probably an ancient Lithuanian named Groak. We will pretend there was. It's very

---

[8] When *How to Die* was originally published Gerald Ford was alive and I thought the joke was to say he died seven years earlier. But now that he is dead is just seemed weird to have the wrong date.

likely that while Groak was lying in his hammock he was eaten by a group of wolves. This is a fact that I dare you to disprove. It can't be done. I put it in the endnotes.[i] Watch, I will do it again.[ii] And again.[iii]

Why do wolves eat people? Simple: they taste good. How do we know people taste good? Easy. What do you taste right now? Probably nothing. Wrong. That's people you are tasting. The way humans are made, the taste buds lie inside of a person. This causes the person to always taste the inside of his mouth. What is the inside of a person's mouth made up of? Person. What is the plural of person? People. What is that you are tasting right now? That's right, people. Doesn't taste too bad, does it? No it doesn't. Wolves seem to agree, and they eat a lot of people.

People don't seem to understand how addicting the taste of people is since they taste it everyday. But wolves don't taste it everyday, and it drives them nuts. The taste of people to wolves is much like nicotine to people, which, according to the state of California, is addictive and causes cancer. So why would wolves continue to eat people even though they know it causes cancer? Why do good looking people wear clothes when they know they would look better naked?

Somewhere between the first and sixth day, perhaps it was the first, God made the earth. This day was October 23, 4004 BC. (I read this in the introduction to a King James Bible once, so it has to be true.) The earth has about 6.5 billion people today. On October 23, 2004 AD, the earth turned about 6008 years old (that no-year-zero thing is a toughie, though). That's 2,194,422 days. Do your math again and factor in leap year. Alright, now we are on the same page. Anyway, now, there are 6.5 billion people today, 6.5 billion people yesterday, and 6.5 people the day before, so we can only assume there were 6.5 billion people every day. (Glad I paid attention in math class when they taught that whole pattern thing.)

That means 14,263,743,000,000,000 people have lived on this earth. Now say that every day, half of them were eaten by a wolf; that's 7,131,871,500,000,000 who have been eaten by wolves to date (well, to date as of October 23, 2004). At these rates, 3.5 billion people get eaten by wolves everyday. If anyone deserves to have President Bush II declare war on them, it's the wolves.

Wolves live outside. People live inside. It's when the two of these get mixed up that people get eaten by wolves. Don't go outside. I repeat, don't go outside. This will get you eaten by a wolf.

Wolves don't like spicy food. You ever seen a wolf hanging around a Mexican restaurant? Me neither. So what does this mean to us? We need to be spicy. Forget about lathering up with sunscreen everyday. It takes 40 years to get skin cancer and only one day to be eaten by wolves. You have to think of the here-and-now. Lather up with Tabasco. Every day. You have to. It's not an option. If you don't, you will be eaten by a wolf. I have seen it happen. Many times. At least eight. Well, once I saw a guy only get his foot bitten off. (Afterwards he went around with only one foot for a few months, then he got a fake one and all he could do was gripe about how heavy it was. Finally I just had to sit him down and say "Look, the burden of carrying around two feet all the time is something that each one of us has to deal with on an everyday basis. Just because you had a two month vacation from the tedious life of walking with two feet does not mean anyone will feel sympathy for you now that you have to have two feet again.) The wolves have to bite you before they know you have Tabasco on you, because wolves, like other canine species, have a very poor sense of smell. Anyway, lather up. Don't be one of the 7,131,871,500,000,000 people; be one of the other 7,131,871,500,000,000 people, the 7,131,871,500,000,-000 people that weren't eaten by wolves.

When people hear the names Clark Gable and Humphrey Bogart, one thing comes to mind: "Why weren't these men eaten by wolves?" This was a question that I needed answered. I did a Google image search for both men, and what I found was startling. First I noticed that the men's pictures were all a shade of gray, and so was the background. Could this gray be a camouflage? No, Marilyn Monroe had the same gray around her. Then I saw it. It was right under my nose. Not mine, but Clark Gable and Humphrey Bogart's. A moustache and cigarette. That's it. The moustache on Clark Gable must have intimidated the wolves, and since the wolves already knew eating people caused cancer, they must have assumed eating a smoker caused more cancer, so why eat Humphrey Bogart? The wolves also probably put two and two together, and instead of getting four, as I usually do, they discovered that moustaches cause cancer. Those wolves are smart.

Henry Kissinger will be eaten by wolves. It's inevitable. It has to be done. The laws of nature are not on his side. However, we can go on in our daily lives knowing that being eaten by wolves is one of the most peaceful ways to die. I have heard drowning was, but that's a lie. However, when the wolves first bite into your flesh, you feel a calming kind of ecstasy, partly due to the narcotics found in wolf saliva, partly due to the roofie I just slipped in your drink. Then you arc at peace, and might even actually make friends with the wolf.

****

OK, that was all well and good, and perhaps informative, but I don't buy it. All that scientific research is fine, but think about it. Ford smoked. Taft and Cleveland had moustaches. Henry Kissinger had neither. And think about the Knights of the Round Table. There were about 30 of them, and none of them were eaten by a wolf.

I decided to take my chances. I mean, years of rubbing Tabasco on my skin had produced many blisters, and just pouring more Tabasco on them only made it worse. I decided just to skip it today.

I stepped outside and, for once, I was able to smell the crisp clean air without it being tainted by the smell of peppers. Then it donned on me. The Knights of the Round Table. I heard before that they impersonated Clark Gable. Could it be that was how they escaped? Then I spotted a wolf in the distance. I tried to turn and run, but it was too late...

CANADA

So, I was starting to get annoyed with Canada. Don't ask me why I was there, or I would have to quote Ronald Reagan during the Iran-Contra Affair: "I don't know."

Don't get me wrong, it's just that Canadians drive me nuts. They think they are all clever and witty with their "unanswerable questions." And not the good kind like "What is the meaning of life," but the dumb ones, like "Why do Americans drive in parkways and park in driveways;" (It's called a parkway because it runs next to a park, not because you park your car there, and it's called a driveway because you "drive" through it on your way from your street to your garage) "Which came first, the chicken or the egg;" (The chicken, you twit, who else would have sat on the egg to hatch it) "Why do men have nipples;" (Same reason 8-year-old girls have training bras: they don't do anything, it just makes you feel better about how your chest looks).

Then whenever you tell them you are American, they claim they are, too, because they live in "the Americas." This is the same kind of logic that makes Europeans think North and South America is one continent. They claim that since we are connected by land, we are one continent. Apparently they have never heard of the Panama Canal or seen a map of Eurasia and wondered where the big gaping ocean is that must be separating Europe and Asia if they are truly two continents.

As you can tell, I was unhappy with my life at this point. Not that I felt I was insignificant or anything like that, just because I was in Canada. Anyway, I once heard an old rancher say that if a bum is sitting on a park bench, and he is happy to be sitting on that park bench, then he is successful. I took that to heart many years ago, and now I was looking for a bench.

I found one.

As I sat down on the bench, I started to think about Herman Melville. That man was a funny, funny man. I love how he would try to write a story about a whale, then get sidetracked by a miniscule detail and talk about that one little detail for pages, even chapters, on end. Oh, that Herman Melville.

Herman Melville was born on August 1, 1819 in New York City to Allan Melville and Maria Gansevoort Melville. His father was a merchant who went bankrupt, insane, and died by the time Herman was 12, leaving his mother Maria to raise him along with his seven siblings.

In 1826, Melville came down with a case of scarlet fever that left his eyesight permanently deficient. In 1835, he attended Albany Classical School. In 1839, he shipped out and became a cabin boy on the whaler *Achushnet*. Later, he joined the US Navy. After his adventures, he returned home to write it all down.

His first book was *Typee,* a firsthand account of his stay with cannibals. He followed it up with a sequel called *Omoo,* which, though it's not as interesting to read as *Typee,* it's much more fun to say the title. He also wrote a couple of "lesser known" works, *Moby Dick* and *Billy Budd.* Apparently, however, he wrote *Billy Budd* after he died. At least that's what I think "posthumously" means.

Melville married Chief Justice Shaw's daughter Elisabeth in 1847. He was also friends with a fellow named Nathaniel Hawthorne.

Nathaniel Hawthorne was born in Salem, Massachusetts, on July 4th, 1804. This makes him 15 years Melville's senior. Hawthorne wrote *The Blithedale Romance, The House of Seven Gables, The Marble Faun, The Scarlet Letter, The Ambitious Guest, The Artist of the Beautiful, The Birthmark, The Canterbury Pilgrims, The Celestial Railroad, David Swan, The Devil in Manuscript, Dr. Heidegger's Experiment, Drowne's Wooden Image, The Egotism; or Bosom Serpent, Endicott and the Red Cross, Ethan Brand, Feathertop: A Moralized Legend, The Gentle Boy, The Gray Champion, The Great Carbuncle, The Great Stone Face, The Hollow of the Three Hills, Legends of the Province House: I. Howe's Masquerade, Legends of the Province House: II. Edward Randolph's Portrait, Legends of the Province House: III. Lady Eleanore's Mantle, Legends of the Province House: IV., Old Esther Dudley, The Maypole of Merry Mount, The Minister's Black Veil, Mr. Higginbotham's Catastrophe, Mrs. Bullfrog, My Kinsman, Major Molineux, Peter Goldthwaite's Treasure, The Procession of Life, Rappaccini's Daughter, Roger Malvin's Burial, The Shaker Bridal, The Snow Image: A Childish Miracle, Wakefield, The Wedding*

Knell, and _Young Goodman Brown_. It must have taken him a long time to write all of these books because it took me a good while only to write the titles.

In his later life, Nathaniel Hawthorne grew a nice walrus style moustache that he occasionally combed into a nice handle bar. And he also had it in his earlier adult life but shaved it off sometime in the middle. He died in Plymouth, New Hampshire, on May 18th, 1864. This was my birthday (only a different year). And Pope John Paul II's birthday (a different year, still). And Mount Saint Helen's eruption day (once again, same day, different year).[9]

As I was sitting there on the bench, a small rodent ran past me with millions of little furry things that looked just like it following him. I decided, what the heck. I have always wanted to do that running of the bulls thing, just never had a chance (actually, I want to go to Spain and do the running of the bulls without telling my parents, just so I can look down from heaven and see the look on their surprised faces when they see me being gored to death on international television). Sure, these little critters (which, for the sake of this story I shall call "lemmings") did not present near the danger, excitement, or ferocity of a bull, but they were a lot cuter.

I had absolutely no idea (or _idear_ as Jack Kennedy would say) where these little things were going, but I didn't care. I was free. I had found my new park bench in these lemmings.

After about four days of this running thing, the excitement started to wane, and I was just plain bored. I had been feeding one of the lemmings, who I called James Joyce, bread I had found in my pocket when we passed a grizzly bear. I felt bad for the bear because I had nothing to feed it, so I fed it James Joyce.

I sensed this caused a bit of a strife between me and the rest of the lemmings, but if they weren't going to say anything about it, then I wouldn't either.

That night when we stopped for camp, I began to regret feeding James Joyce all my bread. I had four American dollars on me (which is a fortune in Canada) so I stopped at a convenience store. I bought a hot dog and soda for $2. I handed them $2 American and received $.60 Canadian in return. Remembering a bum I saw on the street with a sign saying "Punch Me, $1," I realized that if I bought another hot dog and soda, I would get another $.60. That would mean I

---

[9] After the original publication, scholars started to say Hawthorne died May 19. I don't know how that happened, changing death day after 140 years, but I couldn't change it here that would have ruined the whole thing. Some scholars still point to the death day as May 18, and some say May 18-19.

would have $1.20 free, so I would actually get paid $.20 to punch a Canadian in the face. That was an offer I simply could not refuse.

I bought another hot dog and soda, got my change, gave the bum $1 in quarters and punched him in the face. (It was the same satisfaction I had received from looking at the dumbfounded look on a Canadian's face when he asked me what weighs more, a pound of feathers or a pound of gold, told me I was wrong because they both weighed the same, and then completely got put in his place when I pointed out that gold is weighed on the Troy system, which is 12 ounces to a pound, compared to the avoir-dupois system that feathers are weighed with, in which a pound is 16 ounces, making a pound of feathers weigh four ounces more. Stupid Canadians who think they are witty.)

It was about the time this bum pulled a knife out of his pocket and started chasing me that I realized maybe he didn't want to be punched in the face and just thought he was being funny. This Canadian wit stuff is hard to pick up on.

I managed to return to my lemming tribe and become lost in the enormous crowd, hiding myself from the bum. There was a sense of anticipation among the lemmings, as if tomorrow were a big day. Not knowing what the next day held, I could hardly get a wink of sleep. Way more excitement than I'm used to getting.

The next morning we were up at the crack of dawn again, running. Running. It started to seem to me that this was all the lemmings did. It was ok, though.

Pretty soon, in the horizon, I started to see the ocean. This was what the lemmings were excited about! We were going to the beach!

We kept on running. Full speed to the ocean! Finally we came to a cliff and the lemmings started jumping off straight into the ocean. What a wonderful idea. I followed along, and when it came my turn to jump I did a beautiful double back flip that would have made Greg Louganis proud. I hit the water and was about to go for dive number two when I realized that the lemmings just kept swimming away from the cliff. Not exactly the day at the beach I was hoping for, but they seemed to know what they were doing, so I swam with them.

Darkness fell and we were still swimming. By now we were miles away from the shore (in all reality, we were probably only a couple of hundred feet away, but it felt like miles. A lot of miles). I tried asking the lemmings if they thought we should turn back now, but there was no response. They just kept swimming.

I was exhausted and could barely keep my eyes open. I started to nod off, but I stayed awake. I wanted to see where we were going.

But as I kept going, it started to become harder and harder to keep my eyes open, until...

PRUSSIA

I was sitting in a Prussian prison cell waiting for the jailer to come. I know what you are thinking, "Prussia dissolved in the 1930s and '40s, and you were born in 1984, so you could never be in Prussia." Time travel. That's all you have to do. Pick up a book. Read some Stephen Hawking or Douglas Adams sometime. I read a book and now I can go to Prussia. There. (By the way, do you think that it hacks Hawking off that even though he's British his little voice machine has an American accent? It would hack me off if they gave me a voice machine that sounded all British. Unless I was telling a joke that wasn't funny. Those always seem to go better with a British accent.)

Make a note to yourself. Write it down. At least highlight it in this book. (For those of you who are too lazy to even do that, I will put it in bold italics for you.) ***If you ever decide to go back to Prussia in 1904, make sure that the destination you select is not a prison cell.*** (Of course, this could be hard when selecting your latitudinal and longitudinal directions, considering they didn't have GPS in 1904.)

I give you this warning, being that apparently I was not the first present-day person to arrive in this prison cell, because when the jailers discovered me they kept begging me to give them a cigarette with cotton in it. I suppose they meant a filtered cigarette, which weren't around in 1904, because cigarettes didn't cause cancer back then. Anyway, I didn't have any filtered cigarettes, which sealed my death sentence, since the only reason the Prussians could conceive to keep an American from the 21st Century alive in an early 20th Century prison was his supply of smooth, mellow cigarettes. (I could curse that surgeon general, always telling everyone how cigarettes kill you and never pointing out the situations like this when a nice carton of filtered 100's could extend your life expectancy substantially. And what about that guy whose life was saved when he went to the store to buy cigarettes and his house blew up while he was gone? You would think if the surgeon general really wanted to save your life he would put that kind of information on a pack of nicotine gum. Or how about the man who quit smoking, ran outside to breathe clean air for the first time in 26 years, and was killed by a meteor? The surgeon general can just put that bit of information in his pipe and smoke it!)

I had traveled back in time because I needed to give a warning to someone. It was very important. The other day I was watching a fake news show (not Jon Stewart's), and I saw Henry Kissinger giving political commentaries. It struck me that a man like Henry Kissinger, a former US Secretary of State, could be doing so much better, career-wise, right now. It seemed that he missed his true calling in life, and I was going to warn him before he made that mistake.

The way I see it, after the Nixon administration, there was a gold mine sitting in front of Kissinger in the field of stand-up comedy. Think about it; the man could have a plethora of jokes, all ending with the same punch-line—"ME!" "Who vears short shorts? . . . ME!" "Vhat's love got to do, got to do, got to do with it? . . . ME!" Oh man, it would be worth dying if only I could tell Dr. Kissinger this before he made the mistakes he did.

Unfortunately, I had gone back in time to the wrong year, wrong country, and my death was imminent. Not just because of the whole "I'm in a Prussian prison and scheduled to be executed" thing (which was a slight setback on my plans of not dying today), but really because of that Eve person. All she had to do was not "eat" of the fruit of the tree, and then no one would die. Was that really so hard?

Surely if Eve wanted to know what the forbidden fruit tasted like, she could have found a loophole in the whole "Thou shalt not eat" clause. Personally, I would have taken the fruit and blended it into a nice smoothie. You would still get the knowledge attained from consuming the forbidden fruit, but when God sentenced you to death, you could say "Look, you told me I could do anything but eat the fruit, and all I did was drink it. You said nothing about drinking it." But maybe loopholes are part of the knowledge that came from eating of the tree. Then you could partake of the tree and not be condemned on a technicality, but you would have to eat of the tree and be condemned to know of the technicality. It's a vicious cycle (or vicious *circle* in case Daniel Boone has any anal retentive descendents reading this book), but so is life.

Aristotle defines "nothing" as that which a rock thinks about. As I lay on the cold stone floor for hours on end, I found myself thinking of exactly that, nothing. Then it donned on me: if nothing is that which a rock thinks of, vis-à-vis, a rock is that which thinks of nothing. This means I'm a rock, and Prussia can't execute a rock. Think about how much France would make fun of Prussia if they executed a rock. Man, France making fun of you—that's too much. No sooner had this thought crossed my mind when it occurred to me that to be able to figure this out meant that I was thinking and no longer a rock. Curse logic. (And the surgeon general.)

The jailer came back in, discovered that there was no longer a rock, but a prisoner sitting on the floor, and asked me one last time for cottoned cigarettes and led me away to the execution squad.

I was pleasantly surprised to learn that I would be killed by a firing squad today. Ever since I was little I prayed that my last words would be "Whoops," but death by a firing squad was definitely second on my list of ways to die.

I was blindfolded, refused a cigarette, and moved to the nonsmoking execution section. I heard the Sergeant yell out "3,2,1, Fire!" (but not in English, in whatever language he was speaking. Actually, I have no idea what he really yelled, I'm just assuming here.) Then I heard five or six simultaneous clicks. Nothing. I was still alive.

The Sergeant came up to me and informed me that I was to be set free, because it seemed to be God's will that I not die at their hands. I was overrun with gratitude. I lifted my eyes towards the heavens, only to discover what appeared to be a large meteor briskly headed my way. "Oh God, please let this meteor hit in the smoking section..."

But it didn't. It was headed straight t'wards me. Curse that surgeon genera...

SAN ANTONIO

Some people do not know how to take a compliment. And it isn't just the fat girls who don't like to be told they look "less fat" today. No, there are a lot of people who hate compliments. For example, the entire city of San Antonio. They are so smug about having that "Alamo" thing, but they don't want to hear about how nice it is from you.

There was a guard at the entrance of the Alamo, and I simply told him that he had a really nice Alamo here. He tried to inform me that this was "The Alamo." I reassured him that it was "an Alamo," and a really nice "Alamo," probably the nicest "Alamo" I had ever seen, but it was kind of arrogant to say it was *The* Alamo." He tried to argue with me, so I informed him that up in Amarillo we have an "Alamo Carpet," and while it's a really nice "Alamo," it has nothing on his "Alamo."

The same thing happened to me while I was walking on the Riverwalk. When I stopped at this "Last Resort" restaurant for a drink (just a soda, I'm not the type to become a...you know, drunk) the waiter asked me what I did that day. I simply told him that I visited the main "Alamo," and it was the best "Alamo" I had ever seen. The jerk tried to tell me that it was *The* Alamo" and to quit joking around with him because it wasn't funny.

I made it plain to him that I really was impressed with the quality of his city's "Alamo." I was explaining to him that Amarillo's "Alamo Carpet" didn't even have a gift shop. He asked me to leave.

To be quite honest with you, that Alamo wasn't even all that great. Sure, it's a really good Alamo, but it isn't even the best Alamo in San Antonio. I mean, the Alamo Dome is a much bigger and structurally superior Alamo than the main Alamo.

Then there is the Alamo that was built in Brackettville, Texas. They built it to film the movie <u>The Alamo</u>. It looks the exact same as

204

San Antonio's Alamo, but it isn't as old, so it isn't as decrepit. Plus John Wayne made a movie there, which has to give it some merit, and this Alamo has yet to bring sudden death to anyone, so I would hold it in higher regard than the San Antonio Alamo.

And what about the movie? It's a much more portable Alamo than the San Antonio Alamo, making it much more useful in spreading Alamo love across the nations. And if it's on DVD, it's even more impressive. I mean, think about it. There is a small shiny disk no bigger than a (insert your own small object here (what small object did you pick? (I picked a duck))), and you can put it into a machine that shoots lasers at it and obtain both sound and images and projects those sounds and images to a television, a device that projects captured moments in time for my viewing pleasure. That's an impressive Alamo. That other Alamo is just bricks and mortar.

Really, all the Alamo is is a big museum, and if you are going to go to a museum in Texas, make it the Windmill Museum in Nederlands. For one, it has 25-foot revolving blades, and for two, it has the largest collection of Tex Ritter's personal artifacts, and you will never find a more obscure celebrity reference than Tex Ritter.

I decided I would go back to my hotel. It was right across the street from the aforementioned "Alamo," and apparently it's haunted. From what I read on two very reliable sites on the intraweb, I was able to learn that a group of old ladies in blue frequent a smokers' balcony (apparently the surgeon general in the afterlife is more forgiving) and Teddy Roosevelt is a common guest at the hotel bar. Now, I do not care much for talking to dead old women, but I'm sure there is a lot you can learn listening to a former president speak. Quite frankly, I just want to know if you die with a moustache, are you stuck with it for eternity?

I mean, I'm sure a razor will just go right through it, because if you can walk through walls then a razor can't touch you either. But there might be ghost razors, and if there are, can a ghost regrow a moustache? Seriously, what if you had a moustache your whole life, died, and shaved it off? Is it gone forever? Someone might want to change his mind, but it will be too late. And what about all those guys whose wives never let them grow one? The man is dead; the wife is not, it's only fair that he be able to grow a moustache if he wants one.

Needless to say, I retired back to room 3005 without seeing a ghost. My friend Chadrick had mentioned earlier in the night there were some haunted train tracks outside of town. The story goes that a long time ago a bus full of kids had broken down on the tracks, and a train came, hit the bus and killed all the kids. Legend has it, if you stop you car on the tracks and put it in neutral, the ghosts of the children killed in the collision will push you over the tracks into safety.

I called Chadrick and asked if he and his roommate for the night, Steve, wanted to go try out the ghost tracks. Chadrick obliged; Steve declined.

Chadrick had been acting strange around Steve all day, and it was partially my fault. When we first arrived at the hotel, I insisted on having my own room, forcing Chadrick and Steve, who didn't know each other, to share a room. To add some entertainment to the weekend, I called Chadrick (who is black) aside before Steve found their room and told him that Steve came from a very racist family, and he was really struggling to overcome that racism in his own life, but it was a struggle for him. I told Chadrick that as long as he didn't do anything around Steve, everything would be all right, but to watch his step because we want to do everything we can to make sure Steve isn't racist.

Well, that little lie seemed to do the trick, because Chadrick and Steve were both acting very cautious around each other, I was suffi-ciently entertained, and Steve didn't tag along when we went to the ghost tracks.

I was driving to the tracks with Chadrick in the passenger seat when we pulled up next to a car full of black men. Chadrick rolled down his window and yelled "YOU NIGGERS!"

I had heard Chadrick use the phrase "'Sup nigga!" before, which is roughly translated to "How is it going my African American com-padre?" but for some reason Chadrick had developed an inexplicable Boston accent on the word "nigga."

I turned to ask Chadrick why the sudden accent change, but when I turned towards him I saw he was ducked down in his seat, out of view of the car of black men, who at the moment were yelling some very unrepeatable words at me. I was begging Chadrick to sit up, but he refused.

As soon as the light changed I floored the gas and lost the irate brothers. Chadrick sat up in his seat smiling. Apparently he and Steve had known each other quite a long time, and when I informed Chadrick of Steve's "racism" they had decided to pay me back for my deceit. It might have been funny if it didn't almost cost me my life, but hey, what's 30 minutes when it comes to a premature death? Not that much, really. Not even 2 hours.

So we arrived at the tracks, and there was a line 10 cars long of people waiting to park on the ghost tracks. However, instead of parking on top of the tracks and letting the ghosts push them off to safety, the people were parking in the middle of a downward slope on a hill, putting their cars in neutral, then screaming in fear and excitement as their car rolled down the hill. How exciting. And to add to that, some people would sprinkle flour on their bumpers, where mysterious fingerprints from the dead children who pushed them would show up.

I was analyzing the situation, and I could not figure out why these kind ghosts, instead of pushing cars off of the tracks and away from danger, would instead push people who are parked a safe distance away from the tracks onto the tracks and then off again. And the pattern of the fingerprints on the back of the cars had a remarkable resemblance to the pattern left when slamming one's trunk, as if the flour stuck to the oil from the people's fingers. And wouldn't it make more sense if the fingerprints were where the flour was missing, not where the flour stayed on the car? It all seemed stupid to me, but Chadrick was scared, and that was the important thing.

We finally got to the front of the line and started to roll down the hill over the tracks. Chadrick was freaking out, but I personally thought the whole experience was stupid. Chadrick jumped out of the car to see if the ghost left fingerprints, and, sure enough, it looked like someone had been slamming the trunk on a semi-regular basis since the last time the car was washed.

I was getting tired so I hopped over to the passenger side and told Chadrick he was driving. Then I fell asleep. I fell asleep at 12:04 AM. I awoke at 2:44 AM exactly 123.16 miles (for you Canadian people that's about 4,000 kilometers) away from San Antonio, staring at the most magnificent Alamo I had ever seen. It was exactly how I had remembered the Alamo from the movie, not that commercialized crap they had in San Antonio. It was absolutely beautiful. Of course, it was the last time I would let Chadrick try to navigate his way across an arrogant city, but being able to see such a remarkable Alamo after being in a city filled with such mediocre Alamos made me forget the fact I was 123.16 miles away from where I was supposed to be.

It was like my life had gone full circle in a matter of 24 hours. I had gone from seeing a city full of the worst excuses for Alamo to standing in the midst of the most glorious Alamo on the face of the earth. My life had become complete. I think God must have seen the poetic symbolism as well, because he agreed with me that my life had indeed become complete, and decided to take me home before I did something to screw it up again.

Posthumous side note:

My sudden disappearance sure did confuse the trash out of Chadrick.

PARIS

I was standing in the middle of a French cemetery, staring in disbelief at Jim Morrison's grave. I wasn't so much in disbelief that he was dead, or at the genius that once was and now is gone, or anything else. I was just in awe of how feebleminded people can really be. Not even just the French, either. All day I had felt like I was in America (not the entire Western hemisphere as those Canadians would have you believe, but the 46 states and commonwealths that make up the Continental United States).

Ok, 46. That number might not look right, and you might also be wondering about that word commonwealth, but let me explain. I will start with the latter. Kentucky, Massachusetts, Pennsylvania and Virginia, for some reason, call themselves commonwealths instead of states.

Next, as you have noticed, I'm not counting Alaska or Hawaii as states. Reason one: Alaska is just more Canada, and no one wants that. Reason two: Hawaii is just volcanoes. Those aren't states; they are more like malignant lumps in the ocean. If there is one thing I learned in geography, it's that malignant lumps are not states. If they were, I would have referred to the 47 states and commonwealths, being that Mt. St. Helens would have grabbed the coveted no. 47 spot.

Now, Mt. St. Helens, that place is something to be revered, especially for reaching the highest level of canonization in the Roman Catholic Church. Now, I'm not a Roman Catholic (but I did date one in the 80's), so I don't know everything, but I'm pretty sure I have this part right.

When a person (or malignant land lump) dies, he/it gets to keep his/its name, and in our case that's Helens. Then when this person/land lump commits a "posthumous" miracle (like writing *Billy Budd*) he/it becomes a Bl. (if the Pope makes him one.) This is when he/it adds Bl. to his/its name, making him/it a Bl., in our case Bl. Helens.

After a few years, if this person/landmass keeps up the good work, it's possible for him/it to achieve St. Hood. This is done by attaining a majority of the electoral votes of all the states in the Vatican Republic. Elections are held every four years. The person/landmass who receives a majority of the electoral votes is elected the new St. In the case of a close election where one state's vote is disputed, election results are made up and victory is given to the person/landmass whose brother is Governor of the state in question. At this point the person/landmass changes his/its name once again, dropping the Bl. and replacing it with St.

Now, the third level of canonization is the toughest to achieve. I'm not exactly sure how someone/thing achieves it, but surely sharing a birthday with me and Pope John Paul II helps a lot.

Anyway, when someone/thing achieves Mt. Hood, he/it is allowed to keep his/its previous name (St. Helens) and adds the title Mt. to the front of it. It's a very sacred and time-honored tradition that we should not try to overanalyze.

Though a great honor, Mt.-inization does not change the fact that volcanoes are land lumps, so we strike Mt. St. Helens from the list of possible states and commonwealths and we are still stuck at 46.

Now, I'm sure by the time of this publication it will be obvious to everyone what happened to the other two states in the Continental United States. However, in the very rare case that it's still unclear by the time of this publication, I will explain it here.

Apparently New Mexico wants to sue Texas over a strip of land they say is rightfully theirs (as if it's rightfully theirs; didn't we all steal the land from Regular Mexico?). And not just a few wackos either, but the entire State Senate voted unanimously to do so. But the State of Texas has one thing to say to New Mexico: We are Texas. That means we can break off that land you want, make it its own state, and still not give it to you. Then we will name it something nice, like "Other Texas," or "More Texas," or "New Mexico is just like Old Mexico except not as Clean."

If you want to cry about who has rights to land and who stole land from who, I bet we can get at least 38 states to vote saying New Mexico was in fact stolen from Regular Mexico and we want to give it back. Well, sure we stole Texas from Regular Mexico too, and that's why we aren't acting like we are in third grade and pretending that the first-come-first-serve thing is a rule.

Plus, we (Texas) still have the right to leave the Union. In fact, we have the right to take that piece of land you want and make it its own country. Then there would really be nothing you can do about it. In fact, given the choice, I think most Texans would rather give that strip of land back to Regular Mexico over New Mexico any day. Not because we like Regular Mexico better, just because they aren't as whiny. In fact, I bet at least half the population of these United States would rather give Regular Mexico New Mexico instead of Santa Anna's fake leg. Look at how much better this map looks.

Man, that's great. But I was thinking, Regular Mexico wouldn't want New Mexico, that's just like dumping America's trash on them, and that would be wrong. So maybe we could just give them more land. We will throw in Utah. Not that I have anything against Utah or necessarily want to see them leave the Union, but Mexico wouldn't be able to refuse that much free land. So let us look at the new map.

Wow, can you imagine? If that happened, finally, millions of people will be able to sing "America the Beautiful," and for the first time, they will really mean it.

So, needless to say, I'm quite confident that things worked out pretty much as described, and New Mexico and Utah are now part of Regular Mexico.

Now, I was still standing in front of Jim Morrison's grave, in utter awe of the fact that there, six feet away from me, was the biggest sham in rock and roll history. Before Jim Morrison died, he really was interested in faking his own death. In fact, he told his band members that if he died, for them to wait for a letter in the mail. He would mail it to them and sign it with a pseudonym, and if this letter ever came it would mean that he was alive and well. His band members said if they ever received that letter no one else would ever know.

After his death, only two people saw his body before it was buried, leading to further suspicion that he in fact faked his own death. However, this is all a load of crap. He is dead.

The sham is he made everyone think he was a genius; he was not. Sure, the man had a band which made a lasting impact on rock and roll, but come on, have you heard the stuff he is saying? It's not as deep and philosophical as drunk people would have you believe. In fact, it's pretty shallow and meaningless. I read a book of his poetry once—dumbest thing I ever read (until I start to proofread this).

He just gave the image of being a philosophical genius, and people bought it. Here, let me give you an example:
The squid
  Left the earth
  Vaporized by the waste
  Drip
  Drip
  Drip

Well, for making it up off the top of my head, that last little bit was pretty good right? No. It was absolutely oafish; well, it would be if it were a person. I don't know, maybe things can be oafish too. Let's just say that if the poem were a person it would be an oaf. However, if I told you it had some deeper significance you would be in awe of it while I sat back and laughed at how dumb you are. That's what Jim Morrison did.

All I could do was sit there, awed at humankind's fallaciousness. It first occurred to me that day as I was walking along the road and a saw a Chevy Nova drive by. I admit, it was rare sight in France, but ask any American and they will tell you it's an even rarer sight in Latin America because, as we all know, "no va" means "it does not go" in Spanish. There is just no basis for this claim. The first obvious flaw in this statement is the very fact that the Nova did sell in Latin America, in fact better than expected in some areas. Secondly, do you really think people would see a car "going" and read the name and think "ooh that car doesn't go, it says so right on the back." No, of course not. It would be like if I went to a table store and there was a sign on the table that said it was "Very Notable." I wouldn't go around thinking "Man that sure was a nice table, only it wasn't a table. I would have bought it if it was a table." That's ridiculous.

I started to leave the cemetery. The farther I got from Morrison's grave, the less frequent were the spray-painted directional arrows telling me where his grave was. It was probably Americans who painted them, desecrating this sacred, historic ground, and yet, it's the Americans who have a problem with the French. Go figure.

I really don't think the Americans have a problem with the French, they just kind of want to put on a front to make people think they do. Honestly, if we were really sincere about our disappointment and disgust with the French, we would have done something more to show it than change the name of French fries at the Congressional Cafeteria. That didn't affect the French at all; all it did was annoy the Congressmen who had to say an extra syllable when trying to order fries. No, if we really wanted to show the French that we were mad at them, we should have given back the Statue of Liberty. If we are so "Proud to be American" and anti-French, why would we want a gigantic green French statue greeting all the immigrants when they reach America? We wouldn't. If you ask me, whoever made up the "freedom fries" protest didn't get enough attention in kindergarten and needs the attention now.

I caught a cab to the Eiffel Tower to get to my business in France. My friend had a cousin who died and was cremated and asked that his ashes be thrown off the Eiffel Tower. Why the Eiffel Tower is beyond me. I think he saw it on television one time and thought it looked like fun or something. Anyway, my friend had a "job" that he couldn't miss, and I was "unemployed and sat around my parents' house all day," so my friend asked me to do the honors of flying to France and dumping the ashes that the funereal home gave him to pretend were his cousin's off the side.

I wasn't thrilled about the task at hand (and for the record, I can think of nothing I want less than having my remains thrown off the Eiffel Tower—except of course a Thomas Kinkade painting in my viewing room), but when my friend offered me free plane tickets to France, I couldn't say no. Of course, if I had known that I would be arriving in and departing from Paris the same day I might not have been so eager to jump at the opportunity, but at least the airline was providing all my meals for the day. *Side note: If you are ever booking a flight with an in-flight meal, tell the lady at the ticket desk you are a Jew and must have a Kosher meal, and you will get your food first. Just thought I would let you know; you can use that information however you want.*

After waiting in line for what seemed like hours, I was finally at the top of the Eiffel Tower (well, as "top" as they let you go) with an old peanut butter jar filled with what used to be my friend's cousin.

As I stood on the edge, jar in hand, I had no idea what the proper etiquette for dumping ashes off of a large structure was. I hadn't thought about it beforehand, and now I hadn't a clue what to do. Did I simply say a prayer and dump, sprinkle it out slowly, or just drop the jar and run?

I decided I would shoot the ashes over the city of Paris with a long, flamboyant (but graceful) toss, which was a good idea if I would have mastered that "graceful" part. Instead, I tripped over my own foot and flung myself off the side of the tower with the ashes.

I must admit, this was an unexpected turn of events, but with the ground fast approaching, I knew what to expect next...

THE COMOROS ISLANDS

The government of the Comoros Islands has been in a constant
state of instability since the islands declared independence on July
6, 1975. At the time of the declaration, the president was a man
named Ahmed Abdallah. However, within a month he was overthrown by Justice Minister Ali Soilih, which was only the beginning
of the turmoil that was to come to the islands' government. Since
1975, the Comoros Islands have had more coup d'états than any
other country. With so many outside coups, like Les Affreux, coming
in and trying to overtake the small country, it was only logical to assume that sooner or later it would be my turn to try to take this
country as my own. Right?

I sort of had an inside edge as well. I had a friend, who by Comorian standards is from a pretty wealthy family, and who, if the
Comoros Islands were still under its ancient tribal/monarchical system, would be fourth in line to take the throne. The only thing
standing between him (whom I shall call Prince Rashid) and the
throne of the Comoros Islands was three cousins and that whole "we
want to be a republic" thing.

The Prince had come to the States, where I had met him, to
study, and ever since I'd earned the pleasure of his acquaintance-
ship, he had done nothing but fill me with tantalizing stories of this
tropical paradise (mainly the fact that polygamy wasn't only accepted, but expected), enough to give me my own dreams of someday being able to live on these islands and call myself Comorian. The
Prince had aspirations of his own as well, mainly to overthrow the
government and take his (cousin's) rightful place on the throne, so
he presented me with a proposition.

He wanted power, I wanted three wives, and together both our
dreams were obtainable. Rashid couldn't overthrow the government
himself; I mean, what would his mother think? So, here is the deal

215

he presented me with: I get together a coup to take out the ruling party, along with Rashid's three oldest cousins, and he would give me three wives and enough land to live more than comfortably for the rest of my life in Comoros.

At first my conscience was telling me, maybe this wasn't the best thing to do, but then I thought, dangit, I'm an American! And if going to a foreign country that I have no business being in, maliciously overthrowing the ruling power, setting up a new form of government and telling the people that it's the one they want isn't the American Way, I don't know what is. (Toby Keith describes the American Way as sodomizing an alleged terrorist with a boot, but the actions of the US government agree with my interpretation of the American Way over his. Honestly Toby: boot sodomy? That is gross.)

Now it was time to organize my coup. I recruited two guys, Zach and Josh, and we were on our way. (By recruit, I mean I found two guys, said "Hey, want a free plane ticket?" they said "Yup," and I planned to explain the rest of the details on the 31-hours of plane flights and layovers (for you Canadians that's about 3 weeks.))

Studying the previous coup d'états, I learned a lot. Mainly that I need a really cool name for my coup. The other coups had foreign names, so I figured mine should, too. The other names were French, but I didn't know any French, so I decided to name my coup Αλαζονεια. Of course, Rashid didn't point out until later that the other coups didn't pick out foreign names, they *were* French, and that an English name would be foreign to the Comorians. Still, I had chosen a name and I was arrogant, so I decided to keep it.

On the plane I spelled out my demolition plan to Zach and Josh, but they weren't all big on the slaughtering and pillaging thing, so I had to revamp my plans (and quick).

Luckily, I had a plan B. I had a briefcase full of flyers that read:
You No Longer Live in a Republic.
Rashid is King Now.
Sorry For the Inconvenience.

True, my method was unorthodox, but Comorian people are very easy-natured. Maybe they would be relieved to see that there wouldn't be another bloody battle and willingly give Rashid his throne.

We finally arrived in the Comoros Islands, and Rashid (who had taken an earlier flight) greeted us at the airport. Of course, I didn't explain the new plan to him; he really had his heart set on all that carnage, so I played along.

In the car on the way to "massacre the infidels," Rashid explained to us that apparently the government went on vacation this week, so there was really no need to kill anyone, and he suggested we take a more lackadaisical approach, like maybe just passing out flyers informing the people that he was king now. I must admit, his plan was good, but it lacked the zest and ingenuity of my plan. However, people will believe anything they see in writing, so maybe his plan would work. I decided to give it a try.

Along with our luggage, Rashid had found a briefcase filled with flyers just like we needed. Can you believe the luck!

We started posting and passing out flyers everywhere. People seemed to respond well to them. There was a feeling that since the government already changed hands 20 times, what's one more? 21. And that's not a big deal. I mean, the government would change again in six months, and in six months no one is going to care what government is being overthrown, just as long as one is.

So that was it. Rashid was king. I followed through with my end of the deal, now it was his turn to pay up. I had expected him to give me something to the liking of a Russian mail order bride catalog, or maybe there would be a room that I went into filled with girls, like a brothel scene in a movie, and I would pick out three or four women to marry and go on to live my life.

Apparently that was not the case. You see, in the Comoros Islands marriages are arranged when the children are young, and when they reached marrying age they, you know, marry. That sounded like a good deal to me.

Then, each one of the man's wives has her own house. The man (who will be me) lives in one house until he gets tired of that wife, you know, all her nagging and crap, then he packs up and moves in with the next one until she becomes a drag, and by the time he gets back to living with the first wife again, she has calmed down and learned her place, at least for a few days, until she doesn't, and then the man just moves on again. What a nice system. (Now, I am not sure on this, but I would assume the abovementioned wife swapping takes place within a 28-day cycle.)

Now came the difficult part: finding a Comorian man (or three) to want his daughter(s) to marry me. I'm not that bad of a guy, really, but apparently, it's not every Comorian man's dream to raise his daughters so someday they could grow up to marry a guy like me. Who would have thought? Well, besides Rashid, a lot of people apparently thought that, but that's beside the point. I mean, honestly, I successfully overthrew the government; finding half a dozen or so women who would want to marry me *should* be easy, right? Because power is sexy.

Though it was the most pressing issue on my mind, Rashid told me we had more important things to worry about at the moment. Zach and Josh had left on the first plane out of the islands, and Rashid and I were alone to face the old government when they came back from vacation. I don't know what is more stressful, knowing that any day a group of irate former world leaders could come home, see that I somehow got them all fired and try to kill me, or the fact that I was about to have a small harem. Well, definitely the harem, but I needed to make sure the old government didn't come back and try to overthrow Rashid if I was ever going to see that harem.

It's times like this in my life where I usually turn tail and run. If I'm in the US when the old government gets back from vacation, what can they do to me? But this time there was something different. There was a principle at stake that I must hold up. Life is just too short to deny three women the chance to marry me. How selfish of me would it be if I ran back to America (the real one, not Canada) and led a monogamous life that did not allow every woman who wanted to to be my wife? I would just be a horrible person, and I don't know if I could live with myself.

Anyway, there was nothing more I could do that day, so I decided to sleep on it. Rashid was letting me stay at his mother's house, which was nice, at least the bed was very comfortable. The next morning I woke up in the afternoon (I had to fight my editor to keep that sentence in here). I guess I missed breakfast, because when I went downstairs Rashid and his family were enjoying a very large banquet-style meal (fit for a king, hahahah—oh, I need a life(wife)).

Rashid told me to sit down, so I did. The main course for the meal was hedgehog. I must admit that I did feel weird eating the hedgehog, since as a child I had a pet hedgehog, which died of constipation. (Note: Here I'm using two different literary elements, the first and most obvious of which is foreshadowing, which was given off by the keyword DEATH. Being that the reader knows the story is about death, the word death should have set off a mental alarm. The second literary element is irony. It will play in later in the story. You see, I had a hedgehog that died of constipation, a digestive problem, and now I was eating a hedgehog, the first step in the digestive process, and we are already alerted to the death factor, so one can only assume what is coming up soon in the story.)

The meal was absolutely superb, of the caliber that deserved a nice nap afterwards. I had just settled down on the couch and was beginning to drift into a nice slumber when I was awakened by

Rashid. The old government was back, and they wanted to talk (makes you wonder if I was lying about that foreshadowing part).

Rashid and the former leader of the government had decided on a neutral location for their little meeting. When Rashid and I arrived, there was already a round of drinks waiting for us. Of course I didn't drink any of mine, because I was sure they wanted to poison us, but Rashid quickly finished his drink and asked for another. Apparently the poison hadn't taken affect yet. As Rashid and the former government talked, I kept a careful eye on Rashid, looking for any signs of impending death.

Before I knew it, the meeting was over, I hadn't heard a word of what was said, and Rashid was still alive. In the car on the way back I asked Rashid what was said, and he explained to me that the old government had actually been a bit relieved when they came back and discovered they were no longer in office. They had only taken over the country because of the allure of having their names guaranteed to be in history books, but now they were beginning to become a bit nervous that they would either have to start actually doing something, or they would be killed in a violent uprising. Rashid's peaceful ascent to the throne had come as quite a pleasant surprise to them, and they weren't about to argue.

All of this was all good, and Rashid was king and still showing no signs of poisoning.

That evening, as I was lying on the couch, desperately trying to continue the nap that was stolen from me earlier in the day, I began to feel a sharp pain in my stomach; in fact, it felt as if my bowels were on fire. I fell over on the floor, clutched in the fetal position, yelling in agony. Rashid rushed in to see what was the matter with me (actually, he probably just wanted to tell me to shut up, until he saw the condition I was in), and he quickly dialed the ambulance.

I heard the paramedics coming, and I opened my eyes one last time to see a bright light illuminating from...

MILLIONAIRE

In high school the career guidance counselor would always ask me, if I were a millionaire and never had to work again, what would I do all day? I thought the hypothetical situation was absurd and wouldn't answer their question. I mean, if I was a millionaire and didn't have to work, why the aitch (don't you love how the letter "h" looks spelled out?) would I be here asking them for guidance? Really, what were they trying to do, let me see how awesome my life would be with a million dollars right before I'm sent out into the world, penniless and jobless? Have a heart, people; that's just mean.

Well, a few years and one very nice night playing the lottery later, I was forced to answer the question myself. I didn't have to think about it too long and hard because in my heart I always knew what I would want to do if I never had to work: ride a llama down residential streets.

I actually was not surprised that I won the lottery; in fact, I was kind-of expecting it. I know that the odds of winning the jackpot are astronomical, (about 1:178,000,000) but I have beaten much greater odds before. Why, my very presence is proof of that.

Side note: My editor advised my to reduce the six page description of the biological process and attempts to estimate the number of attempts that were made at my conception to the following three paragraphs:

Each individual person (myself included, since I am an individual person) had about a 1:150,000,000 chance of being conceived when he actually was conceived. Sure, the odds of a couple conceiving a child is miniscule in comparison to the figure above, but for that person to be born, he (and I use the masculine pronoun here because I am talking about people) had to beat out 149,999,999 other potential people to become that person.

And then, how many attempts were made at conceiving each person before they were actually conceived? Each time adds another 150,000,000.

Using a calculator and some guess work, I figure that I had a 1:21,750,000,000 chance of being conceived. Put that into perspective: I should have won the lottery 122.19 times by now.

Anyway, at the advice of the lottery officials, I went to a financial adviser, who informed me that a million dollars would not last forever and that I needed to find a way to have some sort of income. (Yeah, I didn't win the jackpot, which was well over 50 million dollars; instead I bought 10 tickets, all with the same numbers, just different numbers on the bonus ball, and while I got all five regular numbers on each ticket, I didn't get the bonus ball, so I had to settle on 10 second-prize payments.) And while I think that financial adviser was a crock (if he cared about my finances he wouldn't have charged me for his advice), he did have some wisdom, and he told me how I could have my dream of riding a llama in residential areas all day and still make money: goat farming.

See, apparently wolves don't only eat people, but they also eat goats (and by wolves I mean coyotes). However, wolves (coyotes) don't know what llamas are, and are kind-of scared of them (and by kind-of I mean really). Because of this, goat farmers like to keep llamas in their fields with the goats, and wolves (coyotes) won't mess with the goats. He also said I could have a donkey, but not an emu.

I must admit that *must admit*, when put together into one word and spelled wrong, can fool spellchecker into thinking that I wanted to say mustard. I also must admit that his plan sounded very good. I could have a flock of goats (or herd or pride, I don't know what they are called. I only wanted them for the llama), ride my llama all day, put it with the gaggle at night and make money off of the hair (or wool, I don't know what it's called, remember I'm just doing this for the llama) when I (by I, I mean someone else) sheer it and sell it. I asked him if I could call myself Mr. Mohair Risen. He said yes. I said deal! I tried to shake on it and he told me to leave.

I tried to find a place that would sell me a school of goats; however, most places downtown didn't specialize in that, but they did like my nametag that said Mr. Mohair Risen. One person suggested that, instead of goats, I get rabbits and call myself Warren of Warren's Warren, but I told him I didn't get it. [10]

---

[10] I originally published *How to Die* under the named Wm. Douglas Warren. That's why that joke made sense.

So, I was still looking for the goats when my "financial adviser" called me and said there was this flea market down by Dallas in a town called "Canton" that had a large area devoted to selling animals, including goats. It sounded good, so I decided to check it out.

I got in my car and started driving to "Canton," but then I remembered that I was rich and didn't have to drive myself. So I stopped at the gas station and saw a guy driving an 18-wheeler with one of those cattle trailers on it, so I asked him if he could drive me to "Canton." He said that he was contracted with a ranch and was on his way to that ranch to pick up some cattle and transport them/it (I don't know what you call it when your cargo is living) to the slaughterhouse. I pulled $20,000 out of my pocket and said I only need a ride to "Canton" and back; then he said something about the ranch that my publisher advised me not to include in this book, and told me to hop on in.

I hopped in, gave him half of the $20,000, told him he would get the rest when we got back, and started on the road. We had barely gone two miles when we passed a For Sale sign on some pastureland by the highway, which reminded me that I probably needed one of those (the pasture, not the sign) to keep my goats and llama in when I got back. I phoned my financial adviser (on a cell phone, because when you are rich you get to have those) and told him to make sure I had one of those (again, pasture, not sign) for when I returned with my goats/llama, and he said ok. I told him to make sure that it was within llama-riding distance from a ritzy residential area, and he told me he would do the best he could, which honestly probably wasn't that much. I asked the mysterious trucker I was riding with (who for the sake of this story I shall call "Ray Charles") if he minded if I turned on the radio, and he told me to go ahead. So I did.

I was listening to the "music" on the "radio" when the broadcaster interrupted with a special bulletin. Basically he said that a convict had just escaped from the psychiatric ward of the prison and to not give a ride to any strangers within a five-mile radius of the prison. Right then Ray Charles turned off the radio and gave me a very suspicious look. I asked him what he did that for, and he said there was no point in listening to that because all it would do is make him think that I was the prisoner and just make me think that he had killed the real trucker and he was the prisoner. I must admit that was a very interesting observation on his part, being blind and all, because that thought had not even crossed my mind. But it did comfort me to see that when he reached over to turn off the radio he accidentally dropped the small dagger he was holding and didn't make any attempts to grab it. However, spending the rest of the six-hour drive in pure silence was a bit awkward.

Finally, we arrived in "Canton" and asked one of the locals where the flea market with animals was. He directed us down to "Dog Alley," which was the area of the flea market with all the animals. However, if we had stepped out of the truck to ask him, we would have realized that there was really no need for such a superfluous question, since the smell of "Dog Alley" would have led us right to the spot.

So, we got to "Dog Alley" and started walking around, and I found a pen with about 35-37 goats in it. There was a sign that read "Goats. $45-$95." I thought, great! I didn't really care about the goats, they were just to make my financial adviser happy, so I told the man I would buy all of the $45 goats. He seemed happy, told me the price, I paid him and he said they were all mine. I asked him which ones exactly, and he said all of them. I told him that I didn't understand; the goats ranged in price from $45-$95, and I only wanted the cheapest ones. He explained to me that some people think that the more you pay for a goat the better it is, but all his goats are the same. Some people just feel better paying more, so whichever ones they think should be worth more, he lets them pay more. I thought that sounded like a good idea.

I gave Ray Charles an extra $50 and told him to load my goats in his trailer. As he was doing that, I decided to stay and chat with the old man for a little while, who for the sake of this story I shall call Diana Ross.

I told Diana Ross that all I needed now was a llama and I would be set. He told me to hold on a second while he went and checked to see if he has anything in his trunk.

Diana Ross came back with a llama and said it was all mine for $15. I told him that the whole reason I bought the goats was so I could have a llama and I didn't want to buy just a cheap run-of-the-mill llama. He told me to wait just a second and he would see what he could do.

Not 30 seconds later, he came back with a llama that I could swear was the exact same one he just left with, but this one was $1000. I asked him what made this llama so much better than the other one, and he said that it was grown in a hydraulic farm and his roots never touched any dirt, just water. That was good enough for me, so I gave him $1000, hopped on the back of The Spanish Inquisition (that's what I named the llama), and road back to the trailer.

Ray Charles was still there loading the goats, which I named William Jennings Bryan (all of them: it saved confusion). He was quite impressed with The Spanish Inquisition, and let's face it, who wouldn't be; The Spanish Inquisition was a stunning marvel of both beauty and intellect.

Ray Charles finally got all the William Jennings Bryans loaded into the trailer with The Spanish Inquisition, and we decided that it was a nice day and we were at the largest flea market either one of us had ever seen, so we might as well do some shopping.

I was getting pretty tired of digging through all these piles of old junk. After the goats and The Spanish Inquisition, all I had bought was some argyle socks and a corn dog on a stick (which sounded a bit repetitive to me too; I mean, who ever heard of socks that weren't argyle).

Then, suddenly, it caught my eye (the left one). Amidst all the piles of the aforementioned junk, there it was: a replica of a medieval knight's horse's armor. It was the perfect thing to change the image of The Spanish Inquisition and make it less vulgar. I bought it immediately and told Ray Charles I was finished; I was ready to go home. But he told me to hold my horses (which I reminded him was a llama); he was still looking.

He purchased a rather frilly-looking sword that the man at the booth promised could cut through a human arm as if it were butter. (Can you imagine how great it must be at cutting butter! It can probably cut butter like warm butter!)

Ray Charles and I got back in the truck and started the all-night journey from "Canton" back to Plainview. I was kind of worried about the fact that Ray Charles kept his new arm-removing sword in his hands the whole time he was driving, but I thought, nah, forget it (yo home to Bel-Air). I was tired, so I went to sleep.

I was awakened when the truck came to a screeching halt. I sat up in my seat to see what had happened. I saw nothing. I became irate and asked him what happened and he responded, "Sh! Tom sees moths." (Did he just say a palindrome? He did, eh?) I looked out of the car but all I could see was a family of opossums crossing the road. I tried to figure out what was going on. First I thought maybe Ray Charles was that inmate who escaped from the psychiatric ward and he had multiple personalities and one of them was named Tom, and Tom was hallucinating and seeing moths while speaking in palindromes, and wanted to kill me, since he was clenching the arm remover awfully tight. Then I thought maybe Ray Charles's name really was Tom, and he speaks in the third person and never learned the difference between opossums and moths. This seemed much more likely to be the case, and it gave me a great idea.

When I had come into wealth I knew that I wanted to do something to help mankind and better my community. At that very moment I had an epiphany, and I knew what I would do. I stepped out of the car, grabbed an empty burlap sack that Ray Charles had in the floorboard and starting grabbing the opossums. I was able to grab the entire family, and had only been bitten three times.

I tied the burlap sack up with twine that I found in the glove box and sat the opossums behind the seats. Ray Charles asked me what I thought I was doing (using words my publisher again advised me not to put in print), and I told him I was going to make my community a better place. He asked me how exactly was I going to accomplish that with a bag full of rabid opossums, and I told him. Simply, I was going to start breeding opossums in a very insecure pen that they could easily get out of. I would breed hundreds, even thousands of them, and they would escape and overrun the neighborhood. And since the opossums would leave me, though I incurred the expenses to raise thousands of them, it would turn out to be a completely selfless act. He seemed to agree.

As we neared town, Ray Charles asked me where we were going with The Spanish Inquisition and all the William Jennings Bryans. I called up my financial adviser and asked him if he(I) had bought me(me) a pasture yet. He said indeed he(I) had, and gave us directions to find it.

It was beautiful. It *was* beautiful. (I honestly do not remember if I meant to write the preceeding sentence twice, but upon discovering that I had done so, I liked it, and then put a different word in italics each time so it looked intentional. Actually, I am thinking about writing it a third time.) It was *beautiful*. It was a quaint little pasture right off a residential block. We pulled up to the gate, which read "437737," and I knew this was the right place. We unloaded The Spanish Inquisition and all the William Jennings Bryans, I paid Ray Charles the other $10,000 and we parted ways.

I went home and went to bed. The next morning (evening) I woke up with a fever, headache, loss of appetite, malaise, restlessness, nausea, drowsiness, sore throat, muscle stiffness, dilated pupils, increased saliva production, increased sensitivity to light and for some reason my opossum bites were itching like a mofo. I decided I might need some medicine, so I looked in my medicine cabinet and found some sleeping pills, and I thought, I might as well take a baker's dozen or so of these and see if I feel any better when I wake up.

So I did just that. I woke up a couple days later to find strong symptoms of anxiety, abnormal behavior, confusion, delirium, hallucinations, insomnia, convulsions, easy agitation and excitement, and for some reason I had developed an immense fear of water. Just the very thought of it would make my throat spasm. I decided I probably needed to go to the emergency room. So I suited up The Spanish Inquisition in his armor and started to the hospital.

It was raining like a banshee outside, and lightning was every-where. The lightning was so close that I couldn't even see it, but every time it thundered I would see an immense blue light in every direction.

Then, all of a sudden, flames burst from The Spanish Inquisi-tion's helmet, and I was flung from my metal saddle int...

THE HOSPITAL

A note to the readers: My editor advised me that you (the readers) by this point are probably getting tired of reading stories that ramble on and on but have no dialogue. I reminded him of the palindrome in the millionaire story, but he said it didn't count. So here you go. A story with dialogue. Enjoy it.

My friend (who I don't feel like naming yet) made me take him to the emergency room. Apparently he thought he was dying, and it was of dire importance that he not do that today, or something like that. I wasn't really listening to him. I sort of tuned him in and out.

We finally got to the emergency room and the attendant at the desk made him fill out some paperwork. When my friend gave it back to him he seemed to be really impressed at how well he filled out the form, like the fact that he was able to spell his name coherently (there, I named him, you happy? He is Coherently.), and he told my friend that he should apply for a job working in the emergency room. (If you haven't noticed yet, I'm not quite to the part where I use dialog, and I'm still generally summing up the main points of the conversation so I don't have to use quotation marks. Publishers charge extra for quotation marks.)

Well, Coherently really didn't care much about finding a job at the moment, since he was dying and all, so he just sat down in the lobby and waited for the doctors to call him in.

Two hours later, I was getting bored with the whole "waiting" thing (Are you happy? I just used quotation marks—that's 50 cents I'm never going to see again.) so I decided to go grab something to eat. As I was leaving, Coherently asked me if I would bring him back something to drink, and I obliged.

When I returned to the hospital, I found that Coherently had already been taken back to the examining room, but the guy at the desk led me back to where Coherently was.

I stuck my head around the door and asked, (this is where the dialog starts) "How's it going?"

"Fine. They let you back here?"

"Yeah, I didn't even have to ask; the guy at the reception table just told me to go on back."

"Okay, did you get the sodas?" Coherently asked, looking at my empty hands.

Realizing that I had forgotten them, I said, "Yeah, I left them in the waiting room."

"Why?"

Still lying, I said, "I didn't mean to." Quickly changing the subject, I added, "So did the doctor like your medical history?" (Knowing the answer should be "NO!")

"He didn't really say much."

"Did he tell you to quit smoking?"

"Nope. He just told me I was overweight."

"As if you didn't already know."

"Really," Coherently agreed. "You think he would assume I realize that every time I take my shirt off at night and see my man boobs."

"So what did he say?"

"He asked what I ate for supper tonight, and I told him 4 Salisbury steaks with extra gravy and a couple of potatoes."

"Then what?" I asked.

"He asked what I had the night before, and I told him a pizza and some burritos; then he looked rather somberly at me and said I need to adjust my eating."

"Somber like he was telling you you were at death's door?"

Laughing, Coherently replied, "Yeah."

I quipped, "I bet he expects to walk in here and see you lying there passed out all like HE'S DEAD!" Then, suddenly remembering where I was, I saw the inappropriateness of what I just yelled. "I guess I might not want to yell that too loud in here, might cause a panic."

"You might make someone cry," Coherently said.

"So, what did the doctor think it was?"

"He said it's either an inflamed pancreas or gallstones."

"Well, which one is worse?"

"I don't know. What's the pancreas for?"

Having no idea, but wanting to make Coherently feel better, I said, "It's just useless, most people get theirs taken out when they are little."

"Isn't that the appendix?"

"Oh yeah. Then what does the pancreas do?"

"I don't know."

"Well, surely we learned that sometime."

"Do you have to have one?" Coherently wondered.

"I think so. Doesn't it filter something, kind of like the liver?"

"Maybe I ruined it with all the tequila last night." Coherently said, as if that made any sense.

"Did the doctor ask you how much you drink?"

"He just asked me if I drank beer or used drugs."

"And what did you say?"

"I told him I haven't in a long time."

"But you drink every day," I argued.

"I haven't had any beer in a month."

"You're half drunk right now. You know they will find the alcohol in your blood."

"They didn't do a blood test," Coherently replied smugly. "He tried to find a vein for about 10 minutes, but he said they were too deep because my arms are so fat."

"So they just gave up?" I asked

"Yeah."

Then we both sat there, in a moment of awkward silence, Coherently slightly embarrassed by his massive rotundness. (Haha, spell check thinks I made up a word!)

"So can you go get the sodas?" Coherently asked, breaking the silence.

"Yeah, sure." Now this was going to be tricky, since as I said, I lied about the drinks, but I had nothing else to do. Might as well say they were stolen.

So I walked out into the lobby, and, to my surprise, there were two sodas sitting on the table. Apparently my lie was only a lie for me, and not someone else, the someone else who left the two sodas in the lobby.

So I grabbed them. They were still pretty full. I poured some from one into the other so I could give Coherently a full drink, so he wouldn't think I lied, and plus, if one was poisoned, I wanted to make sure he at least got some of the poison, too.

I came back into the room to find Coherently studiously studying the labels on the drawers. I didn't want to interrupt him; I mean, he looked so peaceful, and I was about to give him a poisoned soda from questionable origins, but I thought, what the heck, he thinks he's dying anyway.

"Hey, I got the drinks."

"Thanks."

Then I started to feel a twinge of guilt about the whole "poisoning my best friend" thing. "I don't know, there were some people sitting by the drinks, and I think they might have messed with them."

"Why would you think that?"

"Because the lids were off when I got there."

"Oh, I don't care," he said, taking a big gulp. Then he looked back at the drawers he was studying so intently. "What does that say?"

"Which one?"

"The third one from the left."

"Oh. Urethral Sounds."

"What's that?"

"Maybe a high pitched squeaking?" I said. "You know, like when ya pull the lip of a balloon tight and let the air out."

Just then, a Middle Eastern doctor with a very thick moustache and accent walked in, holding a small plastic cup of what looked like milk of magnesium. "Here, drink this very fast. Nasty, nasty drink, drink very fast. It will numb your stomach. Drink fast. Very nasty." Then he stuck his tongue out, squished up his face and started making smacking noises, as if Coherently didn't get the hint that it would taste bad.

Coherently looked at the small glass and threw it back as if it were a shot.

"Whoa, that tasted nasty."

"What did it taste like?" I asked, not really caring to know the answer.

"Gin and chalk."

Regretfully, I knew the taste he was talking about. Feeling that we were in for a long night, I got up and began pacing the floor. I walked over to the open door and began looking out. I could see a police officer squatted down and slowly backing up down the hall. As he came closer, I could see that he had something in his hands.

The longer I watched, the more evident it became that the officer was holding a leash of some sort. Then I saw what the leash was tied to: a pair of bare legs. Obviously, that caught my attention. Then the whole picture came together. This police officer had a rope tied to a naked man's legs, while the naked man (who seemed to be trying to bite his own ears) was sitting bloodied up in a wheel chair being pushed by another officer. I quickly ran back to my seat, hoping no one saw me watching.

"Did you see that?" I whispered to Coherently.

"Yeah."

"I don't think we were supposed to see that."

"Me either," Coherently agreed.

We both sat there for a second trying to take in what we had just seen. Coherently interrupted the silence.

"Did they have him on a leash?"

It took all I had to get out, "Yeah."

"Why was he naked?"

"I don't know."

Coherently, still trying to rationalize the situation in his head, started rambling, "That just doesn't happen. Cops don't bring naked guys into the emergency room strapped to a wheelchair naked every day."

I peeked back out the door to try to see what was going on. "I think they are doing blood tests on him."

"Where is he?"

"They took him into the room across the hall and the blood guy just walked in with them."

I was still trying to see what was going on when the nurse walked in.

"I'm sorry," she said. "I have to close the door. No free shows." With that she gave a hand motion like a bellhop expecting a tip and pulled the privacy curtain so we couldn't see anymore.

I got up and walked over to the window into the hall and started peeking through the blinds. Standing outside of the room with the naked guy was one of the officers, and I recognized him. He was a regular at Coherently's Tuesday night poker games.

I stuck my head out the door and yelled at him, "Webb!" (That's his name.)

Officer Webb spotted me and came over to the room we were in.

"What are ya'll doing here?" he asked.

"What are we doing here? What are *you* doing here?" I replied.

"Huh?" (Webb wasn't the brightest on the force.)

"What's the deal with the naked guy?" Coherently asked. (Which, by the way, was tactful for him.)

Officer Webb realized how absurd the situation must have looked to us, began to tell the story, laughing most of the way through it.

"Oh, he assaulted some people, then he thought it would be a good idea to get butt* naked and run across the parking lot. Then he decided that he was gonna beat up the po-lice. So I hog tied him and brought him up."

"Why did you bring him here?" I asked.

"Oh, he was bleeding on everyone, so we decided to have him checked out here."

"Well," Coherently explained, "we were just wondering what happened; I mean, that's not really something you see everyday."

"Oh, all sorts of things happen here." Webb assured us. "Last month I had to come into the emergency room myself."

"What happened?" I wanted to know.

"I fell into a manhole."

Coherently and I looked at each other in disbelief for a second before he asked the obvious question, "How did you do that?"

Officer Webb looked rather sheepish for a second, then finally broke down and told us, "Got called out to check the hole because a little girl had fallen into it earlier in the day, and they wanted someone to secure it. I got out there and the lid for the hole was sitting by it. I'd say it was about six foot wide, and I put the lid over it, then just to be safe, I figured I would jump on it to make sure that it was on good, and it was. So I went over to the other side and jumped on it there, and when I did the lid flipped over."

Not able to control his laughter, Coherently said, "Oh man, that's rough!"

"That's not the worst part," Webb said. "The worst part is that the camera in the car was running right on me. Caught me falling and picked up the choice word I used."

"Wow, that's awesome," I said, in true admiration.

Looking at his watch, Officer Webb said, "Well, I gotta go check on this crazy guy, nice talking to ya'll though."

After Officer Webb left, Coherently stared at me and very solemnly said, "You know what I was just thinking?"

"What?"

"That crazy guy they brought in, what if he remembers our faces and kills us?"

He had a point, but I wasn't going let him think that. "He won't remember our faces."

"But we remember what he looks like," Coherently argued.

"That's because he was naked."

---

* Personally, I would have chosen the word "buck" to describe his nakedness instead of "butt," but that is what the cop said, so who am I to argue?

"Maybe when you're the one naked, you remember the faces that look at you."

"That's stupid," I replied, but I think he was on to something.

Just then the doctor came back in with the same cheese-eating grin he had on his face earlier.

"Well, I got some good new for you," he told Coherently. "Turns out you were just fat. "

"What?" Coherently said, not knowing whether to be relieved or insulted.

"You ate a little too much," The doctor explained, "had more gas built up in you than a normal person would have in a lifetime, but you are ok."

"So there is nothing wrong with him?" I asked.

"Right, you are free to go, just stay away from fatty and spicy foods for a while." With that the doctor left.

"Well, that was a surprise," Coherently said. At least I think he said that; I wasn't paying attention.

"Hey, steal one of those urethral sounds," I insisted.

"What?"

I repeated. "Steal one of the urethral sounds. The drawer is unlocked."

"No, we'll get in trouble." Coherently is such a whiner.

"Look," I explained. "You are already paying a fortune to the hospital, and no one will know."

"Ok," Coherently said grudgingly, as he opened the drawer and pulled one out. "Wow, those things are huge!"

"Just stick it in your pocket."

"Look how fat it is."

"Just hurry up and do it."

Coherently finally put it in his pocket, and we were able to leave. As we passed the room with the naked man we both couldn't help but look in, and when we did, this time we were sure he got a good look at our faces.

We made it back to my car all right, when Coherently started complaining he was hungry. (Look, I started doing that whole "describe what they say instead of using dialog" thing again. That would have saved me some money with the quotation marks if I didn't just put "describe what they say instead of using dialog" thing in quotes twice.)

So I decided it was better to get Coherently food to shut him up than listen to him for the next three minutes on the ride home. I pulled onto the access road to get to the fast food joints faster when I heard a loud pop, and my car suddenly started veering to the right.

Great. I had a blowout.

I stepped out of my car to assess the damages. As I figured, my front passenger tire was blown. I didn't want to change it right there on the access road because it was dark and to change the tire I would have to sit in the right lane, making me an easy target for oncoming cars (and if you didn't know, you get double points for hitting a fat guy).

I pulled the spare and jack out of my trunk and started to jack up my car. Of course, in the dark, I couldn't see where to place the jack, so I completely bent my frame, and Coherently wasn't coming out to help me because he was still "emotionally unstable from his near-death experience." So, I was able to remove my old tire without any troubles, but as I started to put the spare on I saw a pair of approaching headlights. I yelled at Coherently to turn on my emergency blinkers (which he did) and the car came and drove right past us. It was a police car. I thought they were supposed to stop and help stranded motorists. What happened to that whole "serve" part of "to protect and serve?"

I was finally able to get the spare on, and I got back into the car and started to make my way to some 24-hour fast food joint.

I pulled into the parking lot and, honestly, it was probably the worst parking job I had ever done. I mean, really, there was no conceivable way that the person parked next to me could pull out without hitting me. So, instead of backing up and trying to pull in again, I simply wrote down the license plate number of the car next to me, because I knew it was going to hit me and, more likely than not, the driver wasn't going to stop and write down his information for me, so I did what I had to.

Coherently and I went inside, and I sat down at a booth while he went and got his food. Soon, he was back at the table with three green chile double cheeseburgers, a large fry and a 40-something ounce soda.

"Did you not hear the doctor tell you not to eat spicy or fatty foods?" I asked.

"Oh, well I've already eaten spicy and fatty foods today, so it won't matter if I eat this. I'll start healthy tomorrow."

"Whatever."

The rest of the meal, I just sat in disbelief as Coherently shoved mouthful after mouthful of food into his face. If he wanted to be dead by the age of 30, that was his choice, but I wasn't about to go for that.

When Coherently was about to finish off his last burger, the inevitable happened. (No, he didn't die; I heard a crash outside.) Just as I expected, the car with Texas license plate 31X PP7 had smashed into my car and drove off like nothing happened. Oh well, I thought, I will just report the hit-and-run in the morning and let the owner of license plate 31X PP7 get a pleasant wake-up call from the police in the morning. Of course, I wasn't going to pay to fix it, and obviously I don't have car insurance. To have car insurance, I would have to speak to an insurance agent, and I try not to associate with people in that, most unchristian, of professions.

The way I see it, I can pay an insurance company $200 a month to pay for anything if I can get in a wreck, or I can pay myself $200 a month. If I get in a wreck, I know I can trust myself to pay for it, whereas I know I can trust the insurance company not to pay for it. If I am using my own money and never get in a wreck, it is still there. If I am paying the insurance company, every time I write them a check the money is gone forever, and then when I do get in a wreck, I have to pay them even more a month to cover any money they might have accidently given me. If I do happen to be in a wreck I cannot pay for, I can take out a loan to cover the repairs and pay that loan back at a cheaper rate than paying the insurance company, and then I know the money is actually being used and going towards the said cause. Therefore, I see absolutely nothing redeeming about what the insurance company does. They take your money, keep it for themselves, and then when you need don't give you enough. That is why car insurance sales is known as the most unchristian of professions. At least with drug dealers or prostitutes, they provide some kind of viable service (however unchristian the service is, they at least provide one).

My car was still drivable, so I hopped in. As I got into my car, I suddenly started to feel incredibly nauseated. It was as if having to watch and listen to Coherently scarf up the grease-fest had given me some kind of vicious, artery-clogging contact high. I was beginning to feel a little lightheaded and slightly dizzy as I started driving home, and I also started to become disoriented with my surroundings.

I found myself on an unfamiliar street, in what appeared to be the middle of a police standoff. I tried weaving in and out of the hail of gunfire, but it was to no avail. As bullets started to collect in my engine, I realized that I was not going to be driving out of this situation. With the car rolling to a sudden stop, I looked over at Coherently and realized I had a pretty nice human shield right beside me. Unfortunately, I think he had the same idea because he picked me up, held me in front of him and started to run toward safet...

JOB INTERVIEW

Another note to the readers: I'm still being told this book needs more dialogue, so once again, here is a story full of it. Hopefully though, this is the last one.

I was spending a nice day at the zoo when I walked by the offices and noticed a Help Wanted sign on the window. Needing a job, I decided I would check it out.

I went inside the offices and introduced myself to the secretary, asked her about the job, and she directed me toward the office of Adam Gibbs.

I knocked on the door and heard a voice telling me to come in. I stuck my head in and introduced myself. "Hello, my name is Bernie; I just saw the Help Wanted sign outside, and the secretary told me to come in here."

The stern-looking man at the desk (who I assumed was Adam Gibbs) suddenly got a smile on his face. "Yes, yes, sit down." I took a seat opposite the man and waited for my next instructions. "Do you have any experience working in a zoo?"

"No, never in a zoo, but I did work my way through college in a pet shop."

"Did this pet shop have kangaroo and octopus?" he asked almost hopingly.

"No, mainly just a few birds and some tropical fish."

"So, in other words, you have no practical experience that would be useful in this job," he said somewhat degradingly, obviously disappointed.

"Well, no, I guess not." (I was trying to throw in a double negative to shine a somewhat more positive light on my lack of experience.)

"Well, did you graduate from college?"

"Yes." (No.)

"Maybe a degree in biology or something else that would be of use in a zoo?"

This was when I started to see my job prospect go out the door. "No, I went to culinary school, specializing in fast food cuisine."

"A whole lot of good that degree did you, didn't it?"

"Well, no sir, I suppose it didn't do me much good."

"Well, I suppose we can still find some job for you." He opened a folder and started looking through the files, finding all the jobs I couldn't have. "Not this one...nope, too difficult...we already filled this position...OH, yes, here is a job for you." (I felt some relief.) "We have several college interns here and we seem to have been having a lot of problems with them, mostly vandalism in the women's shower room. We need a monitor to just watch them in the showers and make sure they don't try to break anything."

Did he just say what I think he did? "Well, yes, I can do that job."

The man gave me a good look and kind of wrinkled his face. "Mmm, I don't know if I can give you that job in good conscience."

"Oh, why not?" I pleaded.

"Well, you see, it's such a tedious job; those girls can be very vicious, and you can't take your eyes off them for a second while they are in the shower. If you do, they will do something behind your back, and we will have to fire you for negligence."

"Oh please, just give me a chance. I promise I will work extra hard. I won't take my eyes off them. I promise."

"No, no, it can be really tedious. I mean, some of those girls will stay in the shower for a good hour at a time, and it will be so bland just sitting there staring at them; even if you do your job perfectly, I'm sure you will be bored to tears. Here, let me try to find something in your degree that maybe might be better suited for you."

He started to flip through the folder again.

"Oh, forget my degree! I didn't even go to college. I was only trained for two days at the Burger Joint before I was fired for misuse of the condiments. I want that job, I NEED that job. Please sir, I will do EVERYTHING in my power to be the best woman's shower monitor that you have ever hired!"

The man at the desk appeared not to have heard a single word I said. "AHA! This is perfect for you! Feeding the grizzly bear!"

I made one last plea. "Aww sir, please. I really think that I could be a good shower monitor."

He looked at me sternly. "If you take this job feeding the bear, I will give you a $1000 bonus check right now, plus $15 an hour."

"And you won't give me that offer on the monitor job?"

"No."

I needed a job, and this sounded easy enough for the pay I would be getting. "Well, then I guess I'll take it."

The man's face lit up, and before I could say another word he had a contract in front of me. "Great, sign here." While I was signing his contract, he buzzed the main office. "Judy, could you please send Frank in here?"

"Sure thing Mr. Gibbs." (This confirmed my suspicions that the man in the office was in fact Adam Gibbs.)

"Thank you."

Another man entered the office. He was slightly skinny and had a look on his face suggesting that he might not be the brightest person here, probably working somewhere in mid-management. "Yes, Mr. Gibbs?"

"Frank, I would like for you to meet our new bear feeder, Bernie." I stood up to shake his hand, and when I did he raised my arm and started looking me over.

"Oh wow, look at you!" he chimed in amazement. "You really are a nice one!" He lifted my other arm. "Just look at that! Quite frankly Adam, you have hired some real duds in the past, but he is PERFECT."

"What are you talking about?" I asked.

"Oh nothing," the man now believed to be Adam Gibbs replied. "Here is a check for $1000, and I expect to see you back here at 7:30 tomorrow morning."

I took the check and left. When I arrived at my house it was pretty late, so I decided to go on to bed, and I would cash the check when I got off work tomorrow.

The next morning when I arrived at work, I was greeted by Frank and Mr. Gibbs (I think). Frank was smiling and once again giving me a good look-over.

"The bears will absolutely love him!" Frank began. "I have never seen a person that looked this delicious. If the bears don't finish him off, I call dibs on the shoulder at the company picnic. WOW!"

"What do you mean you call dibs on my shoulder?"

"The bears might not eat all of you in one sitting," the alleged Mr. Gibbs explained. "I mean, you are kind-of tubby."

"You're fat." Frank added, quite tactfully.

This conversation was going nowhere fast. "Well, yes but you don't think the bears will eat ME do you?"

"Well, that's what we are hoping for," the man I would put money on being Adam Gibbs told me.

"What?"

"That's what we hired you for."

This was absolutely ridiculous. "I thought you meant I was going to feed something to the bears, not myself."

"Then why did you think I offered you the $1000 bonus check? It's so you could go out and have a fun time last night, because today you will be eaten by the bear."

"Then what's with the $15 an hour?"

"We will mail your family a check. Usually it only takes the person 3 or 4 minutes to be eaten, and we send their parents a check for a few dollars, accordingly."

"Yes, but last week a man made it a whole 30 minutes," Frank said with excitement. "His family got about 5 dollars after taxes."

I stood my ground. "Well, I'm not going to do it."

"Yes you are," said the man I am calling Mr. Gibbs. "You signed the contract."

"But you can't expect me to be eaten by a bear?"

"Is that not what you were expecting?"

"No! Of course not."

Mr. Gibbs seemed taken back. "Well, I'm sorry, but I don't understand your objections."

"It just bothers me to think of being eaten by a bear."

Now the man charading as Adam Gibbs tried to comfort me. "Everyone is bothered by some things; we just have to live through it."

"That's right," Frank said. "You know what bugs me? Grown men who use the word 'poot.' Who pooted? Was that a poot? I smell a pooty."

The man had a point. Not everyone is comfortable with everything, and if we don't tolerate the things that seem absurd to us, we will never learn to effectively understand other people.

"Well, I guess I never thought about that before." I gave in. "Ok, I'll do it."

Once again, the man who very possibly could be Adam Gibbs seemed pleased with me. "Great! I will get you your stuff."

He came back with an aerosol can of mustard, sprayed me good, and led me to the bear exhibit.

THE ARAN ISLANDS

Third note to the readers: I was finally able to satisfy my editor with the amount of dialogue in the previous two stories, so you do not have to suffer through any of that "dialogue" anymore. If you miss the dialogue, I suggest you make up your own and write it in the margins. Lots of people do that.

When you look at the beauty of nature, you can't help but believe in God. The harmony of living things and the magnitude of all created leaves little doubt in anyone's mind that there is some greater force behind all of this.

But then there are the other people, the ones who see the brilliance and depth of creation and try to make it prove there is no God. They say by carbon dating they can prove the earth is *hundreds* of millions of years old, and they say through fossil records they can disprove the Genesis account. I have many problems with their beliefs on both counts.

First, as I have already explained, the earth is exactly 2,194,422 days old (if today was October 23, 2004). I read it in a very old and out-of-date introduction to the King James Bible, so I know it's true. But, for the sake of argument, let's pretend it isn't. How can someone date anything by carbon dating? Did he keep a piece of organic material, watch it closely and monitor its carbon levels at all times over a couple hundred million years? What was that? No? Of course not, that's absurd, and so is pretending you know the patterns of carbon half-lives over a period of millions of years.

Secondly, I need to debunk the claim that since there are dinosaur fossils and no dinosaurs mentioned in Genesis, we prove that Genesis is wrong. Come on, that's just silly. The Bible claims God created the earth and all that is in it, and if I had to put my money on something, I would put it on God creating *all* that was in the earth, including the fossils. That's right, when God made the earth he made all the layers at once and put the dinosaur fossils in it. Do you really believe that giant 30-foot reptiles roamed the earth millions of years ago? Yeah, right. I'm not even that gullible.

Whether you believe in a god or not, one thing is certain: nature is beautiful. But just as true as that last statement is (very true), there is another truth: people can screw up nature.

It's true. With all of the pollution in big cities, desecration of the rainforests in South America, and miles and miles of waist high stone walls in the Aran Islands, we humans have taken a precious gift (nature) and abused it.

I had taken a ferry from mainland Ireland, where I was on an expedition, hunting down and killing the most dangerous animal in the country,[iv] when a friend of mine told me about the Aran Islands. Apparently, they sell some very nice wool sweaters over there (if you consider a garment that's itchy, can't be machine-washed, and made out of a farm animal's back hair "very nice"). However, I had always wanted to ride a ferry, and I do enjoy clothing made out of back hair, so I grabbed my buddies Heath and Amanda and we were off.

Side note: Well, here is the deal. My editor won't get off my back about the little insignificant stuff, like "making the book readable." So, to keep him off of my back, here is a "character description." If you like the current flow of the story, I will encourage you to skip over the next paragraph, and then you will get to a nice bit of the story about me riding a ferry! But, if you want to know a short, meaningless and superfluous description of Heath and Amanda that will leave you knowing nothing more about them afterwards, then go ahead and read this next paragraph. Don't feel obligated to read it, though; it has about the same amount of relevance to this story as that Herman Melville and Nathaniel Hawthorne part you skipped over in the Canada story.

Heath was the quiet type. Tall and lanky, he was at least seven inches taller than me, but probably 15 pounds lighter. Then there is Amanda. Here is where I have trouble. I've never been able to describe pretty girls. Either I say something wrong and they get offended or I make an inappropriate comment, and I just ruin the whole situation. So, I will keep this simple: her toes looked like pieces of string hung off of a building.

The ferry ride was only about an hour long, but (and don't quote me on this) I loved it! I think I could ride a ferry all day long. The mood changed, however, as soon as we stepped off of the ferry, when we were bombarded by coach and carriage (two different things) drivers wanting to give us a tour of the island.

We kept declining the drivers' requests, and the more and more they told us about the sites we could see on their tour, the more and more we knew what sites we didn't want to see on the island. As far as I could tell, all the island had was a small market area with souvenirs, sweaters, and an "American" bar.

Plus, as far as the eye could see were these walls. Tiny walls. Well, tiny height-wise, but they stretched clear across the island, shore to shore to shore to shore, looking like a very sloppy "Battleship" game board (if Battleship were played on land instead of water. Wait a minute, that gives me a great idea! Battle Beached Whale! When this book flops, I'm going to make and market Battle Beached Whale and make a fortune (by Canadian standards)!).

The thing was, these midget walls completely obstructed the natural beauty of the island. Unfortunately, since the walls were built centuries ago by dead people (well, dead now), no one will tear them down because they are part of the island's "heritage" (an ugly part, mind you).

With the information we received from the coach and carriage drivers, we knew there was one thing on the island to make the ferry ride worth it (actually I thought the ferry ride made the ferry ride worth it (Woo!), but Amanda and Heath needed some more convincing), an old round fort on top of a cliff. These forts were built when someone wanted to protect an area from invaders, but were too cheap/lazy to build a full castle. (Now, what they wanted to protect on this island was beyond me. Maybe they were afraid someone would knock down their walls or something.)

Talking to some locals (and doing our best to figure out what they were saying through the thick accents), we decided there was no way we could walk to the fort from the ferry terminal and retain our current weights, so we finally hopped onto one of the tour vans, giving the driver specific instructions that we were only interested in going to the fort.

On the way to the fort, Heath, who had a video camera, decided that we needed to play a rousing game of "Vikings vs. Locals," casting me into the role of "Viking," with Amanda being the defending "Local."

As we left the market area, the driver started to take us down narrow, one-lane (but two-way) streets, with speeding tour buses constantly coming right at us.

I was rather amused by the whole situation, but Amanda and Heath started panicking like girl(s) (well, Heath was panicking like a girl, Amanda was panicking like herself), so the bus driver turned around (real safe, huh?) and told us, "Don't worry. If you see a bus coming right at us, just close your eyes and say, 'In the name of the Father and the Son and the Holy Ghost...'" Surprisingly, that didn't bring any relief to either Heath or Amanda.

Shortly (it would've had to have been "shortly," no matter where we had gone, because the island is only six miles long), we arrived at the fort. Well, we arrived at the ticket desk to the fort (the fort was still about a half-mile uphill climb), and the bus driver told us he would meet us back at the same spot in 90 minutes.

We bought the tickets and looked up to our destination. It was going to be a long haul. I had seen a sign earlier in the day proclaiming "Guinness for Strength," and, feeling weak, I was regretting not getting a pint (coincidently, Heath, who was feeling a bit dehydrated, *was* regretting getting a pint).

Less than halfway up, I was absolutely exhausted, but Amanda and Heath weren't, so we kept on walking up to this tiny gate at the top of the hill. We ran into a man on his way down from the fort, and I asked him if it was worth the long hike. He said no. When that man was out of hearing distance, Heath assured me that was only because he didn't play "Vikings vs. Locals."

Despite my pleading to turn around and forget the stupid fort, we finally made it to the gate, only to realize we still had a bit of walking to do before we arrived at the fort. In the distance, Heath spotted an opening in the wall surrounding the fort, which would be the perfect location for his production of "Viking v. Local" (Heath decided to drop the S's in "Vikings vs. Locals").

We went through the opening, and Heath directed me to go around the curve a bit, out of view of the camera, and he made Amanda stay in the small opening, telling me to charge on his command.

I was around the bend listening to Heath record an introduction about the villagers who needed a good pillaging when I heard the magic words, "And here come the invading hordes!"

I started to run towards Amanda to give her a good pillaging when I found my path blocked by two American-sized French women who kept walking towards the camera, oblivious to what was going on. Not exactly being the invading hordes he wanted, Heath called cut, and I went back around the bend and waited for my cue again.

Once more I heard "And here come the invading hordes," and this time, there were no French women in my way, so I waved my arms above my head and ran screaming toward Amanda. She quickly picked up an arsenal of small stones and began throwing them at me. I had no choice, so I started to retreat. Score: Vikings, 0; Locals, 1.

Well, we all simultaneously realized what a stupid idea that was (plus, Heath had it on camera, so he could blackmail Amanda and me). We tried to play it off as if nothing had just happened, which would have been a lot easier without the barrage of French tourists giving us a round of applause. Trying to cover our faces, we meekly (so we could inherit the earth) made our way through the aromatic French into the round fort.

Would you like to know the difference in non-Canadian America and Ireland? In Real America (that has a better ring to it that "non-Canadian"), if there is anything that could lead to someone's painful and certain death, there are barriers and warning signs posted everywhere to help keep people safe. Not the case here.

We were standing at the edge of a 1000-foot (for you Canadians, that's 28.6 km.) cliff, with no protection at all to keep us (me) from falling to certain death. (I bet you think you know where I'm going with this, right? Give it a rest. Surely by this point you know you haven't a clue.)

Knowing my luck (and reputation), I took a couple of steps back from the cliff's edge, and, knowing my luck (and reputation), Amanda and Heath got as far away from me as possible.

I wanted to look over the edge of the cliff, but I didn't want to fall to my impending death, so I devised a plan.

I took a few more steps back, laid flat on my belly (perpendicular to the edge of the cliff), and slowly inched my way forward. There I was, hanging my head over the side of the cliff with a completely safe view of the 1000-foot drop.

I took a moment to take in the beauty of the unadulterated natural setting. However, the serenity and peace I was feeling was quickly disrupted by Amanda's shouts of, "There's the invading hordes!" followed by a nice little pelting of stones.

I turned my head to find Amanda still throwing rocks at me, so I flipped around to duck and cover before I thought through the situation enough to realize that flipping around isn't something you can do while hanging over the edge of a cliff.

So there I was, falling off of something tall. This has come to be a familiar feeling (except for me wetting and soiling my pants; I don't remember doing that before).

Well, I see the earth's surface quickly approaching, so I guess I better go. Have a nice life. Goodbye.

ENDNOTES

ⁱ I made this up.
ⁱⁱ Still, making it up.
ⁱⁱⁱ Still, made it up.
^{iv} Bumble Bees. They sure are scary over there, and I did kill one.